BODY COUNT

A ROGUE WARRIOR THRILLER

IAN LOOME

Published by Inkubator Books
www.inkubatorbooks.com

ISBN (eBook): 978-1-83756-515-3
ISBN (Paperback): 978-1-83756-516-0
ISBN (Hardback): 978-1-83756-517-7

BODY COUNT is a work of fiction. People, places, events, and situations are the product of the author's imagination. Any resemblance to actual persons, living or dead is entirely coincidental.

1

PORTLAND, MAINE

The waft of stale urine smacked Bob Singleton first, hitting him between the eyes like an errant tree branch as he pushed open the door to the dingy bar on York Street.

The reek of booze hit him next.

It had been a long time since he'd been in any kind of watering hole, but just three months since he'd briefly fallen off the wagon. The smell set off internal alarms, the immediate notion that he should flee.

Beats being comfortable, Bob thought. *You get comfortable in places like this, bad things happen.*

The music from the club's sound system was ear-splitting, rapid-fire, monotone punk lyrics, the vocalist screaming that people should be exterminated to a machine-gun drumbeat.

It was a narrow room, bathrooms near the doors, a bar along the other wall, a dozen people milling shoulder-to-shoulder in the rest of the space, a few at tables past the bar.

Old posters of sweat-drenched, screaming vocalists sat in

wooden wall frames. They advertised gigs by Black Flag, The Exploited, SNFU, in an era before most patrons were born. At the far end sat a small, empty stage, protected by chicken wire, next to the rear exit.

The smell of liquor grew as Bob approached the bar. The bartender, a strapping young man, was polishing wet beer glasses.

"EXCUSE ME... MIKE SCHULTZ?" Bob said as loudly as he could without yelling.

"WHAT?"

"MIKE SCHULTZ. SERGEANT MIKE?"

The bartender pointed towards the back door, next to the stage. "He went out to have a word."

"WHAT?"

"HE WENT OUT..."

"IS HE SOBER?"

"WHAT?"

"IS HE SOBER?"

The bartender shrugged.

"BUT HE'S OUTSIDE?"

"NO WORD A LIE."

"THANK YOU!"

Bob walked to the end of the room and pulled the door open.

Well... this is familiar.

IT HAD BEEN three months since Sergeant Mike had picked him up off the ground, fresh off his being yelled at and hung up on by Dawn Ellis, his only real friend, but seemingly a million miles away in Chicago.

He'd stumbled, downed a forty ouncer of J&B Whiskey.

It had been an alley, and Mike had intervened just as a couple of lowlifes were rifling his pockets.

Now he needed to return the favor.

The postage-stamp backyard was fenced on all sides, a couple of picnic tables for people ignoring the smoking rules, judging by the butts on the ground.

Mike was hammered. He was in his civilian clothes, his shirt collar unbuttoned, sleeves rolled up. He was backed into a corner, two burly-looking men closing on him.

All three had their fists up, ready to punch it out.

"COME ON!" the sergeant bellowed. "I'll HAVE EVERY ONE OF YA BASTARDS!"

He was swaying in place slightly, his gaze glassy. He took a half step sideways, tripped and fell over. He looked confused, unsure of where he was.

The two men crouched over him.

"HEY!" Bob called out.

One of them turned. He had a wicked scar across his nose, two missing front teeth, fingers missing on his left hand. "This ain't none of your mind," he spat. "He got lippy; now he gets a slap."

"He's a cop."

"We know who he is."

"He's a nosy bastard, is what he is," the second man said. "Jeezum jumped-up Mary and Joseph, he's due, boy."

"Why?" Bob demanded.

"Because he's a pain in my keister," the first said. "We all known Mike going years, and we all know he's suspended. He's got no authority right now. Come over to a cellar party at my uncle Walt's last evening, a wicked pisser, for sure."

"So what's the problem?"

"He gets drunk ass over tea kettle, stumbling about.

Breaks Walt's model of the *Mary E. Olys* in a bottle, leaves it all busted up. Walt gets mad, and number-than-a-post here goes and pulls out his badge and pistol, starts waving it about like an asshole."

Mike had managed to stagger back to his feet. "I..." He waved a finger at them. "I hereby arrest you in... in the name of the law."

The second man quickly raised and lowered the peak of his Boston Bruins ball cap. Bob noticed he was missing two fingers as well. "See, right there, that's the kind of shit what's we're saying. We never judged him, not for being the law. But that's disrespectful right there; he ain't even the law right now. Way I figures, his drunken backside needs a beating to remind him..."

"Touch a hair on his head," Bob cautioned, "and I'll remove the rest of your fingers."

The younger man took a half-step sideways at that promise, his expression nervous. "Now, steady on, boy. We weren't gonna kill the man or nothing." He glanced down at his hand self-consciously, then adjusted the bill of his cap again. "Like I said, he just got a little spanking come due, for all the times he thrown his weight around."

"And like I said: touch him, and I'll guarantee you a lot of pain. Best to just walk away, gents. Plus, he's a cop, and I'm a witness, so this is just stupid."

His bigger friend took exception. He turned fully and took a couple of steps towards Bob. "You might want to take a smarter line of thinking, fellah," he said. Then he frowned. "Don't know that accent, but clear you're from away. Come to our town, start giving us the gospel, you're liable to be next."

Oh, for crying out loud. Bob glanced around quickly. "You

see that red light blinking over there? That's a security camera."

"And you see that club over there?" the bigger man asked, pointing at the nightclub behind Bob. "That's my pop's place. We work hard all day, spends entire summers at sea pulling nets. He knows when we come home, we're dues some respect. That's what Mike forgot. He come up behind Ron here, smacks him in the back of the head, real hard like, and laughs, like it's funny."

"Smacked me good, boy," Ron said.

His bigger friend turned back to Bob. "Now, what'll happen here is we give him some bruises to remember his place. And he can't pull rank, as he got none. And since you're interfering, I'm going to bust you up a little, too, coz anyone defending him is number than my nuts in January, and none the wiser."

"I'm not trying to hassle anyone," Bob said. "But I know how to defend myself. We don't have to—"

"Oh, we sure does! If brains was shrimp, my lad, you couldn't fill a cocktail." He clenched both fists and advanced on Bob.

He threw a meaty cross. Bob ducked backwards at the last second, the slightly drunk patron stumbling on the diagonal. He righted himself quickly. "Oh, think you're a fast one, don't ya!" He threw a swift jab, but Bob saw it coming from the moment his shoulder flexed, bobbing sideways at the last second, sticking out his leg for the man to trip over.

He crashed to the ground.

His smaller friend took a quick step Bob's way.

"Ah!" Bob held up a single index finger. "Now, I'll be honest and say I've been here six months, and I still can't understand a goddamned word you people are saying half the time. I mean, what accent *is* that? Irish? Rural Nova Scotian? Mid-Atlantic? I figure it's all three at the same damn time."

He paused as the first man tried to scramble to his feet, waited until he turned, then tapped him across the chin with a short cross.

His opponent slumped to a seated position, dazed. Bob turned back to Ron. "But I'm going to assume from here on in that you have good intentions, as long as you don't make the mistake of trying to hit either of us. Keep this shit up, and one of you will get hurt. Possibly both."

The young man reached behind him. Bob took a step forward, anticipating him drawing a pistol. Instead, he caught the glint of a streetlight off the blade of a hunting knife.

Ron shuffled forward cautiously. "I'll cut ya, is what I'll do."

He swung the blade in an arc, slashing at Bob's torso. Bob tracked the motion early, focusing on the man's grip, leaning to his right and then throwing a flat-palm strike down, catching the man's wrist bones flush.

Something snapped.

"OH LORD THUNDERING JESUS!" the young fisherman bellowed, dropping the knife with a clatter, falling to his knees and clutching at his broken wrist bones.

"You see?" Bob said. "Now you're off work for a while. Was that smart?"

"Oh, it hurts!" the smaller of the two said. "Oh, jumping Jesus Christ, that smarts a bugger!"

His larger friend scrambled to his feet and lunged at Bob.

He stepped to one side, watching the man pass, his reaction times in the adrenaline "zone," things seeming to slow down. Bob threw the same flat palm strike, this time aiming at the back of the man's passing shoulder joint. Something popped, and the man tripped, falling over face-first.

"FUUUUUUUCCK!" he screamed. "JEEZUM FUCKING CROW!"

"There, now that's two of you off work for a while," Bob scolded. "Who is this helping, exactly? What's the point?"

"Ohhh..." the man whined, grasping his damaged shoulder with his other hand. "Oh God! Oh God, I think you broke my arm!"

"It's not broken, it's dislocated," Bob said. "Doc'll fix you right up. Give it... six weeks of rest, and you'll be back to being an idiot in no time."

In the corner, Mike was sitting up, leaning against the mesh fence. He squinted drunkenly at Bob as he approached. "Bob. Bobbeeeh! Bobster!"

"Mike."

Mike raised both fists haphazardly, one eye closed, the other halfway there. "Put 'em up," he said.

Is... is he really trying to start a fight with me? At his drunkest, Bob had always been a gentle soul. It seemed Mike was the opposite.

He heard a slight scrape on the concrete behind him and began to turn, seeing a flash of movement from whatever it was that smacked him a split second later across the base of the skull.

Ah shit... this could be bad, Bob thought as he slumped into unconsciousness.

THE DREAMS WERE JUMBLED, nonsensical but vaguely

menacing. That was normal, Bob knew, given that he'd just been in a fight.

Wait a second. Am I dreaming? But if I'm dreaming, that means...

His leg began to twitch, nerves overstimulated by consciousness seeping back in. It was old, familiar territory, and even before he'd opened his eyes, he knew what was going on.

Bob kept them closed. Most tough guys he'd ever fought were unaware that unconsciousness is fleeting, usually less than a minute. He let his left lid flit open for a second, just long enough to note someone was leaning over him.

A hand shoved its way into his coat pocket. "Can't find a wallet," someone said.

"Keep looking. They should pays for what they done to Ronnie's hand, like. He can't work none. See if he's got credit cards."

The second voice was coming from maybe five or six feet away. He chanced another quick glance.

Only one more. Damn it. He'd been out of the game for a long time, but it still bothered him when he missed an angle of attack. *Should've clocked the sound of the back door opening, for one.*

The other two had broken bones. That meant the one crouching over him was the guy who hit him.

The man's hand stopped rifling. "He's got a money clip; Lord Jesus, must be a few thousand in there."

Bob took a quick peek, guessing correctly that the man would turn to show his friends. He sprang to his feet, using an extra push with both hands, upright in a flash. It was the truck-sized doorman he'd seen on entering.

The man was less than a foot away, turning in shock as

Bob drove his shoulder into his target's side, thrusting him backwards, both men's momentum picking up.

They were two feet from the door when it opened, blaring punk rock shattering the relative quiet, the barman clearly wondering where the doorman had gone.

They plunged straight through the opening and into the club, the bouncer backpedalling, Bob picking up speed, his weight driving the other man into the room first, then the ground. A crowd of moshing dancers parted around them, strobe lights rendering it all in stop-motion as guitars blared.

The bouncer tried to grab Bob's throat, but he leaned forward, slipping his knees over the other man's biceps, pinning his arms down so that he could hit his attacker with two hard crosses.

The bouncer's eyes rolled up and back into his head.

Bob rolled off him without missing a beat, turning halfway through the motion as he came to his feet. The other two were watching through the back door but wisely staying back.

Damn straight. He suppressed an irritated urge to give the bouncer a good kick. Instead, he leaned down and rifled the man's pockets, recovering his money clip.

Bob walked to the back door. He motioned over his shoulder with his thumb. "If I were the two of you, I'd go help your friend up and maybe make yourselves scarce. Whether your daddy owns the place or not, you're both about six seconds away from a real spanking."

The two men scurried past him, both looking somewhere between terrified and horrified. Bob waited until the door had swung shut before approaching Mike.

"You... you taking me up on that fight?"

Bob ignored his friend and instead moved to the man's

side, using his hands under Mike's armpits to help him to his feet, just as the officer had done for him a few months prior, when he'd made a drunken fool of himself in an alley not so far away.

"Your fighting days are over, champ. Time to go home and sleep it off."

Mike turned his head, his gaze wandering around as he tried to focus on Bob. "Bob? That you, buddy?"

"Yep."

Mike smiled broadly, lips clasped tight, eyes glassy. Then he chuckled. "Heh. Guess... guess you don't think much of me now, huh?"

"I think you need a pitcher of water and a nice sleep," Bob said as they shuffled towards the back door.

"Can't... can't go home. Not tonight. No one there."

"Then it's a good thing my couch is three blocks from here. You can tell me what happened after you sleep it off."

2

Mike stirred and groaned as the morning sun streamed through the apartment's east-facing windows.

Bob glanced over at the old brown sofa. It wasn't much to look at, but it had been long enough and soft enough for the man to get some sleep.

His guest rolled over. "Wha... where...?" He glanced around, making out the details of Bob's one-bedroom apartment. Then he noticed his friend sitting in the corner in a wood-frame armchair.

"Oh." His guilt was writ large. He bowed his head as he straightened upright, blushing. "Oh Lord. Bob, I can't believe..." He pinched the bridge of his nose and rubbed tired eyes. "No one should ever see their group sponsor like this."

Bob shrugged. "Not my first sponsor. Not even my first sponsor to relapse."

Mike averted his gaze slightly, unable to look up. "Yeah...

Still. I'll be handling the embarrassment in due time, but for now, it is what it is, I suppose. Goodness gracious."

He had a softer lilt to his accent, unlike the fishermen. Mike had only lived in Maine for twenty of his fifty years, so it made sense. Plenty of locals, he'd said, still considered him to be "from away."

"Shall we get into it now?" Bob said. "Or would you like something to eat first? I've got bacon and eggs."

Mike snapped to attention, hangover momentarily forgotten. "Erin and the boys..." He had two young sons at home, as well as his wife of twenty years.

"I found her number in your phone and called her."

"How'd you unlock it?"

"You were still conscious briefly after we got here. I said you fell asleep on the couch after we watched the game. I don't think she believed me."

The broad-shouldered cop buried his face in his hands. "Oh, Jesus. What have I done?"

"Had to be a catalyst," Bob said. "Want to talk about it?"

Mike glanced sideways at him. "Not your problem. Not here, dragged into your life, anyway. We can talk about it at group."

"Uh-huh. No pressure, of course. But you slept on my couch, and I'm curious. One of those jagoffs last night said that everyone in your neighborhood knows you're suspended. What was he talking about?"

Bob's own life had been looking up. It had occurred in the weeks after getting sober again that whether Dawn talked to him or not, his trajectory was fatally nihilistic.

She'd been angry after being questioned by police in connection with the death of a hit man in Bakersfield.

A man he'd lied to her about letting live.

She'd said she didn't want to talk to him again, not then, maybe not ever.

Figuring he'd gutted the only worthwhile relationship in his life, he'd retreated into the booze. Mike had turned things around for him, sent him to talk to a local shrink.

The antidepressants had probably made most of the difference, if he was honest with himself.

He'd avoided them for so long, and now it seemed impossible to believe he'd been so dumb. They hadn't changed his personality, hadn't altered his skill set. They'd just allowed for a little daily optimism, a little more humor, fewer racing thoughts. They'd helped dispel the constant train of self-criticism and doubt.

He'd met some locals, found a good pool hall that didn't serve booze, and hooked up a volunteer gig with a local kitchen.

Life seemed strangely – almost surreally – normal.

And that was mostly down to Sergeant Mike Schultz.

But that Mike and this Mike seemed worlds apart. Bob could smell him from eight feet away, for one.

"The last time we saw each other... man, it was only two weeks ago."

"Lost my job, I think," Mike said. "Maybe. Hard telling, not knowing. Erin... she moved down the street to her mother's with the boys."

"Ah, geez."

"Oh, it's been a couple of weeks now already, and I think maybe she was considering coming home."

"Then you went on a bender."

"I did, that."

At that precise moment, the alarm on the apartment's clock radio kicked in at full volume, an old Rupert Holmes song set to piano, the chorus demanding to know if he liked piña coladas.

Bob strode over to the coffee table double time and turned it off. "Sorry. It's done that since I moved in. I can't figure out how to stop it or why it even exists as a function. Or why the times seem basically random. Jesus H. Bad timing."

Mike chuckled wryly. "It's par for the course, bub. When it all goes wrong, it really all goes wrong. And I'm not so sensitive that I'm just going to crack on you over a song about drinking, okay? All this nonsense has been building for a while."

That's cryptic. "You know why they suspended you, I take it."

"I do."

"And you intend on sharing with your sponsee..."

"At group. If I feel the need. Bob... I don't know you as well as I'd like because you've got all sorts of secret military stuff going on in your past, and we tried getting into that without success. But I know you well enough to know you're still looking for a fight half the time. I don't want to be the one who gets that going."

Bob studied him quietly for a moment.

Mike caught his inquisitive look and fidgeted. "What?"

"Oh, nothing. I mean... it just seems to me you're one of those guys who will give anyone else the shirt off your back, but when people try to help you—"

"I don't like to be anyone's problem."

"Yeah... the tough guy's lament. Remember what you told me about helping others, my fear of making things worse?"

Mike squinted against his hangover and the natural light of the morning. "Yeah."

"I believe it was 'Better they know someone cared, even if you fail.'"

"Yah, that was my pop's favorite expression. Something his mother gave him."

"Yeah... So..." Bob said.

"So what?"

"So what happened? How'd you get suspended?"

Mike sighed. "You're not going to let this be, are you?"

"Not likely. It's the most interesting thing I've been involved in in months."

"I'm glad my suffering is entertainment for you, Bob."

"You know what I mean. Spill."

"Well," Mike said, "it all started when I lost a body."

Bob's eyebrows rose. "You... lost a body? You mean, like..."

"A corpse. Yeah, that's what I'm saying. I lost a dead guy."

PORTLAND, Maine
TWO WEEKS EARLIER

THE DISPATCHER'S call for the nearest car wouldn't have normally reached him at such an early hour. But Sergeant Mike Schultz was playing designated driver, taking a bunch of his fellow serving members home after celebratory drinks.

They'd partied while he'd gone down the road, grabbed a few coffees, headed home for a few hours, returning just after midnight to ferry eight inebriated cops.

Then he'd turned the car northwest, heading towards his

family's house in North Deering and a deserved good night's sleep before a day off.

"Dispatch, this is 3699, go ahead. Over."

"Roger, 3699, we've got a multi-vehicle at Read Street and Quarry Road, called in by a passer. Caller believes at least two have gone 10-48. Medical examiner and EMTs are en route. Over."

Ten forty-eight was the code for an unattended fatality. "Roger, dispatch, put me 10-8 and en route. Over."

Mike hated accident scenes. All cops did, particularly fatals. There was no one to be helped, no wins to be had. Just misery.

He approached the intersection. *No shoulder on Quarry, and there are always trucks parked in the lot to the right side; might as well pull over here.* He parked the cruiser fifteen feet from the turn, next to a brick industrial building, a low-rise office of some kind. He turned on his flashing emergency roof lights.

He walked up to the intersection and turned the corner.

Ten feet away, an old Pontiac station wagon had slammed into the first in a series of temporary concrete medians down the middle of the road, set up to slow traffic around a manhole repair. Its back end had fishtailed into the oncoming lane.

The line of two-foot-wide concrete blocks ran for about fifty feet, with gaps along the way so that people could turn.

A parking area, to the right side of Quarry Road and behind the brick office complex, had been cordoned off, its asphalt churned up and waiting to be replaced.

The station wagon was a big old boat, Mike figured, something from the 1970s or early '80s. A second vehicle, a recent-model sedan, appeared to have then slammed into the first car's protruding tail end.

Good thing it's an industrial park. No foot traffic or neighbors. Nobody needed to see that sort of carnage, he figured.

He walked back to his cruiser and around it to the trunk, removing the accident scene kit and the big roll of yellow tape. He walked back to Read Street and placed a lit triangular hazard warning sign twenty feet from the median and nearest wreck, then looked for two posts, stringing the bright yellow tape across the road. In black letters, it repeatedly warned, "Police Line. Do Not Cross."

He walked back towards the scene. The streetlights were keeping it bright and clear, but he projected his penlight ahead of him anyway, to ensure he didn't tread on any evidence. The scene was strewn with broken safety glass and hunks of body panel, most of it near the two cars.

He followed the perimeter to the other side, up Quarry Road, and blocked off the street again, using a lamppost and a bus stop sign as posts for the tape. Then he made his way back to the station wagon.

The driver was half hanging out the door, thrown sideways and through the broken window.

Body's momentum probably caught the release, popped the door open when the head broke through the glass and the body slammed into it, Mike figured. He looked up Quarry Road, noticing the forty-mile-per-hour speed signs, designed to slow traffic in an area that saw a lot of truck traffic. *What the hell was he doing speeding down here? There's nothing along Quarry at this time of night.*

Mike crouched slightly to study the driver. The man's face was badly lacerated by glass cuts, smashed in, likely by impacting the steering column, the life and light gone. A large bloody puddle had formed under him on the asphalt, suggesting a nicked artery somewhere. He checked the man's pulse to be sure but got nothing.

He looked past him to the steering wheel. Chunks of flesh were partially hanging off the plastic, confirming his face had slammed into the wheel at high speed. It looked as though the other car had then struck the station wagon, the equal-and-opposite reaction throwing his unbelted torso into the door.

Mike moved carefully around the vehicle, making sure there were no other passengers. He placed a hand on the hood. *Still slightly warm. Must've been in the last fifteen minutes.* They'd be able to narrow that down later, he knew.

He made his way to the other vehicle. A man and a woman had been thrown through the windshield and lay in a pool of blood ahead of the sedan, the latter just a few feet from the station wagon's driver. She'd gone head over heels, her short red hair pointing back at the sedan.

Mike kneeled and cautiously looked at the other side of her skull. A deep indentation suggested the impact had partially caved it in.

He checked her pulse. Then he rose and walked over to the second man, just ahead of the sedan's front wheels.

Nope. Looks like a bad one tonight.

Goddamn it. What a goddamn waste.

He peered back at the wagon, wondering why the driver hadn't seen the concrete median. *Probably one too many wobbly pops. But you never know.*

He made his way back to the first vehicle. He was two feet away when the man's body slid, the cautious balance across the ajar door giving way, the door swinging wide, the body tumbling head-first to the concrete.

"Jeezum crow!" Mike exclaimed, jumping back at the sudden movement.

The body looked undignified, as if someone had toppled over while kneeling in prayer.

Can't leave him like that, arse up in the air. It wouldn't matter to the accident investigators, he knew. Once the man had fallen from his original position in the car, any link to speed and direction of travel had been broken.

He crouched next to the man and rolled him over. *A senior, maybe seventy, seventy-five.* He avoided eye contact; he'd been a cop too long, seen too many vacant gazes, the spark of life gone. The state of the man's crushed nose and cheekbones didn't help. A jagged piece of glass stuck out of his neck.

That explains the puddle of blood. At least he was already dead, based on the impact. Poor bastard.

He checked the man's inside pocket and found a wallet. It was empty save for eighty dollars in cash and a driver's license.

Huh. Now, I haven't seen one of these before.

The license was ancient, expiring in 1962. "Domas Petrauskas," Mike muttered. *Maybe that's why he crashed; maybe this was the first time he'd tried driving in sixty years.*

But it didn't seem likely. The car had to be later than that despite being old itself, from the 1970s, just based on the size.

He put the license back into the wallet and put it back in the man's pocket. Then he stood up and took a deep, cleansing breath of night air.

You never get used to it.

Mike made his way back to his police cruiser and opened the door. He keyed his mic as he punched the station wagon's license plate into his display terminal.

Matches to an '08 Ford Mustang. Stolen plate. Curious. What the heck is a senior citizen doing with a stolen plate? He keyed the mic set on his epaulette. "Car 3699 to dispatch. Over."

"Dispatch to 3699, go ahead, Mike."

"Yeah, we've got a bad one here, Jeanie... looks like three gone 10-48; vehicles are all stove up. No point wasting the EMTs' time. Just send the ME and let traffic know. I've secured the scene, over."

As if on cue, an ambulance approached, coming up Read Street, sirens blaring. It parked just ahead of the scene.

"Never mind, dispatch," he said. "They're already here. Over."

"Roger, traffic has been alerted. They'll spot you off shortly. Over."

The traffic investigators would spend hours there, cataloguing every shred of glass, taking photos from all angles to allow for later speed modeling.

"10-4. Between you and me, Jeanie, I really have to get to bed earlier. Late night horror shows are a young member's game. Over."

"Surprised you were still out and about. Didn't you book off earlier tonight? Over."

"Yeah, taking some of the boys for a few PBRs, giving them a sober ride home. You know the deal. Over."

"I do indeed. Non-drinkers get all the lousy jobs, Mike. Over."

"I'll look out for the traffic boys. 3699 out."

He got out of the cruiser and headed back towards the scene. The ambulance's emergency lights continued to rotate, red and blue flashing across the red brick wall of the nearby warehouse.

By the time he turned the corner, the two EMTs had already rushed out of their vehicle to check the victims.

Mike looked around. "Evening, boys."

"Middle of the morning, more like."

"Where's the other one?" Mike said. "You moved him already?"

"What other one?" The tech looked at him sideways.

"The one driving the station wagon. He was right there, by the door."

The tech rose slowly from his haunches. "You all right, Sergeant? There was no other body here."

What the hell is he talking about? "But... there's blood, there, by the door."

"And there's two drivers, thrown from their vehicles, lying right between them," the tech said. "What..." He looked around quickly, as if worried someone might watch him being embarrassed. "What am I missing here, exactly?"

Mike looked at the position of the sedan's passenger. She was only about three feet from where the old man's body had fallen, and she was pointed in the same direction as the station wagon. He could see why they'd assumed...

But that doesn't make any sense. "Now, boys... I'm telling you true, there was another body *right here.* I walked over to my cruiser, not twenty yards away on Read, called this in, chatted with dispatch, and when I got back, you two were here and the third victim was gone."

The second EMT was still crouched, a young man with sandy brown hair cropped tight on the sides. "Sarge... I'm telling you, there weren't no other body here, no way."

Mike felt a flush of indecision. He jogged back a few yards and looked up and down Read Street, but there was no one else in sight. He jogged over to the tape and lifted it, climbing under, then looked down Quarry Road.

No one.

"Look, it's probably been a long night..." the first tech said. "You... had anything to drink tonight, Sarge?"

"I *know* what I saw, boys," Mike insisted. "I checked the man's ID."

A second cruiser approached, coming their way down Quarry.

Traffic. They'd get to the bottom of it, Mike figured. He was a thirty-year veteran, decorated multiple times.

They'd see the sense in what he was saying.

3

"But I'm guessing they didn't," Bob said.

"Yes and no." Mike got up and walked over to the window and looked down at the street, pensive. "Traffic techs figured out there was a third person present as soon as they realized the female vic was from the other car. Blood from the steering column couldn't produce a DNA databank match."

"So… he just vanished?"

Mike nodded curtly again. "The fact that someone took the body of the station wagon driver somehow, with me right there…"

"They blame you."

"The department knows about my history, about me beating the bottle. Or… dodging it for a while, I suppose. The higher-ups think I let a drunk driver walk away, that he wasn't really dead."

"So where did the puddle of blood come from? Nobody bleeding like that usually wanders away. There'd be a trail a mile wide."

"That's what the traffic guys said. But I've got a few higher-ups who don't like me much, truth be told."

"You probably figured they'd see the light if you could figure out what happened?" Bob suggested.

"I made a lot of noise, had traffic hunting for a 'Domas Petrauskas.' Turns out there's no sign he exists. No address, no social security number, no license since records went digital in the eighties. Ticket database only goes back to '97, but there was nothing there either. Worse, we checked with the feds, and there was no social security number assigned either, not back for decades, not even in '62."

"Cameras?"

"Only one, above the front doors to a storage depot on the corner, and cut off by the angle of the building."

"Ouch. That didn't help, I imagine."

"Nope. The internal politics aren't good, either."

"You mentioned the higher-ups."

"One of my superiors was embarrassed a few years ago when I pulled over his drunk-driving brother, and I think he saw a chance to stick the knife in. He told me he was going to see me disciplined for gross negligence. So now I'm suspended, with pay, until my hearing in two weeks."

"That's..." Bob just shook his head. "If I'm being straight with you, Mike, that's the craziest story I've come across in a while."

Mike turned sharply, angered. "Is that supposed to be reassuring!? I mean... what are you saying, Bob? That you don't believe me either?"

Bob kept his tone gentle. "You didn't start drinking again until after this all happened, I'd guess?"

"Yeah... Sorry, bub, it's the pressure, you know?"

"I do."

"When Erin said she was going to her mother's, about ten days ago, I just sort of lost it. I'd been ranting about the unfairness of it all and maybe got a little too hot. She said something, trying to sound casual about me not slipping, and I just screamed at her, Bob. Lord jumping, I just lost my temper. I was downright harsh, a child."

"She storms out..."

"And I figure, in the moment, no one's with me nohow. No one's got my back. I've got a bottle of Allen's we were given for Christmas from her cousin, who doesn't know about my drinking..."

"You kept it?"

He lowered his head, blushing and ashamed. "They dropped it off at the station and... you know?"

"That little voice said 'just in case. Just hide it in case you need it.'"

A firmer nod. "At least you understand, stupid as it was."

"That I do. Used to hide mickeys around the apartment so my fiancée, Maggie, wouldn't toss them, right before she passed, around the time she was imploring me to get help."

Mike's eyebrows rose. "I assumed when you said she died in a car accident..." He let the unseemly thought tail off.

Bob shook his head. "A lot of people thought that because of my bad habits. No. Maggie drank, but not to excess, not really. And she wasn't drunk that night, just angry at me, not paying attention because I'd been such an ass, and because she didn't pay attention when she drove angry. I should've stopped her from going, apologized. Instead, I was an arrogant dick, and she took off. Pulled away too quick from a stop sign, is all."

Mike crossed his arms and gazed out into the early morning sun, then sighed audibly. "Jesus Christ, but if you don't mind me saying, that's a fucking sad statement. Quite the pair, aren't we, bub? Paragons of virtue, you serving the country, me fighting crime... both of us fucking up everyone we get close to."

"Not everyone," Bob said. "Helped a few people in the last couple of years. You too, as a cop, on the regular, despite the rep you get."

"But that's my duty. My job. In my own life..."

"In your own life, you took me to group, got me sober. That wasn't on duty. Stopping the fight maybe..."

"Technically not," Mike said. "Shift was over. I was walking to group when I caught a glimpse down the alley. Instinct, is all."

"Instinct to do right by someone, to help someone. Instinct to take your own time sobering me up, then spend three months mentoring me back to some sense of self-worth. Stop beating yourself up. You did the right thing all along the line until the yelling and the drinking. And that stuff can be fixed."

"But it hasn't happened yet. Traffic's already buried in caseload and is confused by the scene anyhow, figuring there was too much blood and tissue for the injuries to be minor. Hospitals didn't turn up any mystery injury cases. The chance of them even making headway by the time my hearing comes around... well, it doesn't look good."

Bob felt a sudden, strange surge of energy. He'd been listening to people tell him the same thing – that trying and failing beat the hell out of not trying at all – for two years. It was always tempered, however, by that alcoholic's self-doubt, all the time, that impostor syndrome that said he was just fooling himself.

But using the same rules for Mike seemed to make it clear.

It made a lot of things clearer.

"I've been wallowing in my own bullshit for months, ever since the closest I have to family told me to fuck off," Bob said. "Without you, it might've taken me down. But that ends today. I owe you, Mike, but more than that, it's just the right thing to do. We're going to figure this thing out, and we're going to get you your job back and maybe some peace of mind for whoever that old man left behind, before he vanished."

Mike was bobbing his head gently in agreement, but his expression was bereft of hope. "Okay... although you're going to have to forgive me for being skeptical."

Bob rose to his feet. "I might surprise you," he said. "All that military training you found so interesting a few months back, when I needed an ear, and you were lending one. Now, I'm going to cook us some eggs and bacon. Then you're going to start repairing your marriage by calling Erin, by apologizing and promising it won't happen again."

"And you'll what... change the captain's already made-up mind?"

"Possibly. But first, I'm going to find your dead man."

ACROSS THE ROAD from the apartment block, in an otherwise empty laundromat, a man sat at a table by the broad rectangular window, partially obscured by its film of dust and dirt, partly by the giant painted letters offering full same-day service.

He'd gotten good images of both men with a 300mm zoom. The policeman they already knew; that was why he was there in the first place, with the sergeant refusing to let the issue drop. The embassy had provided documents showing Schultz was facing disciplinary proceedings, yet still wouldn't budge from his claim.

That made keeping tabs on him essential, he'd been told. Shoot close-ups of where he goes, whom he meets.

The second man was an unknown, not making an appearance in the two weeks since the accident. The photographer had gotten a good side profile as they'd left the bar, as he'd held open the building door and helped his drunken friend in the night prior, then another of each man through the apartment window.

Now, the younger of the two, the tall friend, was taking a hire car somewhere. He held down the SLR camera's shutter button, the power-winder whirring as it fired off six frames in rapid succession.

He waited until the hire car pulled away, then set the camera down on the faux-wood table by the window. He opened the laptop that sat just beyond it and plugged the camera into it using a USB cable. A few moments later, he was sending the photographs to his handler.

That should keep them happy. They'd told him to stay with Schultz, and he couldn't do that and follow the hire car. Perhaps once they knew whom Schultz had been talking to, his instructions would change.

The photographer hoped not. Like most of his colleagues in the region, he was usually inactive, just living his life like any Portland resident, coaching Little League and teaching history. It had all come about suddenly, the need for his time and involvement, and he didn't much like it.

He checked his email.

A confirmation tick said the message had been received.

He closed the laptop and retrained the long lens on the apartment window.

WASHINGTON, DC
2650 Wisconsin Avenue

Colonel Igor Yaremchuk sat at his desk near the centre of the Russian embassy's upper floor and stared at the high-res image of the man in Portland, Maine, his mouth slightly agape.

Yaremchuk's official title was "chief cultural attaché to the Russian Diplomatic Mission." In fact, he'd been an officer with the Sluzhba vneshney razvedki Rossiyskoy Federatsii – the Foreign Intelligence Service that replaced the KGB – for three decades.

In his time with the FIS, he had seen feuds with the Americans come and go, agents swapped, others deported from either country. But there had been only a handful of operatives considered so dangerous or injurious to Russia that they were supposed to be eliminated, if possible, on sight – what the British and Americans termed an "expedient demise."

One, the man in the photo, had murdered the son of a powerful oligarch, had wiped out multiple Russian mercenaries in Iraq, had killed their agents in Africa and South America.

Robert Singleton.

It seemed surreal, and a moment of panic set in briefly as he considered their options. Should they try to do as told by Moscow and eliminate him at the first opportunity? That would leave open the question of what such a dangerous man – a man they'd thought long dead before his appearance a year earlier in Memphis – was doing in a small city in Maine.

And it couldn't be a coincidence, he knew. A decorated CIA agent was not in Portland on vacation, not when he was talking to the policeman who'd already interfered.

They had decades invested in the community, years spent gathering intel along the Eastern Seaboard and from the Bush family estate at Kennebunkport, just forty minutes south, the retreat of one of the nation's most powerful political families.

Soon, they would pull one of the best undercover operatives ever to walk on US soil. They were just a week away, only requiring a name be officially added to their diplomatic list approved by the US State Department. The operative, code-named Uncle, would assume the identity of a real Russian, the paperwork immaculate.

Protected by diplomatic immunity, Uncle would be taken to Boston, put on a plane and be back in Moscow hours later.

If Singleton exposed or captured Uncle – a service legend – he stood to gain intelligence on dozens of assignments, on undercover agents and sleepers across the US and Canada.

And Singleton had a huge price on his head after killing the son of former KGB deputy director Ivan Malyuchenko, a powerful oligarch.

But eliminating him would set off alarm bells in Washington. Where there was one, more would come. They needed to know what he'd learned first, what his handlers knew in sending him there.

He picked up his desk phone and hit the extension line for encrypted calls, then speed-dialled 76.

It was answered on the second ring. “Yes?” The sound was mechanical, filtered through alteration software that disguised the speaker’s voice.

“We have a situation,” Yaremchuk said. “There’s a new player... Robert Singleton, a friend of the policeman, Schultz. He’s known to us, a significant fly in the ointment. Put someone on him, get back to me when you know what he’s doing. I will arrange intervention. We don’t want this to get messy, but that may be unavoidable at this juncture. We shall ensure there are close family relatives ready.”

4

PORTLAND, MAINE

The Lincoln sat parked in front of the downtown public library branch, on Elm Street. The second-hand car was twenty years old and nothing pretty but was mechanically sound.

Bob had avoided getting a car for months. He'd been spotted twice already by the National Security Agency using its access to public cameras, while driving in Arizona and New Orleans.

But working on Mike's case was going to mean getting around town quickly; the dealer's reassurance that traffic cameras were banned in Maine had helped make his mind up.

Inside the library, Bob sat at the research desk and pored through old phone books. He took them to the desk from the reference section three at a time, returning each pile less than five minutes later.

He'd found what he was looking for almost immediately, a mention in the 1961 phone book of a "D. Petrauskas," with an address in Bangor, a small city nearer the Canadian border. But none of the ensuing three decades had offered a second, more recent listing.

He slapped the cover closed on the 1999 white pages. With records going digital after the turn of the century, there wasn't much point in continuing. A search at the reference desk for any other "D. Petrauskas" mentions turned up nothing.

No wonder they came up blank. If D. Petrauskas existed in Portland, the sole indicator was the 1962 license. *But he was in Bangor in 1961.*

HE WAS HALFWAY BACK to the car when his phone rang. Bob checked the sidewalk traffic, then stood near the library wall to prevent blocking pedestrians.

"Hi," he answered, recognizing the number immediately.

"Hi," Dawn said.

"It's been a while."

"I had a lot to think about," she said. "You're okay?"

"Fine." There was nothing positive about sharing his fall from grace, he decided. At best, she'd feel guilty and, at worst, doubt him further.

And it was good to hear her voice. It was the first time since fleeing Chicago that he'd gone more than a month without talking to her. She'd found out about California; he'd lied about killing Geert Van Kamp. There was nothing to be gained by intruding on her deliberate silence.

"You?"

She was silent for a moment. "This feels awkward, all of a sudden. I've made it awkward."

"No, I made it awkward by lying to you in the first place," he said. "I should've just told you the truth. Because how I handle a guy trying to kill me – and by extension you and Marcus – is up to me, not you."

She paused for a long beat. "That's... unlike you. Normally, you'd be racked with guilt over what the other person wants—"

"I'm back in group. Even saw a therapist a few times. He thinks my deference to the feelings and concerns of others is something I use to handle the guilt of avoiding responsibility, by forcing that guilt onto others."

"He might be right," she said. "My friend Justine is late all the time. Her therapist says it's actually a way to maintain a sense of control over others' time."

"I just thought I was being nice. But if that's what the experts say..."

"Bob... you know how much we care for you."

"I do. Found family are still family. That's another one of his."

"Fine. I was worried from how harsh I was that you might do something risky, like drinking again or taking on someone's troubles."

"Nope," he said, shame preventing the truth yet again. He cursed inwardly. *Just be honest, Bobby, you fucking coward.* "I mean... I had a little slip."

"Oh! You mean..."

"Yeah. Went on a bender. Got some help, got back on the wagon. Now it's all good. I am helping someone out, though, working on stuff you wouldn't much like."

"Uh-huh." She managed to make a murmured, neutral response sound skeptical.

"Relax. As far as I can tell, it's not dangerous. More or less weird than anything else. My group sponsor is a local cop. He claims he lost track of a body at an accident scene and has been suspended."

"A body? How does someone 'lose' a body?"

"Good question."

"Isn't that... you know... looking for trouble and all? He's a police officer; you're on the run."

"I'm okay with it. He needs help, and I owe him. Plus, I'm Bob Bennett to him, a laborer."

"You think you owe everyone..."

"No... but I definitely owe him."

"Do you want to talk about our fight? Maybe we should—"

"Not really," he interrupted. "I had to sort of put it out of mind, or it would've eaten at me constantly. I just figured... I just figured maybe you wouldn't call anymore."

She took another moment to compose herself. "I... worry about you. I worry you'll forget how much progress you've made since Chicago, getting along with others, working normal jobs. Normal work. A normal life. You'll start blaming yourself for orders you followed, decisions in the past that were never yours to make."

"Fixing roofs these days," Bob said. "No worries there. The only damage I'm doing is to my aging knees, and the only thing getting hammered are shingles."

"No more 'it was him or us,' then, I guess?"

Bob figured he had to stick to his guns, keep it honest. "There was one, in New York, before heading up here. You don't want the details."

"Unavoidable?"

"No. Preventative. A psychopath claiming they had no problem killing whoever got in their way, someone who'd already shot and injured an old friend, almost ended his life."

"I... don't know what to think about that. I don't know enough..."

"Nor will you," Bob said. "It's not your business."

He said it gently, but it didn't matter. "That's... I mean, I'm trying to apologize for how I acted," Dawn said. "But you're shutting me out."

"No, I'm not. I promise I'm not. But you shouldn't have to live your life through the filter of worrying about a middle-aged man," Bob said. "I will always love you like family, unconditionally. I hope you feel the same. But the mistake I've made is leaning on you to keep me sane, inserting my problems, my moral challenges, into your world."

"I've always been happy to—"

"I know. But that's part of the problem. You care about me, but to your own detriment sometimes. And I'm tired of being the guy who causes that."

She inhaled sharply. "What does that mean for us?"

"From now on, unless it involves the two of you, I'll be keeping the harsh details to myself. There's other stuff we can talk about."

"Okay," she said. "It doesn't feel right, though. You saved me—"

"From a situation I put you in to begin with. You owe me nothing. I'll just... be happier if you're happy. Okay?"

"Okay. And this new thing..."

He chuckled. "Even with me telling you I'm going to hide the worst details, you still want to help?"

"Well... it's like you said: found family is still family. And we love you, Bob."

After talking to Dawn, Bob drove the Lincoln north, following I-95 as it snaked north out of Portland, past miles of dark green pine trees, through the smaller capital, Augusta, past working-class small towns like Pittsfield, the tonier lakeshore village of Newport, and into Bangor.

He felt better for the conversation. He knew he'd become accustomed to not crying on her shoulder, and keeping the nastier details of his life from her was the easiest way for both to get what they wanted. She could rest assured she'd done the right thing. He could still do what had to be done.

It took a little over two hours, the pint-sized city picturesque and low-rise, like a smaller Portland. Its downtown consisted of just a few blocks but looked busy. Multilevel apartment and office blocks – none much higher than six or seven stories – quickly gave way to family homes and bungalows in neat rows.

The address in the old phone book had included a unit number, meaning he was looking for an apartment building. Instead, the location on State Street was occupied by a newer-build A-frame house, home to a sleep clinic.

Bob parked at a coffee place across Fern Street. The front door jingled as he pushed it open.

"Hello!" the woman behind the counter greeted. "What can we get for you today?"

"Just a question," Bob said. "I haven't been in town for years. Didn't there used to be an apartment building here—"

The woman appeared bemused. "Been gone for years!

Torn down – oh, I'd say must have been twenty-five years ago."

"Ah. Okay. Shame."

"But... the coffee's still great! Can I interest you in an Americano? Just got the new beans..."

"Thanks, I'm good." Then he felt guilty for wasting her time. "I'll get a green tea, I guess."

He headed back outside with the paper cup.

Well, that was a bust.

But something didn't quite fit, Bob figured.

They didn't have "unlisted" numbers until 1971. So why did D. Petrauskas have a 1961 address, but none the next year? If he'd moved out of state, he wouldn't have had a Maine license. *And if he moved in state, that license wouldn't be in a dead man's pocket in Portland.*

He drove back to Portland, stopping for gas and wincing when the pump turned over fifty dollars.

He was back at the library reference desk twenty minutes after getting back, a clerk helping him pull newspaper "fiche" – rolls of old editions stored on film strips that could be read on-site with special projectors. With no ability to "search" the papers using keywords, like a modern website, it would mean going page by page.

Bob limited it to a ten-year stretch, from 1960 to 1970.

The theory was sound. They'd learned in CIA training that the most common way for an undercover operative back then to build a realistic background was to "tombstone" an identity. The term referred to fraudsters taking the birth and death dates off new tombstones and then using that information to get a person's real birth certificate in another jurisdiction before the individual's death was registered there.

Once they had a genuine birth certificate, real government documents in that name were easy to obtain. Initially, they'd done it with infant deaths, as the person wouldn't be remembered. But as time had passed and officials had become more wary of tracking those death certificates, they'd moved on to other recently deceased.

Modern technology and awareness had made it much harder to accomplish. But in the sixties, deaths weren't even always registered, depending on the individual and family, and certainly weren't shared with other US states or Canadian provinces unless requested.

Given that the elderly man using "D. Petrauskas" had died in Portland and a man with a similar name had once lived in a nearby city, Bob figured it was possible the death was never noted.

He'd gone through the entire decade of obituary listings with no sign of an initial death notice. He traced his finger through the last column of tiny newspaper type, with no sign. *Without that, there's no evidence Petrauskas ever—*

A thought occurred. Petrauskas was a European name, maybe Latvian or Lithuanian based on its old Latin sound. *Maybe his church was foreign, orthodox. Maybe they handled their listings differently.*

He went back to the first year, 1960, this time zooming out to full-page size on the elongated reader screen so that he could look at the half-pyramids of display advertising that surrounded the columns of type. By the third week of January in, he'd found something similar to what he was looking for, a regular display ad that went in every so often, with "In Memoriam" in English and Cyrillic.

It seemed to be a Russian Orthodox church, in the city's west end. A handful of names in Cyrillic script were under a short note mourning their loss. There were others, too, one for a local synagogue, another for a Dutch Reform Church.

None contained his target.

It took another fifteen minutes to get through papers from 1961. Bob was about to give up when he saw the small display ad in the lower right corner of a page. "St. Anthony's Eastern Orthodox Church, Bangor" listed five names, each followed by a date and time for their service. The last jumped out at him.

"Domas Petrauskas, 18. Suddenly, on the 21st of October. Domas leaves behind family in Lithuania and will be missed."

That's it? It wasn't much, but it was something. He flipped the pages back a few weeks until he found the related news story:

City youth dies
in head-on crash

A Bangor resident is dead after a head-on collision last night between a car and a semitruck.

Police said the young man, 18, had been working late, and his vehicle crossed the center line shortly after midnight, giving the truck driver no chance to avoid the crash.

The truck's driver was taken to Eastern Maine Medical Center in serious but not life-threatening condition.

Police said the young man was a recent immigrant and had been in America for less than two years, working as a manual laborer.

He is survived by family in Lithuania.

It matched the age, the sudden nature and the orthodox church notice.

Bob returned the fiche to the reference desk and headed outside. He needed Mike Schultz to make a call, find out whom the station wagon had been stolen from. Maybe there was something there to connect the two.

5

CASPER, WYOMING

Nikolai Ivanovich Grusin followed the line of the tall hedgerow, ensconced in its shadow. The sun had just gone down, the nearest light source on the main building of the training facility forty yards away. Its ten-acre rear gardens were divided, segmented off by a maze of hedges, trees, low-slung brick walls and small earthen hummocks.

He knew he had to be quiet, and he kept half an eye on the downtrodden path ahead. Even stepping on a small twig would be sufficient to identify his location in the extreme still of the evening.

He heard a rustling of leaves, saw the branches trembling gently about ten feet ahead, where there was a gap in the hedge. *Careless fool. Less than two hours in the field and he ignores his surroundings, how they can betray him.*

He slowed his pace, creeping towards it.

The figure wheeled around the corner, a double-barreled shotgun in both hands.

Before he could even make out who it was, Nikolai was

diving sideways on instinct as both barrels roared, spraying the very edge of the hedge behind him with red paint.

He rolled over sideways twice and came up on his knee, his suppressed Sig Sauer pistol drawn. He fired twice, slugs from the modified gun striking his attacker in the forehead, green paint covering the spot.

The man lowered the shotgun and dabbed at his forehead with his free hand. "Ti shutish, shto li?" he muttered. *Are you kidding me?*

"Speak English," Nikolai demanded. "Always remember that whether it is stressed in the assignment or not, your last resort is to operate in public."

The man shrugged. "Da, da... I mean, yeah, yeah, of course."

At least his accent was getting better.

Nikolai had been an asset of the Russian Foreign Intelligence Service for more than twenty years.

The occasional training sessions, at a rental facility acquired through front companies, were among his few tasks during a typical year, keeping unofficial agents-in-place sharp.

Most were officially cultural attachés of the embassy in DC or another urban consulate. The titles were unimportant except as a conduit to being assigned diplomatic immunity, protecting them from arrest and detention without the permission of their embassy.

In most cases, anyway.

Nikolai, whose cultural knowledge was limited to violent pornography and videos of people dying online, was offered no such protection. He and his team operated under aliases, anonymously. If something went wrong, they had no protection and would be fully deniable.

"Where is your partner?" he asked the trainee.

The man shrugged.

"Good. Don't offer anyone any help."

Nikolai wondered how seriously they took him, given his disgrace. Surely they knew. The botched mission that had cost him his rising career at the FIS, and his Moscow office was infamous in the service.

Officially, training was all he did. Once or twice a year, on a timetable never explained to him, he carried out remote training, trying to hone and maintain the skill sets of fighting men who rarely got a chance to use them.

But he had other tasks. When his government needed someone in the United States to die – an exceedingly risky endeavor and therefore rare – they contacted Nikolai.

Occasionally, on a difficult job involving high security, other disgraced former FIS acted as his backup and support, seconded from menial jobs as drivers or bodyguards at the embassy or consulates.

They were mercs, ex-spooks, former soldiers. Like any spy, their assignments would be infrequent. Unlike sleepers and deep-cover operatives, they knew their work would be dangerous, with the risk of arrest or death and no legacy to honor them back home.

No diplomatic immunity or even an acknowledgment that they served their country. It was the only offer, the only chance they'd be given to prove they deserved to return to the fold one day.

"Just remember," he told the trainee, spotlights near the main building casting long shadows across the training ground, "if you're not paying attention one hundred—" Before he could finish the sentence, a wire loop arced over his head.

Nikolai's hand shot up to the gap between it and his neck, the thick garrote defeated by his leather glove.

Decoy, stupid, flashed through his mind. He wrapped his trapped hand around the wire and threw his right shoulder forward, forcing the man to either hold on or let go. His attacker chose the former, and Nikolai jutted out his right leg slightly, unbalancing his opponent, using it to hip toss the man to the ground.

Before he could react, Nikolai raised the pistol and shot him four times, center mass, the green paint splattering across a bulletproof vest.

"And remember," he said, the second man defeated, "to act without hesitation. Had he closed that garrote instantly or used it as I was rising from my knee, he might have taken me."

The two men looked despondent. "Almost," the one by the hedge said.

"Almost is usually fatal," Nikolai said. He nodded back toward the main building. "Go, clean up. We debrief in thirty."

There had been four men hunting him for the last two hours of the last training day. It had taken him forty minutes to eliminate all of them using the fullness of the compound's natural cover.

His phone rang. He answered it on his earpiece. "Yes?"

"It's me. We need you."

"You understand what you have to do?"

The voice was electronically altered and encrypted. Chris Jefferson had hoped he would never hear its mechanical drone again.

But that ship had sailed. "I understand," he said.

"Remember, keeping your distance is essential, as it was yesterday. We'll have further instructions for you before redeployment."

The line went dead.

Jefferson hung up the phone in his home office. He slowly wiped a hand across his bald scalp, the skin damp from sweat.

Redeployment!?

His heart was pounding. His breath felt shallower. He hadn't felt so nervous in years, such abject panic.

Remember your training.

Slow breaths in through the nose, out through the mouth.

He counted to ten, then repeated the process once more.

"WHO WAS THAT, HON?" his wife, Carly, called from downstairs.

"NOTHING! WORK," he yelled back.

That would require a better explanation when he went down to the kitchen, he realized. The school rarely bothered him on Fridays because the team nearly always had a practice or game, and the Portland Privateers had been State Little League runners-up two years running.

Everyone knew Coach Chris was a winner. There had even been approaches from Single- and Double-A ball.

It had never occurred to him when they'd embedded his family four decades earlier – because he'd only been seven years old – that a prized spy ring in the Soviet espionage firmament would eventually simply become redundant.

Their fate had been sealed by the exit of the Bush family from national politics and the declining popularity of the fishing and hunting lodges that once drew so many monied Americans to Maine.

Their legendary handler, Uncle, had called it "casual access," placing everyday Americans, true sleepers with no other intelligence or diplomatic ties, in the proximity of important people who talked too much.

Jefferson had known nothing but being American. But he'd been born Roman Ratachkov, raised in an experimental training town called "New Haven" near Severnoye, on the Chinese border. From the McDonald's drive-in to the anything-you-need drugstore and two-bedroom, fifties-style bungalows, everything had been modeled after the America of 1985.

It almost seemed dreamlike, a life he'd almost forgotten, as if it had never happened at all. And now, a day after his sudden activation, with the prospect of everything changing in the length of a phone call, he'd come to realize how much the life that he'd built since meant to him.

I have a family, I have a career, kids who depend on me, school parents who believe in me. Why? Why now, for God's sake?

Now? Now he was American.

His father had been operational, spending summers working as a handyman and general helper at the Bush family compound in Kennebunkport.

Conversely, until running surveillance on the cop a day earlier, Chris had done just one task for their paymasters in forty-seven years, more than twenty years earlier. He'd dropped off an envelope containing rolls of film on his father's behalf, his mother out of town on her regular trips to the state capital, Augusta, where she worked on a state senator's team.

They'd used a "dead drop" – a marked public location where people could pass information anonymously – to exchange the envelope. Despite his father's instructions, the young gym teacher had waited in the adjacent Payson Park and watched from a distance to see who picked it up, hoping the get a glimpse of "Uncle," the legendary KGB handler.

Instead, a woman in her late teens or early twenties had done so. In retrospect, it had made sense; Uncle hadn't gone undetected for over a half-century by being reckless, and had sent someone else.

His parents had died a decade earlier. His own call had never come.

Until now.

"HON? ARE YOU COMING DOWN?"

"YEAH! JUST A SECOND!" he yelled back, trying to sound polite about it. "JUST... I'M JUST GOING THROUGH EMAILS!"

What would he tell her? How would explain a sudden move, a sudden job change? How did they intend on repurposing him, a forty-seven-year-old man who had been teaching gym and coaching ball for two-plus decades? If they had to move him, he'd always figured it would be to a city, because a pro ball coach was more of an advantage than a high school coach in Portland, Maine.

And how did it relate to the man he'd been asked to watch?

He turned on his computer and double-clicked a desktop icon labelled "Baseball Manager 2009." It immediately rebooted the computer using software set up by his father not long before his death, switching to a secondary hard drive that used eighteen-bit encryption.

He placed his finger on the first button of the adjacent mouse, and it read his fingerprint, preventing the drive from wiping itself and the computer's modified BIOS from suddenly ramping up the voltage and blowing the motherboard, processor and power source.

The desktop image on the monitor was blank save for a single folder. He double-clicked it, and a PDF-style document opened. It was labelled "Private." He knew standard operating procedure was to memorize the contents. When he turned off the machine, it would automatically destroy any trace of the file.

He flipped to the second page. It was a full-page black-and-white photo, high resolution, of a man leaving a diner.

Robert "Bob" James Singleton, forty-four years old, six three, operational weight estimate eighty-eight kilos, ambidextrous.

Jefferson's mouth gaped slightly in surprise as he read the man's history and why he was a target. The list went on for several inches. But despite Foreign Intelligence's obvious desire to see Singleton dead, Jefferson's instructions from Uncle were clear, to keep his distance but maintain surveillance. A team would arrive in town within hours to assist.

After the mission, Uncle had said, they would repurpose him to a new community where he could be more useful, part of a general wind-up in Maine.

Jefferson felt a hollow sensation in his stomach, butterflies kicking in. There had to be a way out, a way to safely defy them and preserve what he had, to protect his family and be rid of the burdens of his past.

But he couldn't see what it was.

And he knew what they expected for his FIS pay. It was

less than four thousand dollars a month but a healthy supplement to his meagre teacher's salary.

Any failure to comply or attempt to run would result in the cleanup team dealing with him, as well.

Or maybe Carly.

He took a few more deep breaths to compose himself and went downstairs. She was in the kitchen, putting away the last of the dishes. "What was that about?" she asked.

"Just work stuff."

"Work work, or baseball work?"

"I'll let you guess."

She sighed and leaned back against the counter, crossing her arms. "You let the league push you around, sweetie, because everyone's busy praising Coach Chris and showing him the love. They could bug you earlier in the week, not on Friday."

He held up both hands in a resigned wave of surrender. "Eh... last-minute details. But... I told them it didn't matter. I have to deal with a Tony issue, so Jim will handle the team tonight."

"Tony" was his fictional best friend from high school, years before Carly relocated to Portland from Vermont. He had a meticulous backstory... and a cabin in the woods, miles out of town, where occasionally Jefferson dropped by to minister to the poor, wretched alcoholic.

It was the kind of last-minute, drop-everything problem that would make a good cover if sudden absences were needed. His name came up no more than once a year, to maintain the fiction, because Tony had never really been needed.

She rolled her eyes. "Jeezum crow, hon, that fella's had the radish. Are you ever going to be done helping him?"

He shrugged. "He's like family. Now, it's no big thing, a few days of sitting in his dooryard, sipping lemonade on the porch once I get him off the liquor, and hearing someone gives a darn, that he hasn't been forgotten by the world."

She took a few steps and hugged him. "You're a good man, Christopher Jefferson." Then she gave him a peck on the forehead. "I'll go cheer them on for you tonight, okay?"

He watched her walk to the back door and out into the sun. He loved her so much that he could become lost in the idea of it, breathless as a statue in her presence, as if the slightest kiss of air from her lungs could bring him back to life.

All he wanted was to be good for her.

But he didn't feel like a good man.

He never really had.

6

Bob sat in the dented black Lincoln, parked at the curb, and watched the house from across the road and slightly down the street.

Mike had gotten an address on the stolen station wagon, just in case. He'd also told Bob to watch his language because it was in a pricey part of town.

Munjoy Hill was a historical neighborhood of century-old, two-story A-frame houses, with minimal front yards, most little more than a front flowerbed. But within a few blocks were parks, beaches, docks and the Atlantic.

It was the kind of place that had been a cheap dump once, then became quaint and artistic, before finally being gentrified, attracting politicians and the kind of idly privileged who never quite seemed employed, folks who described themselves as "artists" without requiring the income from actually selling anything artistic.

The A-frame in question was a deep navy blue with white trim. Its listed residents for at least three decades had been Tom and Rose Peters. He'd run both their names and come up with an obituary from July for the latter. Apparently, she'd had a heart attack in her sleep at seventy-eight.

That hadn't sounded too bad to Bob. He had no fear of death, not anymore. Just hope that there was something more after it. Going in his sleep, he figured, would be a mercy.

He'd swung by the house, intent on making up a plausible premise and door-knocking them as a utility official. Finding the obituary at the last second, and a reference to Rose volunteering at a nearby seniors' center, had changed the approach to one a little softer, just a friend from the center stopping by to wish Tom his condolences.

Instead, he watched as a twenty-something woman with short brown hair climbed the front steps and checked the mailbox by the door.

He thought about crossing the street and engaging her, seeing if she knew them well enough to let something slip.

Daughter?

Granddaughter, more likely.

He watched her straighten up, seeing the slight bulge at the back of her waistband. *Hmm. She's carrying.* Despite the nation having so many open-carry laws, he rarely ran into young women with pistols in their belts.

It made the connection doubly interesting. *Police, maybe.*

Perhaps we'll just keep tabs on Ms. Curious here until we know what's she's up to, he thought. He reached down and retrieved the Styrofoam cup of green tea from the holder under the radio. He had no more roofing work lined up for another ten days, and that meant plenty of time to spare.

7

Rachel McGee took a handful of coupon flyers out of the mailbox and unlocked the front door.

Then she paused and turned suddenly, looking around. She'd had that slight chill on the nape of her neck, like someone was watching.

But the street was deserted.

Maybe it was just the worry setting in again, the black void that had visited her daily since her grandmother's heart attack a month earlier.

Or maybe you're just looking for a fight. For a reason to lose your temper.

It was hard to believe Grammy Rose was gone, still. Her grandmother on her mother's side, Grammy Rose had been there for her when Rachel's father had abandoned them nearly twenty years earlier.

She'd been just seven years old, plunged into sudden doubt. The emptiness, the void from his lost presence, had been crushing.

It had all been made a little easier by Grammy Rose's

kindness. She'd stayed with the older couple for nearly a year while her mother regained her sanity and reversed the effect drinking had had on her business, a tiny community health clinic on Peaks Island.

Each day with Grammy Rose had had a sort of magic; she'd told her granddaughter stories about fairies in her abundant wildflower garden behind the house. She'd known Rachel was a tomboy and regaled her with exciting battles by famous pirates right there, off the coast of Maine. They'd watched *The Princess Bride* together and picked berries that Grammy Rose made into pies, and watched the sunset down the block, where the road seemed to run directly into the inky water of Portland Harbor.

She hadn't seen either of them in two years, not since moving to Baltimore. But she missed Grammy Rose no less for the distance. If anything, distance had driven home the fact that she was gone that much more bluntly.

Gramps had been different. He was a quiet, studious man. But he could erupt fiercely if his concentration was disturbed while reading. He helped Grammy Rose tend her garden with a loving, gentle touch and respect for the flowers. But if his dinner was not exactly to his liking, he could be harsh to her, making sarcastic remarks about her ability in the kitchen after so many years together.

He was tall and sturdy, a retired dockworker at the harbor who'd found a second career as a travelling salesman. He took plenty of trips, but he always returned, reliable as the tides.

Until two weeks earlier, when he'd vanished.

She glanced each way down the street again, then turned back to the house and let herself in, letting the door swing loudly closed behind her.

The house seemed surreally quiet.

She feared Gramps was dead.

How and why was another question. Their old Pontiac, a powder-blue-and-faux-wood car about the size of a speedboat, had been involved in a fatal accident. Rachel had been lucky enough to spot it on the evening news.

Despite insistence that almost got her arrested, police had been unwilling to share information with "anyone other than next of kin." Her mother had apparently already been contacted about reclaiming the car and assured her father was not one of those at the scene and had reported the car stolen the day before the accident.

And that, incredibly, was that. Police said they'd consider a missing persons report and file it if her mother, the legal next of kin, filed it. And her mother, Liz, who had been effectively estranged from Gramps for more than twenty years, had no intention of doing so.

"He's on the road somewhere, trying to flog whatever cheap Chinese junk he's decided to import this time," she'd said. "He doesn't care that your grandmother is dead, and he doesn't care about us. So don't get your hopes up."

And despite Rachel ranting until her ferry left Peaks Island two hours later, she hadn't changed her mind. "He's a selfish man," Liz had said, a glass of neat whiskey in hand. "He left town to make money, he left the garage unlocked, and some unfortunate joyrider stole the Pontiac. Then they died. That's it, that's all," she'd insisted.

Rachel was still angry, still frustrated at Liz's dismissive attitude. It had been building, her sense of futility and her resentment. Nobody seemed to give a damn that a man who'd lived in Portland for sixty years was missing.

Rachel flexed both hands into tight fists, trying to ward

off her tension. Then she wrinkled her nose. Gramps's house always smelled slightly of rug cleaner. They'd kept dogs for most of their lives, and the place always had a pet odor, so Rose had tried to cover it up, the chemical scent of fake flowers growing to a critical mass.

In recent years, Grammy Rose's infirmity and Gramps being on the road had prevented them adopting new furry friends. She frowned at the thought. It must've hurt the older woman; she'd always had a special place for pets.

The front hall opened into the living room to her right.

She checked the telephone table by the door, to see if the old-fashioned answering machine had any messages. It flashed "0."

Rachel knew the heart attack hadn't been Gramps's fault, but somehow, she still wanted to blame him, wanted to hear him admit how he hadn't been worthy of Rose for all those years.

Instead, it was like he'd ceased to exist. Suddenly, she'd been hit by a strange yearning to find someone she'd resented on some level for years. It was confusing.

The fridge was stocked, the piling-up mail suggesting any departure was sudden or supposed to be short. He'd seemed strong and determined the last time they'd talked, a month earlier.

She crossed the living room to the bookshelf and looked around. Her mother had already collected Rose's jewelry, photos and clothes. The rest, she knew, would be left here for whoever bought the place.

On the lowest bookshelf, a dark gray, square cardboard box jutted over the edge. She opened the lid. *Bills, it appears. Maybe some other legal papers.* She flicked through a few. A water meter reading and reminder of rate changes in

January; a receipt from a dentist for a new bridge for Gramps from earlier that month; a letter from their book club offering a subscription discount.

She put the lid back on and picked up the box. Her mother wanted the bills, wanted to keep them paid up until Gramps made an appearance.

Rachel looked around, drinking the room in. *So many years, and so little left that really means anything.*

She hadn't been sure what to make of it, where to turn. Then she'd done a Google search on the accident intersection, not really expecting anything.

The report that it returned, from city council's Police Review Board, was fourteen pages long and almost entirely redacted, a PDF of already-blacked-out pages. A stamp cited the Freedom of Access Act's privacy provisions in disciplinary proceedings.

But whoever redacted it had made one mistake, leaving the name of the defendant in the case uncensored: Schultz, Michael, Sgt.

Rachel realized it was possible the two were unrelated, that the officer in question had some perfunctory, bureaucratic reason for being written up at that scene, on that day.

But he was the only lead she had.

Machine's empty, no mail. You've searched every room, the garage. There's nothing else here to find.

She felt her heart ache a little as she left, feeling like maybe it was for the last time.

I need to suck it up. I need to suck it up and toughen up. That's what Grammy Rose would want.

. . .

Outside, Rachel walked back to her Toyota pickup and got in. She took out thc pay-as-you-go phone she'd bought a day earlier and speed-dialled her friend and neighbor, Abby.

"Hello?"

"Hey. It's me."

"Where are you!? Why aren't you answering your normal number!? I've texted you six times in the last two hours!" Abby exclaimed. "This place has gone nuts! They've had investigators from your office over here all day today! They said you were supposed to have a disciplinary hearing this morning with the commander and didn't show. They've got you as AWOL."

Her commander in the Navy's Judge Advocate General program was a notoriously distant man, barely acknowledging his staff of legal aids and lawyers. He seemed to spend most of his time in DC on business and was rarely seen at Fort Meade, near Baltimore.

He'd refused her request for emergency leave, then put her on a second caution for threatening a superior officer.

"They're upset because I'm on the rotation for cases now," she said. "They've paid for my education, and I've messed up careful planning for a lot of people and case scheduling for more."

"Is this more about your grandfather? You can tell me; they're not going to go looking for you right away." Abby was always a sympathetic ear.

"It's better you don't know," Rachel said. "Look... I'm about to miss an appointment, so I have to go. If they ask, tell them I'll be back as soon as I can. I apologize, but personal business took precedence. I can't say more, as they wouldn't understand. Okay?"

"Wait! They're going to ask for your number..."

"It's a pay-as-you-go, a burner," she said. "Just... don't worry. Okay?"

Rachel ended the call. She got out of the truck and strode over to the nearby trash bin. She tossed the phone in.

They might get a warrant for Abby's phone. That would give them her general locale. A new phone would prevent them easily triangulating her, at least. They'd get to Munjoy Hill eventually if they kept looking.

Too much to take care of, she thought as she walked back to the truck.

Down the block, she saw a slight shift in the shape of a shadow by the driver's seat of an older-model Lincoln, behind partially tinted glass. The car was jet black and stood out; she hadn't seen it when she'd pulled up, she was sure of that.

Probably just a hire-car driver, pulled over and waiting for a trip.

The street was empty, so she pulled the truck around in a U-turn to head back to her motel room. She'd promised her mother she'd visit the island later in the evening, drop off the box of bills.

The pickup passed the Lincoln. The driver turned away as she passed.

The hair on the nape of her neck stood up a little.

Got to cool it. Starting to see things.

Rachel had driven another four blocks up Atlantic before she spotted it again, following behind her, tiny in her rearview mirror but difficult to hide, with only one car between them and light traffic.

If I take a minor side street, it'll force him to speed up or potentially lose me and tip that I know he's there. Instead, she turned left at Forest Avenue, a major thoroughfare. If he was keeping tabs on her like a police officer, he'd keep his distance, maybe close a little based on natural driving patterns. But he wouldn't rush to catch up.

Sure enough, the Toyota had passed by another four blocks when she spotted the Lincoln again.

Yep. I'm being followed.

8

Bob's hackles were up.

The truck had taken a left onto Forest Avenue, then continued for another klick. But she was driving too evenly, her speed not going up and down regularly. He'd tested it for a couple of blocks by maintaining the exact same pace, forty yards back.

Surveillance training was that people tended to maintain one precise speed in two circumstances: when they thought they were being watched by police, or when they thought they were being followed.

He didn't plan to underestimate her because of her age. She carried a piece of some sort in her belt, and the furtive glances down the road when she'd entered the house had almost suggested she wasn't supposed to be there, was worried about being watched.

The truck continued on Forest past Mayor Baxter Woods, a massive, treed park to the left, and a low-rise strip mall of quirky businesses to the right: a Vietnamese restaurant, a photo studio, a sign advertising a Museum of Beadwork.

The truck slowed and turned left at Walton Street, following the park's western edge.

Bob touched the gas, aware side streets could be short, branched, taking her into a suburban maze in which he'd be easily lost. The Lincoln turned left.

Where is she headed? He'd studied the local map enough to know they were somewhere near the community gardens and the massive Evergreen Cemetery.

He realized there was every chance following the woman was a dead end. But the house she'd visited had once been home to someone claiming – a year after his death – to be Domas Petrauskas. At the least, he figured, she might have contacts for a previous owner, or an explanation.

More than that, he didn't have any other leads.

And in a few weeks, Mike probably loses his thirty-year career.

The truck had clear road ahead. The driver stood on the gas, the Toyota suddenly shooting forward.

Shit. She's doing a runner.

The truck's brake lights came on, and it nearly slammed to a halt, slowing down to take a hard right at Stevens Avenue. With a car between them, Bob knew he had to be careful or be seen while trying to keep her in sight.

He hit the gas, the Lincoln tailgating the older model Honda Civic ahead of it. He got just close enough to see the truck turn again, off Stevens and into the cemetery entrance. It disappeared behind a line of trees.

Bob swerved the Lincoln around the Honda and back into the lane, ignoring the stop sign, the sedan fishtailing to the right, onto Stevens, as his foot shifted quickly from brake to gas. He repeated the maneuver a moment later, turning left onto the cemetery property.

The truck had disappeared. But he could see a parking lot in the distance, maybe five hundred feet ahead. He slowed the car.

The lot was empty save for her truck and a couple of other cars parked at the far end. Five separate narrow roads, little more than pathways, twisted like tentacles away from the parking area, between trees and past the rows of gravestones that covered the massive cemetery.

He parked the Lincoln and got out. He couldn't see which she'd taken.

Start near her car, I guess. He turned left and followed the asphalt.

Bob had walked about twenty feet before he heard a hiss from a copse of trees to his left.

"Pssst..."

Oh, for crying out loud.

Clearly, she wanted to ambush him, or she'd have just stood on the road. "Yeah... I'm not wandering into a thicket so you can take a crack at me," he said loudly. "Maybe just come out, and we can talk?"

Tree limbs were pushed aside momentarily so that she could get a look at him. She exited the copse, her hand near the back of her belt. "Whoever you are, you should know that I'm armed." She drew a .40-calibre Colt, bracing the grip with the palm of her left hand but keeping the barrel pointed down and away.

"Is that really necessary?" Bob said.

"If I need to shoot you, sure," she said. "In that case, it's very necessary."

"I just want to talk," Bob said, slowly closing the distance between them.

"If you just wanted to talk, you'd have approached me rather than following me," she said. "I saw you at the house."

"Yeah... about that..." He moved closer, to within about six feet.

"Hey! Back up!" She raised the pistol to his chest height.

Bob stopped moving.

Her hands were trembling ever so slightly.

She's nervous, and I have no idea what the pull on that trigger is.

"Miss... if you could put that down, I'd feel a whole lot better." He took another step her way. "If you twitch a little too hard and that goes off..."

"STOP!" she bellowed. "You move an inch, and I promise that'll be exactly what happens."

I need to de-escalate this, quickly. Bob glanced past her, then widened his eyes, not saying a word, hoping she'd turn to find a potential source. Fate lent him a hand: somewhere behind her, past the trees, they heard the crack of a tree branch.

She turned her head quickly, glancing backwards to make sure Bob wasn't bait. The moment she began to move, Bob took one big step forward and snatched the pistol out of her hand.

The woman took a few shocked steps backwards.

"Now, let's just relax..." Bob began to say.

The kick was fast, accurate. She turned side on, taking a quick hop forward on her planted foot and snapping her other leg outwards from the knee, the toe of her cowboy boot catching the pistol flush, the gun flying out of Bob's hand, landing with a thumping bounce on the turf a few feet away.

Bob stared at it, wide-eyed and eyebrows raised.

Been a while since someone surprised you, Bobby.

She squared off in a fighting stance, feet spread slightly apart, hands up, ready to defend herself.

"I really don't want to—" Bob managed before she charged in, snapping a side kick towards his midsection. He blocked it away easily with both hands, but she was fast, relentless, her torso twisting, her fist whipping around in a backwards punch that caught him flush in the temple.

He shook off the blow just as she pivoted on her left leg, the spinning kick aimed at his head. Bob used a cross-arm block to prevent it from hitting him, then dropped low, shooting a low kick at her calf, the force unbalancing her. Instead of following instinct and hitting her with a blow as she fell, he caught her by the collar of her shirt and lifted her back to her feet.

She ignored the save in the anger of the moment, throwing a left elbow towards his head that forced him to duck backwards, the back of her arm harmlessly smacking him in the forehead.

"NOW JUST HOLD ON A DAMN SECOND!" Bob yelled. He stepped to one side and brought the flat of his palm down on her shoulder, a counterweight as he kicked her feet from under her.

She slammed to the grass, flat on her back. She rolled over quickly, scrambled to her feet, coming back up in a fighting stance. Then she stopped and peered at him, puzzled.

"Why didn't you ground-and-pound?" she asked. "You had me. I was down. You could've easily pinned my arms—"

"I TOLD YOU... I told you I'm not trying to hurt you! Jesus tapdancing Christ, will you give me a minute to explain!?"

She stared at his right arm. "That's a Marines unit tattoo."

"It is."

"You're an MP."

"I'm not."

"Yeah, bullshit!"

She turned and ran, heading in the opposite direction from the parking lot.

Ah, shit. She's quick, too.

Bob took off after her. *This is going to look greeeat if we bump into anyone.* "HOLD UP!" he yelled.

She ignored him, gaining distance.

Of all the people to follow, I pick a runner. "OKAY THEN," Bob yelled, slowing to a stop. "I'LL JUST GO WAIT BY YOUR TRUCK."

She slowed, then stopped, already fifty yards ahead of him. She turned and walked back towards him. Then she came to a halt and crossed her arms, staring at him coldly. "So this is the part where you arrest me."

She sounded resigned to it.

"I'm NOT an MP," Bob said. "No bullshit! I mean... really!? For crying out loud, do I look like shore patrol? I'm not even carrying."

She frowned again. "Really?"

"Really." *Is she AWOL? That sure sounded like it.* "I mean... I have a piece, but it's in a bag under the front seat of my car. I've been trying to avoid trouble, only carrying it when I know I might need it."

"Sounds dumb," she said. "What about the times you don't know but you still wish you'd had it?"

"Hasn't happened yet. I can usually handle things. Maybe we could start—"

"Keep any smart-ass questions until I'm done asking mine, please, as you're the one acting like a stalker," she said. She walked back over to her gun and retrieved it. "Now... why were you following me?"

"Okay, that's fair," Bob said. "But I have to give you the backstory, or it'll just sound weird. Okay?"

"We'll see."

"It started a couple of weeks ago, when my friend attended an accident scene."

FIFTY YARDS SOUTH, Chris Jefferson crouched by a headstone and watched the pair fighting through a camera's zoom lens.

He'd been following the man for hours.

The woman had been a surprise, but Uncle had insisted she was not to be contacted if avoidable. She was a "complication," he'd said, whatever that meant.

He thought they'd spotted him when they'd first confronted one another, Jefferson's foot cracking a large twig near the headstone. But the distraction had been momentary. Now the fight seemed to be concluding, Singleton shoving the woman to the ground, then giving her a chance to get up.

They began talking.

Jefferson stayed low and scurried due east, towards the parking lot. He walked across it casually, looking out for bereaved visitors and seeing none. At Bob's Lincoln, he reached down and under the frame of the car, adhering a radio frequency tracker.

Now at least he can't give me the slip.

He wandered casually over to the path and glanced down it. They were still near the trees, talking about something. She'd holstered her gun.

He took a few more steps to the south and concealed himself behind a tree.

The woman's role was "uncertain," Uncle had insisted.

Jefferson didn't want to know. He wanted the whole thing to be over, for some rationale to present itself so that he could extract himself, so that he and Carly could stay in Maine. He also wanted the growing sense that he was acting like a traitor to just go away.

Even though I am one.

But it had never been his choice, he rationalized. He'd been forced into it by his parents, and they were both dead. He wanted to run, but having a family complicated everything. In point of fact, everything that made him happy – everything he wanted outside of a job in the big leagues – was right there in Portland.

9

Nikolai Grusin pushed through the swinging doors, the cooler air outside Portland International Airport's main terminal refreshing after his flight.

He scanned the curb. A Cadillac sedan was parked twenty feet away, the man by the driver's door familiar.

He approached, and the man used a key fob to open the trunk. The driver held up the lid while Nikolai stored his bag.

"Sascha," Nikolai said.

"It's good to see you, Nicky."

"Hmm." The two men had served together in Moscow.

"I'll take us back to the motel the local asset booked, yes?"

Nikolai nodded. He opened the back door and climbed in. He liked the idea of Sascha having to drive him.

The notion was an amusing and welcome break from stewing about their assignment. He'd taken one look at Yaremchuk's encrypted file a day earlier, in his Maryland townhouse, and realized what an opportunity he had.

The Cadillac pulled out into traffic, Sascha maintaining a respectful silence.

The town looked small, pedestrian, from the air, Nikolai thought. What on earth was a man like Bob Singleton doing here?

Singleton had had a price on his head for several years, ever since wiping out a Ferak Group team in Iraq. That bounty had been upped to a hundred thousand US dollars just a year earlier after the death of Victor Malyuchenko, son of Ivan Malyuchenko, the KGB legend.

He knew how pragmatic and corruptible some of his paymasters were. The money would go a long way if he wished. *Enough to buy my way back to Moscow.*

If Yaremchuk was aware of the bounty, or cared, he hadn't mentioned it. But Yaremchuk was rich, connected.

He doesn't need this. I do.

The key would be to act swiftly and ruthlessly, in case Sascha and his associate Boris got curious and started asking Yaremchuk questions. If they connected the dots, they might want a cut, he knew.

And that wouldn't work for Nikolai.

THE YOUNG WOMAN stared at Bob like he was crazy.

"Who?"

"I'm telling you, there's a driver's license in that name that leads back to that house."

"And I'm telling you, I spent twenty-four years, off and on, visiting that house," she said. "It belonged to my grandparents. And nobody named Doormouse Petr... what!?"

"Domas, Domas Petrauskas."

"No one by that name lived there, and neither of my

grandparents ever mentioned him, nor my mom," she said. "But... your friend Mike, he and I have business because that was my grandfather's station wagon at that accident scene. And maybe his body was the one that disappeared."

But if that was the case, Bob knew, there had to be a connection between that house, its occupants and the disappearing corpse. Mike had seen that driver's license.

"I was told your grandfather reported his car stolen."

"He did. But he also vanished within hours of that. He hasn't been seen since, not for more than two weeks. I don't believe in coincidences, not of that magnitude," she said.

She had a point, Bob thought. There had to be a reason why Mike hadn't mentioned the car owner disappearing. Maybe the cops didn't even know.

"You've talked to the police?"

"They won't help me because I'm not his next-of-kin. My mother is. And she insists there's nothing wrong, he's just gotten wanderlust. He's... he was a travelling salesman. He spent a lot of time on the road."

"Without his car?"

She rolled her eyes. "He has a Subaru that's also missing."

Bob frowned. It sounded like the police version made sense, the man's car had been stolen, and his own daughter wasn't worried.

She sensed his reticence. "My mother's not a reasonable woman sometimes, and she didn't get along with him. His wife died recently, he'd just had a break-in... and he disappears without a word for two weeks, at the exact time that his car is involved in a fatal crash and the driver disappears? Like I said, there are coincidences and there are coincidences."

She had a point. It was possible they were looking for the same accident victim.

"I'll take you to meet Mike if you can trust me enough to work with me a little," Bob said. "The only way we can find out if your grandfather was involved in that crash is by figuring out where that body went, and why."

"Fine. Where do we start?"

"Names, maybe?" He held out his hand. "Bob Bennett."

She shook it perfunctorily. "Rachel. McGee."

"McGee? Not Peters?"

"McGee was my father's name. He fled when I was little. I have no idea what happened to him. But my mother loved him a lot. So she kept it."

"That's rough. I'm sorry to hear it."

She shrugged. "It is what it is. But I didn't want to be a Peters anyway. Grammy Rose worked in government. I didn't want anyone thinking I'd traded off her name."

Bob nodded his head towards his Lincoln. "We need to check something out at the scene. Follow me?"

She looked unenthusiastic. "Sure… fine. Lead on."

THE ACCIDENT SCENE had long been cleaned up; just a quiet street corner on the edge of an industrial park.

Rachel looked at the buildings on either side of the road. It was clear why police had no video; one was at the back of the back side of a building, without access at the time due to construction. The other, a vast brick storage depot, was on an angle to the road, its front doors not quite visible from the corner.

She looked across the road. Bob was standing next to a warehouse of some sort, waving for her to join him.

She jogged across the road.

He pointed up the block. "Pizza joint."

"Okay." They started walking towards it. After twenty feet or so, Rachel asked, "Why?"

The accident intersection was perhaps a hundred feet away.

Bob pointed up, above the restaurant's front door. "See that camera? It rotates to each side. That means it probably got video of the accident scene."

She frowned. "The police didn't check it?"

"Mike didn't mention it. It's so far away they probably wouldn't be able to use it as evidence, so it's possible it wasn't checked at all. I'm not even sure what we'd get from that far away. But it's worth trying."

"Okay, so we see if they have a recording from that night, and we take it," she said. She headed for the door. She glanced through the small rectangular inset windows. Then she began to push it open.

"Whoa! Hold on a sec! Geez," Bob said. "We need to figure out the best approach."

"The best approach!?" She peered at him like he'd gone soft in the head. "Here's the best approach: we march in there; we demand that file; we make it clear that turning us down would be a mistake."

"Uh-huh," Bob said. "Look... what you said at the cemetery, thinking I was an MP. Would I be right in thinking you're AWOL from somewhere?"

"That's none of your business."

"If we're working together, what I say is my business is my business," Bob insisted. "I need to know who I'm depending on."

She released the door. It swung shut with a light clunk. She crossed her arms. "I'm a junior lieutenant with the JAG unit in Bethesda."

"You're a lawyer," Bob said, not hiding the tone of disappointment. "What are you, twenty-five? Seems a bit young to sell your soul."

"I'm a quick study. And people like me – your condescending tone notwithstanding – spend a lot of our time keeping people like you out of the brig."

"The JAGs I've met are usually a little cooler under the collar."

"What's that supposed to mean!?" Rachel snapped. "Maybe they like that I'm aggressive. Maybe being driven means I don't take unnecessary shit. What, I'm supposed to be dainty and restrained because I'm a girl, is that it?"

"What!? No! Why the heck would you..."

"Because that's what guys your age do; you judge younger people by old standards and—"

"Your imagination is clearly healthy, even if the attitude isn't," he interrupted. "The reason I judge you aggressive is because you tried to ambush me at the cemetery, and now you want to charge in here without a plan and, from the sounds of it, bust heads."

She peered at him plaintively. "Have you listened to a *word* I've said since we met? My grandfather is *missing!* First off, *you* followed *me* to an isolated area. So... yeah, that'll make any woman nervous. You're a guy with unknown intentions. Second, my grandfather could be *dead,* and he's definitely gone, and NOBODY GIVES A SHIT!"

She reached for the door handle. Bob leaned on the door so she couldn't open it.

"Please... just listen," he said. "I'm not trying to get under your skin, okay? I just want us to consider what the best way to handle this is rather than—"

"I don't need interview technique mansplained to me by some hard charger," she said. "Which, given your age and that you're up to your neck in some weird fucking stuff, I figure fits you to a t. You're already lucky I didn't kick your ass at the cemetery. Stand aside."

Bob sighed. She clearly wasn't in a mood for reason. "Fine." He removed his hand from the door.

He watched through the glass as she strode up the main aisle to the front counter. *Thank God the place is empty*, Bob decided. He couldn't hear what she was saying, but she was animated, pointing towards the intersection, talking with her hands.

The young man at the counter shrugged in resigned fashion.

She said something angry, coming up off her heels. He shrugged again, hands up in a "what can I do?" pose, his answer just a few words.

She pointed at the intersection and yelled something muffled, almost loud enough to be heard outside.

Then she pointed at the clerk, and her hand went to the back of her belt as if she was going to draw the Colt.

Ah, shit. I might have to...

Before he could finish the thought, the young man reached under the front counter and produced a sawed-off shotgun, which he placed on the counter between them, his hand on the grip.

Rachel turned around and stormed out of the store.

"DON'T say it," she cautioned.

"I mean... you're a *JAG*!? *You're* the best legal mind the Navy could produce?"

"I figured I'd save us time. And I didn't technically threaten him. I implied. I figured he'd wilt."

Bob nodded to the restaurant's interior, beyond the glass. "Yeah, well, you figured wrong, counsellor. He's picking up the landline, probably to call the cops. *Stay here*."

10

Bob pulled the restaurant door open and went inside.

The server shrank away from him, towards the phone hanging from the wall, the receiver in his left hand. But he kept his right on the shotgun. "I'm calling the cops," he said. "Don't you try nothing!"

Bob held both palms in surrender. "Not her friend, just an associate coming in to apologize."

"Yeah?" The server paused. "Well, you can just screw right off, is what you can do!"

"Or I could compensate you fairly for the stress you just suffered, if you'll hear me out."

He was unsure, the handset still aloft. "What?"

"Say... a hundred bucks, up front, for two minutes of conversation." He was too young to own the place, and the name tag just said "Tyson," no title. A young man working a Saturday morning in a pizza joint wasn't making a ton of money, Bob figured.

He took out his money clip and peeled off five twenties, then slid them across the counter.

The server looked at the money, then at the handset. He hung up the phone. "Okay. Two minutes." He kept the shotgun in view.

"There was an accident, two weeks ago Friday," Bob said. "Two people died."

The kid nodded. "Sure."

"Did you see any of it?"

"The next morning. Road was a fucking mess, though. Bits of glass and metal and shit everywhere. They had it shut down for a few hours, like. While they cleaned up and stuff."

The doorbell jangled, and Rachel walked back inside. She was moving quickly.

"Oh, no!" the youth said. "She's not coming back in, no, sir!"

Bob turned quickly and glared at her. He took out his clip and peeled off two more twenties. "She'll be quiet, I promise. RIGHT? Because everyone's getting along right now. Right?"

Rachel inhaled sharply through her nose but kept her pursed lips tightly shut. She crossed her arms again, clearly not happy at taking direction.

"Now… that night, you have the security footage from your front camera still?"

The kid nodded. "It's recorded onto a solid-state drive in the back."

Bob smiled as warmly as possible. "Great. How would you like to make another hundred bucks?"

. . .

IT TOOK the kid about five minutes to find the file from that night and cue it up on a backroom computer. When he was done, he opened the room's door and let them in. "Okay, it's ready to go. Don't know what time it was, so I just set it to the start, at twelve-oh-one."

Bob sat down and used the mouse to scroll the video ahead. At just after 1:35 a.m., with the road otherwise empty, the station wagon came into view. It rounded the corner of Read and Quarry, immediately crashing headlong into a temporary concrete road divider, the kind set up by work crews.

He leaned in, the detail fuzzy, a connect-the-dots black-and-white image, and at a distance. The driver's side door opened, and a man got out, walking around the back of the car and disappearing from view, cut off by the camera rotating away.

"Was that your grandfather?" he asked Rachel.

She leaned in over his shoulder. "I mean... he's in shadow. He's the right size, but he's moving pretty easily. Gramps had arthritis."

The camera rotated to a central view of the empty street ahead of the storage depot. Then to the right, to a parked car on Read. Twenty seconds later, it panned back to the intersection.

A few frames passed with no movement, just a slight rocking motion to the station wagon. Then another person seemed to come into view, through the back windshield, shuffling into the driver's seat. *Maybe it's a shadow.* "Or maybe... is that someone in the back seat?" Bob wondered.

If they had law enforcement resources, he knew, they could use software to try to slightly improve the image. But without it, the car was too far away to gain much clarity.

Rachel traced the image with her fingertip. "There. That's someone's head, alright. But is that in the back seat or front? Hard saying, not knowing." It rotated away again, and they waited another forty seconds.

The clerk was getting nervous, looking over his shoulder and out the door to the store. "Is this going to take much longer?"

"A few minutes is all, I promise," Bob said. "There's another fifty bucks in it if you can be patient."

As the station wagon rotated back into frame, there was more movement across the back seat, someone disappearing to the right, out of frame. The driver's seat appeared to be occupied. The car shook slightly, as if someone had slammed a door.

Headlights approached in the other lane. The station wagon's tail end had fishtailed a few feet into their path. The other car didn't swerve, the driver clearly not paying attention to the road curve ahead.

The sedan's front bumper slammed into the station wagon's rear left corner, pushing the vehicle straight, glass shattering and a head momentarily protruding from the station wagon's driver-side window.

The driver and passenger of the sedan crashed through the sedan's windshield as it slammed to a halt, their crumpled forms left lying ahead of the car.

The station wagon's door popped open from the force, a body half falling out, its momentum arrested by the head getting caught in the window frame, so that it was hanging half out of the vehicle.

"Jesus H," Bob muttered. He looked over at Rachel. Her mouth was hanging open in shock, fully aware she might have just witnessed her grandfather's death. "You okay?"

She pursed her lips and nodded, then composed herself. "Why did he get back into the car?" she said. "And who was in the back seat? Because someone else clearly got out of it before impact."

The scene was still, no one moving, both vehicles disabled, the second car's headlights still on. Bob forwarded the video. Less than nine minutes passed, and a policeman walked into frame. "That's Mike Schultz," Bob said. "He was just a few blocks away when the call came in. Someone passing on Red Street must've spotted it and dialled 911."

Schultz could be seen carefully approaching the station wagon, walking around it. Then he walked back towards the camera and out of frame for a few moments. The camera rotated to the straight-ahead image. Twenty seconds later, it caught him behind his cruiser, retrieving a large roll of tape to cordon the scene off from any other traffic. He slung it between two posts, placed a red hazard triangle on the ground midway, then returned to the station wagon.

He was about two feet from the suspended driver when the man's body slumped to the ground, the door opening fully, the body crumpled in a pile. He knelt with the body for less than a minute. Then he checked the man's ID and repeated the pulse check on the other two. He stood up straight and paused.

Then he began to walk back towards the camera. They lost him again for a few seconds until the third angle kicked into place. He was sitting in the cab of a police cruiser parked along Read, fifteen feet back from the corner, talking to someone.

The camera rotated 180 degrees, back to the scene.

"Wait a sec... what's this now?" Bob wondered.

A pair of men appeared at the bottom of the camera frame, from behind and to the right of station wagon, off screen. They crouched by the driver's body, next to the station wagon door, lifted the body from under its arms and dragged it out of frame.

He looked over at Rachel. "Well... that might explain Mike's disappearing victim."

She was chewing on a knuckle. "But I can't tell if that was Gramps."

As the camera panned away, Bob caught the flash of lights strobing across the scene and the buildings. "Ambulance showed just as Mike was calling it in, not twenty seconds after they grabbed the body."

The right-side view showed Mike getting out of the car and walking back. The camera angle tilted back to the intersection, showing him lifting the tape to duck under it. A pair of EMTs were crouched by the two remaining corpses.

"Look..." the young man said, his tone nervous. "I can't afford to get fired."

"We need this file," Bob said. "How much to buy it off—"

"Oh, no, no way! Seriously, I can't afford to get fired. I've got school in a month. I don't even know how to download this stuff."

"Can you copy it and mail it, maybe?" Bob asked.

The kid looked at him, dumbfounded. "This app is bananas complicated. I can't even tell how you find the individual file."

"When do they erase these?" Rachel asked.

"End of the month," the kid said.

"Fine." She turned Bob's way. "Give him another hundred to make sure it doesn't happen before then."

Bob glared back at her. "What, are we on a date?"

"I don't have it on me," she said. "Pay the man."

Bob pulled out his clip. He had cash in the bank but no idea how long it had to last. Helping Mike was getting expensive.

11

The night was setting in, stars abundant as they stood on the sidewalk outside the business.

They'd both missed dinner.

"There's a diner a mile from here," Rachel said, nodding southwest. "Get a coffee, maybe a bite, compare notes? They usually have a quiet booth or two."

Bob nodded. "Works for me."

The restaurant was a single-story whitewashed chunk of concrete perched on a triangular lot. Bob figured it had probably been a Country Kitchen once upon a time. They parked both vehicles in the side lot, using two of twenty empty spaces, accompanied only by a giant steel dumpster, its green paint fading from age.

They met halfway to the door. "Not a popular spot, then," Bob said.

"They have their regular crowd," Rachel said. "But they're mostly older, coming in for breakfast and brunch, not up for an evening meal at nine o'clock."

Sure enough, the place was empty save for one older

customer near the doors, sipping his coffee while he read an old hardcover missing its jacket. The hostess showed them to the rear corner booth. She was older, in a flamingo-pink dress and squarish, sensible white shoes.

"Just to let you folks know we do close at eleven," she said, handing them each a brown plastic menu. "The specials today are Salisbury steak with mash and California veg mix, or the Monte Cristo sandwich with fries. And we've got a real nice French onion soup to start. Now, what can I get you to drink?"

"Coffee, please," Rachel said.

"Green tea," Bob answered.

The waitress headed towards the kitchen.

Bob knew he had to be honest with her. "Look... I know you're upset by what was in that video."

"Who wouldn't be?"

She had that annoying youth habit, Bob had noticed, of trailing her voice up at the end of sentences, like everything was a question. It was irritating even when it *was* a question.

"The thing is, from my friend's perspective, that video at the store might be enough to clear him already. It shows he told the truth, that a body was lifted from the scene."

Her eyes widened and flashed anger. "So... what? You're just going to tell him and walk off before I have any answers?"

"Hey... I can't get access to the video any more than you can. But Mike will be able to; he's a cop. And I owe it to him—"

"Oh, I think I get what you're saying. You're saying you don't need to work with me anymore on finding Gramps, because your friend's alibi is somewhat covered now, would that be right?"

For some reason, the lilt of a Maine accent made him feel that much more guilty, like he was being scolded by a nun or something. "Look, I didn't get into this to solve the mystery of a local car accident. I'm not preventing you from going ahead—"

"No, you're not," she said. "I never asked for your help in the first place. But you promised me you'd introduce me to Mike Schultz if I trusted you. Now I expect you..." She tailed off, the waitress returning to take their orders.

"What can I get you?" She didn't have a pad to write down their order, and Bob figured she'd long been accustomed to memorizing everything.

"Egg-white omelette, two slices of turkey breast, green salad," Bob said. "Thank you."

"Jeezum crow, even your meal choices irritate me," Rachel muttered. "Quarter-chicken dinner, fries, gravy."

Rachel handed the waitress the menu without breaking Bob's eye contact. She waited until the older woman had turned and was walking away. "Now I expect you to fulfill your part of the bargain. Once we eat, we go to Mike Schultz's place. I tell him my side of this. Maybe a cop will care enough to help when you clearly don't."

"It's not like that," Bob said. "You don't know me or my life. I've got a fairly large tower of serious shit to worry about already, and I don't want to drag you into that. Okay? This... whatever it is... is just not my problem."

"Whatever. Like, just... whatever!" She shook her head, the expression verging on disgust. She looked away and sighed, then muttered, "Goddamn, boomers suck."

"Boomer? I'm forty-four!" he exclaimed. "Technically, I'm a fucking millennial! I'm barely old enough to be your father."

"Okay, Boomer," she muttered, gazing off towards the front of the restaurant.

Jesus H, this food can't get here fast enough, Bob thought.

THE MAN behind the wheel had a neck thicker than a fire hydrant.

From the back bench of the rented Cadillac, Chris Jefferson watched the driver, Sascha, as his attention flitted between the road and the satnav on the dash.

Sascha had been in Portland since the night before with Boris, in the front passenger seat. Nikolai, the mountainous, bearded man sitting next to the coach, had arrived just a few hours earlier.

They'd spent a few hours getting ready at a motel room, the air conditioning having kicked out, the shared quarters stifling. The coach had made it clear he didn't want to get involved in anything heavy and that Uncle wanted discretion.

But Nikolai had rebutted that Moscow called the shots. And Moscow wanted Bob Singleton dead.

The woman, they said, had made an unfortunate choice in friends, a man with a bounty on his head.

"Shouldn't we at least call Yaremchuk?" Coach Chris had proposed, only to be shouted down in Russian.

"Vperedi. Vot ono, da?" *Up ahead. This is it, yes?* Nikolai asked in Russian.

"Da," Chris said. He put away his phone, the tracker having done its job.

"Speak English," Boris said, his tone as flat as it had been since they'd met.

"The parking lot on the corner," Chris said.

Boris leaned in towards the dash slightly as he studied the lot. "Why here? It is tactically difficult."

"What? Why tell me that?" Chris asked. He knew there was no percentage in showing any fear in front of them. "I didn't pick it for an ambush or anything. We're just following the tracker on the car."

"Is three open sides, so hard to defend. Is two exit streets, so hard to pin them down. Is bad, tactically."

"It's what we've got," Jefferson said.

"Where do I park?" Sascha asked.

Boris nodded to their right, to St. John Street, running behind the restaurant. "Best location for a quick exit, if required."

Sascha turned the car right and pulled it over.

"Now what?" Chris asked.

"Now we retrieve our gear from the boot of the car and wait for targets," Nikolai said.

"Trunk," Chris said absently, rueing that he'd picked up the phone two days earlier. Why couldn't they just fuck off back to Washington, leave Portland in peace? They were going to ruin everything.

"What?" Nikolai demanded.

"Trunk of the car, not boot. That's English."

"I know is English. Is why I said it? What are you trying to say?"

"No, I mean it's the term they use in England. In Maine, we say trunk."

Boris turned and looked over the back seat at him. "Maybe you shut up until we ask questions, okay?"

Fine by me.

. . .

NIKOLAI LISTENED to the hum of the Cadillac's big engine, the weight of the KP-9 machine gun welcome in his hands, the cold steel assuring.

Yaremchuk wanted them to be cautious, careful, tail both targets until they were isolated, put them away quietly. And everything in Singleton's file suggested that would be a mistake, that every attempt in the past to take him quietly had failed terribly.

What he would not expect was something rapid and public, in a safe area, where he would not see it coming. *And I want that hundred thousand.*

He had at least acquiesced to the sleeper's request that they don't just walk into the restaurant and open fire. Nikolai wasn't really concerned about innocent civilians, but they drew massively more attention than killing a single man.

Instead, he'd agreed they'd wait on the road, giving them instant egress in the case of unwanted attention. Even if police response proved slow, Jefferson/Ratachkov had noted, there might be other customers carrying weapons.

Nikolai did not consider himself a greedy man. It was enough money to get him access to people in the senior bureaucracy who could clear his slate, get him back into the field for the FIS.

And all I need to do is kill one man.

There really was no choice in it, Nikolai figured, despite the sleeper's hesitancy. He turned to look out the side window, watching the parking lot, eager for the blood rush of battle.

12

They plowed through dinner in silence, Rachel taking an occasional break from chewing to glare at Bob.

Eventually, she said, "Did you ever really plan on helping me?"

Bob sighed. "I don't know you. As much as we could help each other, sure. But you're not offering me a whole lot now other than a bunch of neato conversation."

She hung her head slightly. Bob sensed a whiff of defeat in it. "I just don't understand any of this," she said. "He was never a nice man, Gramps. My mother always sort of hinted that he could be mean to both of them when she was growing up. But I don't believe he just hit the open road, a month after his wife of fifty years dies. I don't buy it."

Hang on now...

Bob had a thought. "As a kid, did you ever hear them speaking a different language?"

Her head snapped back to attention, her gaze narrowing.

"Why would you ask that? I mean... There was a moment, when I was very young. I'd have been seven or eight. How—"

"Working on a theory," Bob said.

"A theory?"

"Yeah... please... enlighten me."

"I was in the living room, and Grammy Rose was talking to someone on the phone in the kitchen. And it just sounded like nonsense, like when a kid puts on a French or Greek accent without really knowing what the real words sound like. I asked Gramps what she was doing, and he said it was just something she'd learned, to talk to family in the old country."

"The old country?"

She shrugged. "The Peters side of the family is from England originally. It didn't make any sense. I just... you know, stored it away as one of those things I probably should know but embarrassingly didn't, like you do when you're a kid. A regional dialect or something. How did you know to ask me that?"

He took out his phone and tapped letters for a few seconds. He handed it to her. "Would it have sounded something like this?"

Rachel took the proffered phone and tapped the "speak aloud" prompt. The phone read a few lines of text back. She leaned back a little. "Yeah... I mean, it was nearly twenty years ago. But... yeah, maybe. Similar."

She frowned and used her index finger to scroll quickly up the browser page. "Lithuanian?" She handed him back the phone.

"The name I mentioned earlier, Domas Petrauskas, was Lithuanian," Bob said.

"Okay. Weird."

He tapped the name onto a note on the phone screen and handed it back. "Look at it again."

"I don't..." She trailed off the thought, shaking her head. "You've lost me."

"If you were forced to translate those two names into English..."

"Okay. Well, Domas could be..." The thought tailed again as realization set it. "Thomas Peters."

Bob shrugged.

Rachel leaned back in her chair. "So... what are you telling me, Bob? That my grandparents lied about where they were from?"

She wasn't seeing the whole picture. She was going to have to hear it eventually, Bob figured. "Back in the sixties, Lithuania was part of the Soviet Union," he said. "Emigrating from there to here was forbidden, officially. Generally, only refugees were accepted into the US, people who managed to flee or get out before the Soviets took over."

"And you figure they'd have gotten in trouble or maybe been deported if they admitted where they were really from."

She still wasn't seeing it.

"Rachel... that name belonged to a kid who died in a car accident in Bangor a year before your grandfather began carrying around an ID with that name on it. Your grandparents weren't Lithuanian refugees fleeing persecution, and they sure as heck weren't from England."

"What?! Yes! Yes, they were."

"I think they were spies."

"WHAT!?"

The restaurant was almost empty, just the elderly patron reading his book near the door. But Bob used both hands to offer a "lower the volume" gesture anyway. "The pieces fit, is all. They used a stolen identity from a dead person to gain new papers; they anglicized their names. You said your grammy Rose worked in politics?"

"GRAMMY ROSE WAS NOT A RUSSIAN SPY!" Rachel bellowed. Then she realized the other patron and waitress, far across the room, had turned to look. She raised a hand. "Sorry... sorry about that."

She turned back to Bob. "My grandmother was... why would you even *say* something like that!? Goddamn! I'll have you know that my grandparents were both registered Republicans! They loved America! They voted for Reagan and George HW!"

"All of which would be a solid cover if—"

"DON'T say it!" she warned. "I'm not listening to that nonsense for a second longer!" She rose to her feet. "Fuck this! I'll find Schultz on my own." She opened her purse, struggling with the snap in her anger.

"It's because the buckle is—"

"I DON'T NEED YOUR HELP!"

She took out a twenty and tossed it on the table. "You know what? I don't need your help, and I certainly don't need you insulting my family with this bullshit fantasy you've concocted. I know about the tape. I can talk to your officer friend on my own. Goodbye!"

She got up and stormed towards the front doors.

Fine, let her go.

Hotheaded idiot.

But Bob knew that if he was right, there could be more to the man's disappearance.

You followed her and freaked her out. Yeah, she's angry. But you're upending her world. She's steaming out of here, mad as hell. And her grandfather may have been an agent or asset.

This is not going to end well.

He remembered Maggie again in that moment, angry at him, shoving her way out of their apartment door in Chicago. He pushed the morose sense of loss down deep again, then got up, jogging to the front counter and throwing down another ten with Rachel's twenty. "Keep it," he said before the waitress could protest.

The doors had just clunked shut. He ran over and opened them.

"Rachel! Please! Wait a second!"

She stopped walking, her arms crossed defensively. "That was some kind of bullshit, springing that on me."

He hung his head slightly. *How do I do this tactfully?* It had never been his strong suit. Bob had always found the easiest way to offend people was to just state facts. Eventually, he'd hit one that clashed with their beliefs. "I realize something like that could be difficult to hear when you've maybe just lost both of them. But I wasn't trying to upset you."

"Oh really? You have a strange way of showing it."

"I raised it because I used to work in government, after the Marines. We were trained to look for signs—"

"My grandparents weren't spies, Bob." But this time, she said it more quietly, like she'd begun to think about it a little maybe.

"Look... I'm not trying to intrude, and your life is for you to figure out," he said. "But I promised you I'd introduce you to Mike. I can at least do that... okay?"

She took a deep breath, still so annoyed that eye contact

was out of the question. "Fine." She nodded towards the parking lot. "Let's go."

A Harley-Davidson Softail pulled up at the curb, the bearded biker in a leather vest and a Star-Spangled Banner headscarf. He turned off the ignition and locked his handlebars, wheel towards the sidewalk.

"Nice bike," Bob murmured as the man climbed off.

The rider held up a fingerless-gloved palm, like a policeman directing traffic to stop. "Don't touch it."

"Oookay," Bob said as they passed him and headed towards the parking lot. Bob turned and added, "They're closing at eleven."

The biker stopped and turned again, glaring at Bob, then his bike. "Just... don't fucking touch the Harley, okay, asshole!?" Then he turned back towards the door and went inside.

Rachel glanced back quickly as she walked. "That was bullshit. That was totally uncalled for."

"Yeah, real charmer," Bob said matter-of-factly. "Just don't assume it's a biker thing; I've known more nice than nasty."

She stopped walking. "We should go back inside and have a word."

He stopped walking. "We what now?"

She turned back towards the restaurant, still scowling. "That guy was really rude. I just think we should—"

"NO. No, we shouldn't!" Bob interrupted. "Jesus H! Why on earth would you want a confrontation over something that unimportant!? Who put such a large burr up your backside, exactly?"

"Maybe I just believe in sticking up for myself."

He looked at her, aghast. "How did you make it into the JAG office, with that kind of temper?"

"It's a new thing. I usually hold it in more. That doesn't feel right just now," she said. "I'm... I'm tired of tact! I'm tired of nice! I tried that, and nobody listened. But... you know what? It's not really your problem anymore, given that you have no intention of helping me, not any more than one meeting with Schultz."

Bob gestured vaguely ahead of them, not bothering to rein in a sour look. "Just... let's get going, okay?"

She reached for the truck door handle.

The volley of gunfire shattered both of the truck cab's side windows, shards of safety glass flying, bouncing off her jacket.

Bob was moving as soon as his brain registered the sound, diving forward and dragging her down to the ground.

They both scrambled to a seated position. Machine-gun fire echoed off the restaurant's wall, bullets chewing through the truck's body panels as if they were so much crepe paper, exiting the other side, both of them lucky not to be hit.

"We can't stay here!" Bob stressed. He grabbed her by the wrist. "When I say go, we run for the big dumpster along the back wall. That thing is quarter-inch rolled steel, actual cover. Ready... GO!"

They rose in unison and sprinted across the narrow lot, hurling themselves behind the dumpster as bullets kicked off the ground behind them.

Rachel drew her Colt.

"Are you good with that thing?" Bob demanded, another volley of gunfire half drowning him out, bullets pinging off the sides of the giant container.

"Good enough. I qualified," she said.

"I'm a former sniper," Bob said. He held out a hand. "Maybe...?"

She handed him the Colt.

Two more bursts of gunfire echoed, slugs kicking up small chunks of asphalt, others flattening against the dumpster, dimpling its surface, then tinkling on the asphalt like wind chimes.

Bob ducked his head around the side of the dumpster long enough to sight them, avoiding another barrage. "They're at the far end of the lot behind a dark sedan, Caddy or Lincoln, maybe, about fifty feet away," he said. "I counted three, two carrying KP-9s."

He leaned around the edge of the dumpster and fired back twice, spotting movement as the men ducked behind a black Cadillac, leading one of them and firing a third shot. From the distance and in the poor light, he knew his chances of hitting anyone weren't great.

"Might've winged that last guy," he said optimistically.

"What do we *do*!?" she snapped.

"I guarantee you that waitress has called the cops by now," Bob said. "But we're outnumbered and outgunned. We can't really 'do' anything except defend our position and wait for the cavalry."

She took a deep, centering breath and regained her composure. "I could try to sneak back around the front of the building," Rachel said. "Get behind them and get the drop on them that way."

Bob turned his head slowly and glared at her again. "Okay, Rambo. You do that. Meanwhile, there's fifteen, maybe twenty feet from here to the corner. Should one of them not blow your head off, when you get around the building, there's another forty feet from the far corner of the restaurant to their car. And we only have one gun, so in the meantime, I'm stuck—"

"OKAY! Okay, I get it! Damn!"

She was going to get them both killed, Bob figured.

Still, at least this time she didn't call me boomer.

He leaned around the corner and fired off another shot. *Better take it easy, preserve ammo.*

He glanced over at the old Lincoln beater, thirty feet away. *She had a point about carrying a piece.*

JUST SHY OF sixty feet due north, Nikolai ducked below the Cadillac's hood line again.

Coach Chris looked over at him and wondered what he'd been dragged into. The man was aggressive, but also stupid. It was a terrible place to ambush someone, with three roads offering routes out.

Maybe this is what happens when FIS agents are shit at the job. Maybe they get sent to places where a disposable asset can come in handy.

They had anticipated one of the targets might be carrying a weapon. The report sounded like a standard nine millimeter.

The steel dumpster, on the other hand, had been unanticipated. Instead of perforating the pair, they'd wasted ammunition for several minutes, barely getting a glimpse of their target.

And they think I'm the idiot.

These guys are going to get me killed.

The whine of police sirens seemed to get louder.

"What is the local response time?" Nikolai demanded.

"For what?"

The Russian was stoic. "Police."

"I don't know. Maybe fifteen, twenty minutes?"

"Or maybe seven. If you do not know, you do not know. So that could be for this?"

Coach Chris cocked an ear and listened to the siren. "Sure. I mean... Portland is really small. It doesn't take long to get from a to b."

"I could flank," Sascha suggested. Then he stood, emptying a clip at the dumpster and the brick wall beside it.

Nikolai waved his hand for him to sit. "Stop wasting ammunition. Yes, flank. But you must go a block over, a block up. Everyone in this country is armed, remember, so keep head down, keep the weapon under your jacket."

Sascha nodded and crouched low before scurrying towards the back of the car and the road behind the restaurant.

Bob's alarm bells were going off. There'd been no gunfire for a solid two minutes. "Something's wrong," he said.

"No shit!" Rachel hissed. "We're being shot at in the middle of goddamn Portland!"

"No, not that. It's just gone too quiet. They should've either advanced on us or..." He turned and glanced over at her truck. "Do you have a remote starter for that thing?"

"I do. Why? We're pinned down."

"One of them is flanking us. They can't penetrate our cover, and they haven't retreated or tried to get a new angle on us. That leaves them waiting for someone to flank, push us out of cover."

Her eyes widened. "What do we do?"

Bob chanced a quick glance around the edge of the

dumpster. "I'm going to create a distraction, and then you sprint for the truck. I cover you. You jump in and peel out of here, then turn back onto Brighton Avenue, by the front doors. I use the cover of the building to join you."

"Why aren't you the one running into the open?" she demanded.

"Because I'm the one who has to create the distraction. There's a streetlight directly above their car. Those bulbs create a nice pop and shower of glass when you shoot them. If you think you can hit one ducking out of cover in a split second..."

He let the thought hang. Rachel scowled and turned towards the truck, crouching behind him. "Say the word," she said.

"GO!" Bob said. He leaned around the dumpster and fired one shot, the streetlight exploding in a shower of glass and sparks, the three attackers ducking behind the black sedan.

Rachel sprinted for the truck, staring at it en route. A head appeared above the Cadillac's hood line, and Bob opened fire, sacrificing two bullets to keep them honest.

She jumped into the truck and peeled out of the lot, turning hard right as soon as its wheels found the street. Bob turned and sprinted back towards the front doors.

The man coming the other way down the sidewalk stopped, wide-eyed, at the sight of him. He reached under his jacket and withdrew the Kalashnikov just as the doors to the restaurant swung open.

The biker poked his head out and saw the massive man carrying the machine gun. "Oh shit!" he exclaimed, his head disappearing back inside.

Bob broke into a run, swerving his path slightly as the bigger man took aim.

The Toyota's engine picked up, Rachel gunning it, the quarter-ton pickup mounting the curb, clipping the big gunman with its oversized wing mirror, his body dashed to the sidewalk.

Bob jumped over him and climbed in.

She gunned the engine.

"Are they…?"

Bob looked over his shoulder. "Not quickly enough. Just keep your foot down until we're well clear."

"Who in the hell—"

"Later," Bob said. "For now… sirens. Cops approaching. We need to book."

"Okay. Where to?"

"JUST HIT THE GAS!"

Bob looked over his shoulder and through the truck's undersized back window. They were perhaps fifty yards up Brighton when the Cadillac squealed around the corner by the restaurant. The big man she'd clipped had raised himself off the sidewalk, and they slowed just long enough to let him in.

"Step on it," Bob said. "That Caddy's probably lighter than your truck, and they'll be faster."

"I am!" she said.

Up ahead, traffic had slowed, a line getting ready to turn right, towards a baseball stadium. Rachel began to slow down.

"Just go around them in the other lane!" Bob instructed.

"The ONCOMING lane!?"

"There's no traffic in it, and the road is flat for a half klick. No one's going to hit us."

She did as requested. "Jeez, this feels wrong."

"Yeah, so do bullets, generally speaking," Bob suggested. He glanced behind them. "They're gaining on us."

"I can't turn a quarter-ton Toyota into an Indy car, Bob."

Bob looked back once more. They'd taken the wrong lane, right behind them. The man they'd knocked over was leaning out the back window, pistol in hand.

The sound of the shot was muffled and far enough behind them that Rachel didn't immediately realize what it was. Then she gave Bob a quick, terse look. "Are they..."

"They are. Not much chance of them hitting us from—"

The back window shattered, safety glass spraying the cab.

She glared at him. "You were saying?"

Ahead, Brighton Avenue ran directly into a traffic circle, each of the five spokes already busy with traffic. "What do I do?" Rachel demanded.

"Just go straight through it. Ignore the cars, the road. Just aim us at the park on the other side."

"But—"

"Trust me, and maybe we make it out of this, OKAY!?"

She stepped on the gas. Bob could feel doubt seething from her every pore. The truck mounted the circular sidewalk surrounding the roundabout, narrowly missing the stone-and-wire modern art in its middle.

It bounced back onto the road, slipping between two cars using the traffic circle, over the curb and into the park.

Bob glanced back in time to see the trailing Cadillac grind to a halt, cut off by traffic from five directions. "Keep going," he said. "On the other side of Noyes Park, hang a hard left on Bedford."

She did as requested, the Toyota covering two more

blocks before he told her to turn right, then left again. "Slow down," Bob said. "We're just regular traffic now."

Rachel chanced a look back. "We're clear?"

"Yeah, we're clear."

"Jesus Christ." The Toyota stopped behind another car at a red light. She bumped her forehead against the wheel. Then she looked over at him. "I mean... holy shit, that was nuts."

"You okay?"

She nodded. "Now what? I mean... normally someone would go to the cops. But..."

"But you're AWOL, and I'm disinclined to be the center of attention. But we can still get back to work. Mike lives in North Deering, and I promised I'd introduce you."

13

The drive to Mike Schultz's house was taken in silence for the first five minutes, both recovering from the sudden rush of adrenaline.

Eventually, Rachel said, "Who ARE you, Bob? Exactly. Because prior to the last few hours, I'd have figured you were a construction worker helping out his buddy."

"Which I am."

"Yeah... but you're also an expert marksman..."

"Ex-Marine, remember?"

"And you worked in a field that teaches you to flag enemy agents? And you just happened to be in Portland when my gramps disappears, a man you're now suggesting was a Russian spy? That's a hell of a series of coincidences."

"I mean... it is what it is," Bob said. He didn't want to lie to her, but he didn't want Rachel prying too deeply, either. "People in the Marines often work in security when they get out, and they often get sick of it and find something else. I found Portland and fixing roofs."

"Uh-huh. That's all?"

"Pretty much. I fell off the wagon. Mike got me into group again. So I owe him."

She let it go for a couple more minutes of silence. Eventually, Rachel said, "You realize he's still going to lose his job, right?"

"Because..."

"Because when the shit hits the fan, he's still the guy who lost the body. He was still in charge of the scene, right? Having evidence someone took it doesn't really change that. I mean... maybe they see that video and they give him a break because he was right around the corner. But..."

Bob hated to admit it. "You might have a point there."

"So maybe what you really need to do," she suggested, "is help me find Gramps, or his body if he's dead, and whoever took him. Maybe then your friend Mike can build a case that he didn't fuck up, that someone who knew what they were doing set that crash up. That they did it so they could make Gramps disappear."

Bob mulled it over, looking for an easy out.

But she still had a point. Even if the original charge didn't stick because they had the video, Mike had still left an accident scene unattended, even if only for a few minutes. Mike would argue he couldn't park nearer, that the scene was right at an effectively blocked-off intersection, that normally being fifteen feet around a corner wouldn't be a problem.

They'd counter that, as the road was temporarily closed down, he could've just blocked the south side of the intersection with his cruiser instead of using tape.

It was a hindsight position. But they wouldn't be wrong. *Damn it. Why did I have to end up working with a lawyer?*

They pulled up outside Mike's house. Bob noticed Erin's red Kia Soul still wasn't in the driveway. "I think he's alone."

They got out of the car.

Mike answered the front door on the second knock. He had bags under his eyes, an exhausted expression. "Bob... it's late."

"I know, sorry. This is Rachel McGee. She's helping us."

Mike opened the door wide and invited them in, then closed it behind them. "Just... go straight ahead there, Rachel, and you'll hit the kitchen. I figured this late, you've probably got something?"

They reached the kitchen. Bob and Rachel sat down at the breakfast table. Mike gestured towards the counter. "You want a coffee or anything?"

"I'm good," Bob said, checking the functional U-shaped kitchen out. The fridge door was covered in art from a budding young crayon specialist.

Rachel shook her head. "I'll pass."

Mike took a third chair. "Okay, spill," he said.

"We've got some good news," Bob said.

"And some bad," Rachel added.

Bob breathed deeply, in through his nose, out through his mouth, the cycle reducing his stress. *Just... don't get in an argument with her in front of him. That's helping no one.*

"The good news is we've found a security video that proves you were telling the truth," Bob said. "The body was taken in the two-minute period after you walked back to your squad car."

Mike sat up straight, his incredulity obvious. "I mean... that's great! That's great, right?" He frowned a little. "Why aren't you both acting like that's great?"

Bob explained the dilemma.

Mike slumped in his chair. "Without knowing how or why, I still wear it. Maybe even then. Jeezum cripes." He hung his head. "At least... I mean, I guess at least Erin will believe me now."

In the moment, Bob remembered his other responsibility. He scanned the room again, looking for any signs of booze.

"If you're looking for what I think you are, you needn't," Mike said.

"All good?"

"Not a wee drop since you found me at the club."

Rachel leaned back in her chair and crossed her arms. "So?" she asked. "Am I right, or am I right?"

"Hard saying, not knowing," Mike said. "You come rolling up in my dooryard at eleven at night; suddenly I've got more problems than I started with."

"That station wagon belonged to my gramps," she said. "I think he may have been the man they kidnapped."

"You mean..." Then Mike caught himself, realizing how insensitive it was going to sound. "Beg pardon, miss, but I should be clear if Bob hasn't. There's no way that individual was alive. They didn't kidnap a living driver, they—"

"I know what you saw, or think you saw. But this whole thing is strange as hell. Maybe... I don't know, maybe he was just unconscious, maybe—"

Mike interrupted her by leaning over the small table and putting a giant hand on hers. Then he shook his head gently. "Been doing this for thirty years, dear. That driver had already passed. He was in a state, and I checked his pulse and all to be sure."

Rachel swallowed hard, her eyes welling slightly. She wiped them away quickly with the back of her hand. "I don't know why I'm letting it bother me. He was a real bastard to Grammy Rose. To everybody."

"But we can still figure out what happened to him," Mike said. "Right, Bob?"

Ah hell. It's not like you had a roofing job coming up or anything. "Yeah. Yeah, of course we can."

She brightened a little at that. "Then maybe we both get what we want. You get an explanation to hand to your superiors. I get closure on Gramps. But not on the basis that he was a Russian spy. Right?"

Mike's face contorted into pure bewilderment. "Eh!? A what now you say!?"

Bob explained Gramps's stolen identity. "What it wouldn't explain is why here, in Portland, hell and gone from any major cities. The closest we've got is Boston, two hours away. And we're a hell of a long way from DC."

"That... and the fact that my grandparents weren't traitors," Rachel added.

"She's right that we shouldn't jump to any conclusions," Mike said. "There could be any number of reasons we just haven't considered yet."

Bob glared at him for a moment. She was difficult enough already without an ally. "True. But my theory makes sense. They're the right age; they followed standard procedures during the Cold War for embedding agents. And outside of the fact that your grandfather was clearly headed somewhere at one in the morning, there's the fact that someone grabbed his body and shot at us."

"Someone shot at you?" Mike asked.

Bob told him about the restaurant. "Trying to catch us flat-footed, in public. They probably tagged my car with a radio frequency homing device. Whatever your gramps was up to, I get the strong sense it wasn't legal. Or... you know...

some jagoffs with Kalashnikovs wouldn't have tried to blow our heads off."

"Or maybe they were shooting at you," Rachel said, "and just followed me because I followed you." She turned Mike's way. "How much has he told you about what he used to do? Because if you'd seen him at the restaurant..."

Mike scowled a little. He clearly didn't like the tone of her intervention. "Bob's business is Bob's business," he said, "and I leave it at that. If you want him to cut your gramps some slack, maybe return the favor, Ms. McGee."

"They weren't shooting at me before we met up in the cemetery," Bob said, getting back on topic to cut the tension. "So the question is, when did they tag me? There? We'd only just met. I was at your grandparents' place but didn't leave my car, so it had to be either the cemetery or at the accident scene. But that also means they followed us there somehow. They could've been watching your grandparents' place, but they wouldn't have made me, also, or known what I was driving in order to tag the car."

Rachel saw where he was going. "Then that means they already knew you were involved, helping Mike. That also means they must've followed you to Atlantic Street in the first place. And that, in turn, means they know you're helping Mike and were already keeping tabs on both of you."

Mike looked unsure. "Yeah... but how? Disciplinary hearings are private until they issue a judgment, typically. How would they even know I was involved?"

"Maybe the same way I did." Rachel told them about the poorly redacted file.

They needed to understand the gravity of their situation, Bob realized.

"If these people are as organized and resourceful as I

think, they probably have police informants or other local law enforcement on the payroll," he said. "There are independent information brokers who can scrape together enough to bribe their way into classified government records; I highly doubt it would take someone well resourced more than a day to find you, Mike. You've been here three decades, and that's a big footprint. And if they had you under surveillance, watching this place, they'd have seen me come and go, and that would have given them where I live."

All three went silent for a moment, recognizing the implication. They were all in danger, all in someone's sights.

"We should go," Bob said. "If I'm right, my car is tagged. But it's back at the restaurant, which means we have a few hours where they're unsure of our location. If we find a motel tonight, we might be able to throw them off us for a while."

"Assuming they're not out there already," Mike said, nodding towards the front door. "Watching."

Rachel eventually said, "Maybe. Maybe you're right and this is something bigger than all of us. But... outside of knowing my family, there's one thing working against your spy theory, Bob. That scene at the restaurant: would a Russian agent be stupid enough to try to gun us down in the middle of Portland, Maine? Wouldn't they try something quieter, a little Novichok on a door handle or umbrella tip, maybe, like in England a few years back?"

Bob rubbed his chin stubble. She had a point. There had to be a reason, though. Something had set them off.

Or someone. He glanced over at her. They'd already been following him, which meant they'd probably ID'd him already, if they were FIS or had its support.

Maybe she's just the latest unlucky winner of the meet Bob Singleton lottery.

THE MOTEL ROOM was still stifling. Sascha was smoking French Gauloises cigarettes, dark tobacco in maize paper giving off an acrid hue that drifted across the rooms in cloudlike strata.

Coach Chris felt slightly nauseated. He hadn't been in an enclosed environment with a smoker for years. It was tense, too, because Sascha didn't say much, and Boris – lying propped up by pillows on a twin bed, reading the local paper – said even less.

Nikolai was out getting food while they waited to hear from Yaremchuk.

"He's going to be pissed," Coach Chris muttered.

"What?" Sascha turned his head and blew out a plume of blue-gray smoke. "Who is going to be pissed?"

"Yaremchuk, over this debacle tonight."

The big Russian scoffed a little at that. "He favors Nikolai because he gets the job done in the past, and because he knows Nikolai was FIS star. He will not care, not too much."

"You didn't question his plan tonight. But you're clearly not an idiot. You must've had reservations about a public shoot-out."

On the bed, Boris lowered his paper. "Because Sascha is a good soldier. He follows orders." He returned to his reading.

Whether he agreed or not, Sascha kept it to himself. He butted out the cigarette on the saucer from his coffee cup. "We are comrades. We have worked together a long time."

"You owe him."

"Sure. He got us all sacked by the service... but he also got us replacement gigs with the diplomatic security corps, and that eventually got us back in with the service. So we go full circle."

"Except, unlike Yaremchuk and his ilk, you're now disposable, without diplomatic protection. The same as me," Coach Chris said. "Even when he left you in this—"

"Even when, even when," Sascha groused. "You are a part-time asset. You cannot understand."

Boris lowered the paper again. "There are always political considerations in what we do, internal, external. But with Nikolai, you know what you get. Yes, he can be like the bull in the china shop when on target. But he succeeds. And as brave as you may think you are in your role as a schoolteacher and baseball coach, do you really mean to tell me you would say no to him?"

He waited for Coach Chris to contradict him. After a beat, he raised the paper once more. "I did not think so."

Across the room, the door handle began to turn just as the phone rang.

14

Igor Yaremchuk was seething as he berated them over the encrypted line, put on speaker for all four men to hear.

"Bozhe moy!" Yaremchuck spat. "Now, not only do we have to worry about whether any cameras nearby caught images, we have the cops nervous... AND THE TARGET IS ALERTED!?"

From the sofa, Nikolai said, "We know where they live. We could set up ambush, wait for them to return. Quick and quiet."

"This... this is not good, for any of us," Yaremchuk said. "When the director hears of this, I will get my balls cut off maybe, yes? Which means maybe I should cut your balls off."

"It was poor luck, nothing more," Nikolai said. "We are slowed down by having to babysit the sleeper."

"Nikolai... you know I trust you to do the job. But this..."

"So we go out and next time do it right, is all," Nikolai

said. "We are more cautious this time. We can find them today, I promise this."

"Perhaps. But Uncle is concerned about who they've talked to, how much they know. I think maybe he's right. He thinks it cannot be a coincidence that Bob Singleton is here. He wants us to find out how much exposure we face... which, if your new friend recalls, is what I suggested in the first place, not to just go in guns blazing."

He had said nothing of the sort, Nikolai knew. But he would not be able to prove it. Ever the politician, Yaremchuk was preparing to sacrifice them as solely responsible if they ultimately failed at their task.

It was nearly midnight. "Where are they now?" Yaremchuk demanded. "Have they gone home?"

He took out his phone and loaded the app. "He left his vehicle at the restaurant."

"So the girl and Singleton are working together, for sure," Yaremchuk said. "But at least if they are still on the move and haven't given up, they are still there. Portland is small."

"Singleton's apartment is downtown," Chris said. "The girl we haven't figured out yet. She was at the old man's house, though."

"The old man had a grandchild, yes?" Yaremchuk said. "You read his file."

"I did," Chris replied. "But she's supposed to be in Baltimore, working as a Navy lawyer."

"Stupid! Of course it's her! She's found out the old man has disappeared, and she's looking for him," Yaremchuk spat.

"Wouldn't Uncle have known, flagged us?" Chris said. "After all, the girl is—"

"Uncle lets us know what Uncle needs us to know," Nikolai interjected. "What next, then?"

"We'll find them again tomorrow. This time, handle things quietly and with discretion," Yaremchuk ordered. "Uncle leases a warehouse near the airport. It is functional as a safe house or for other purposes."

"We won't fail again," Nikolai said.

"You had better not. I know you, Nicky. I suppose you know there is a bounty on his head, yes? You figure that money will buy you favors a back home."

Nikolai could feel his two comrades glaring at him. "Of course, you know full well I would split this with my men," he replied.

"Of course, Nicky," Yaremchuk said. "No doubt you were thinking of them."

Bob and Rachel left the motel with the sun barely risen and the streets still quiet.

He stuck to the speed limit. They were in no hurry, and the truck had been parked behind the building, with little chance of being spotted.

At the first traffic light, he glanced over at his passenger. She looked sluggish and sleepy.

"I'm glad you let me drive," he said. "You're not exactly coming across as a morning person right now."

"It's six freaking twenty," she muttered.

"Navy doesn't have JAGs up at the crack of dawn? It must seem a charmed life to the average able seaman, watching you rouse out of bed whenever—"

"I normally get up at seven," she said. "We were working late, remember?" She rubbed her forehead and sipped on the Styrofoam cup of coffee rescued from the motel lobby before they left. "Why so early?"

"Ferries are already running, and I suspect we only have a couple more hours before our pursuers from last night track us down. We just have to hope they don't know enough about you to figure out where we're headed."

The Peaks Island Ferry was already busy at six forty-five in the morning. After buying a ticket in the office, they drove the pickup on board, a traffic controller waving them into one of two empty lanes and onto the ship's lower level. After parking, they walked back to the stairs leading up to the main deck.

It took less than twenty minutes to cross. Bob leaned against the rail throughout, enjoying the smell of the ocean, the slosh of waves against the sheet-metal hull, the stiff breeze that rustled passengers' windbreakers. Rachel sat a few feet away on one of the cherry-red metal benches.

He turned back towards her. "Now, doesn't this beat driving in traffic? A bracing breeze, salt in the air."

She squinted at him disdainfully. "Can't you just be a grumpy schlub in the morning like the rest of us?"

"Oh, come on!" He strode over and sat down next to her. "Look how much better off we are than eight hours ago."

"A boat ride beats machine-gun fire, yes. Not a high bar."

Bob's pitch at the motel had been simple enough: if Rachel's grandfather had been involved in anything dangerous, there was a solid chance her mother knew something about it. And they needed to explain her grandfather having Domas Petrauskas's ID.

"I just hope she's in a good mood," the young lawyer said.

"I'm sure she's not that bad," Bob said. "You seem to have turned out okay." He glanced at her again and remembered the temper from a day earlier. "Generally speaking."

Rachel sighed. She downed the last of her coffee and chucked the cup into the adjacent bin. "If I'm angry sometimes, it's because we're not much of a family. She's always shown disdain for my grandparents. She wasn't..." She let the thought hang there for a moment, unable to figure out quite how to express herself. "She's a good person, but she wasn't a good mother. I think... I don't know... I think maybe she thought it would be more fun for me after my father left if we were more like girlfriends than a mother and daughter. So she let a lot go."

"And she left you with them for a year?"

Rachel nodded. "When I was seven. She never really explained it to me, at least not properly. Her clinic license was nearly suspended after she slipped up and overprescribed an older gentleman. He was okay, but they investigated, decided she was drinking too much, working 'unreasonable' hours."

"But she kept her license?"

"Yeah, barely. She quit drinking completely, for about three years."

"It didn't stick."

"Nope. I'm sure she hides it from her regulars. The island's really small, but there are still about a thousand people full time, so she still gets plenty of traffic at the clinic. They'll know, though. Everybody there is up in everyone else's business. Gossip on the island is a cottage industry, and her next-door neighbor is one of the worst."

"So perhaps there are other people there who knew your grandparents?"

She turned abruptly and fixed him with a hard stare.

"Are you going to raise the Russian spy nonsense with her? Because something like that might set her off, especially if she thinks you're talking to the neighbors. I don't want you to upset her, or anyone on the island, more than is necessary. As I'm pretty damn sure that you're wrong—"

"I don't think I am," Bob said. "Look, whether you want to accept it or not, your grandfather was wrapped up in something, and it wasn't good. A man driving his car, after he disappeared, died and was then removed from an accident scene. Your grandmother spoke another language, possibly from a Soviet state, Lithuania. Your grandfather carried false ID based on real government paper."

"None of that is proof he betrayed his country," she said sullenly. She hung her head as the ferry approached Peaks Island, heading towards a tiny port and the neighboring two-story, A-frame houses. From a distance, they seemed haphazardly spread, wood-sided structures in pale blue and yellow, ochre red and forest green, from the era before kit homes.

"No, it's not," Bob conceded. "But those guys shot at us last night for a reason. And I'm not going to figure out exactly what was going on or what happened to him if you continually lose it out of embarrassment or shame. Look... I get that none of this is easy for you. My life hasn't exactly been smooth sailing either. But maybe let's try to look at the bright side: we have leads; we just need to connect them. And I'll take a boat ride and some family squabbling over bullets in a restaurant parking lot."

"If you mean visiting the island is less troublesome than being shot at, I guess," she said. "Although... you haven't met my mother yet."

. . .

Liz McGee lived on Seashore Avenue, a long, winding road that almost encircled the island's four-mile perimeter. Rachel drove, the asphalt winding between trees for a few minutes, then past small family homes before exiting into a steep, sweeping curve, the ocean just twenty feet or so to their left, whitecap waves crashing against a short, sloping rocky beach.

"That's Spar Cove," Rachel said. "I used to come here with my mom when I was little and skip stones. The land you can see in the distance is Long Island, which is sort of like Peaks for manic-depressives. Not as many people choose to live there."

Bob sensed a little friendly rivalry. "It's not as nice, then?"

"Not at all. Not many services, and the locals are sort of reserved about strangers."

"But not on Peaks?"

She clucked her tongue a little. "The problem here is the overnighters, the short-term visits. Lots of houses that people used to live in full time have been converted into Airbnb rentals, that kind of thing. The visitors come over with their cars, even though most aren't here long enough to need them, so the road congestion is increasing, and the parking problems near the terminal are getting worse."

"Then this is like Nantucket, I'm guessing, with lots of monied types having a second home here?"

"You'll see. When we drive back to the terminal, I'll take the other half of Seashore, where the bigger homes are." She gestured ahead towards the shore. "You see that rock jutting out of the water? That's Whaleback Ledge. I used to sit out there as a kid when my mother was being difficult, just let the sound of the waves shut it all out."

She turned the car right, down a short gravel driveway.

Her mother's house was modest and couldn't have been much more than two bedrooms, a living room and kitchen, Bob figured. It was the only bungalow among a group of about eight houses.

"You're sure she'll be home?"

Rachel nodded towards the back of the house, where they could just see the tail end of a red hatchback protruding. "Some folks here use golf carts, but Mom never really took to them. And it's Sunday; clinic's closed on Sunday."

They climbed the front steps, and Rachel rang the bell.

They waited.

No answer.

After about a minute, Rachel got impatient. She rang the bell twice more.

Still nothing.

"Are you sure—"

"HELLLOOO!"

They both turned towards the call. On the house next door's porch, a short, elderly woman in a yellow flowered sundress was waving at them.

Rachel spoke under her breath. "Remember the gossipy neighbor I mentioned?"

"This is her?"

"In the dress that looks like it was made from seventies curtains? Yeah, that's Mrs. Arbogast."

She waved for them to come over. They went back down the steps and crossed the twenty feet or so to the property line. "Hello, Mrs. Arbogast," Rachel offered with what Bob figured was uncharacteristic warmth. "How are you, dear?"

"Is that you, Rachel? My eyes aren't what they used to be."

Bob figured she had to be eighty if she was a day.

"And who's this you've got with you? Did you meet a new feller?"

"Ugh, no," Rachel said. "Sybil, this is Bob. He's just a friend. And he's Mom's age."

"Well now, in my day there wasn't nothing wrong with finding a fella who's a little older and has the means to take care of you," she said. "But I suppose times have changed. Come over for a quick visit? Or are you staying a while?"

"Just a visit, Mrs. A." Rachel nodded back towards her mother's place. "How has she been? You know, with the... issues."

"Now, I don't like to get involved in the business of others, as you know," Mrs. Arbogast suggested.

"Of course not."

"But if I'm being honest, she's been drinking pretty regular. Had a go at me for waking her up last week. Came out in the dooryard in her bra and knickers, but it was already noon." Mrs. Arbogast turned towards Bob. "She likes a bit of the..." She made a drinking motion. "Not that I'm paying attention or it's my business."

"Mrs. Arbogast used to babysit me when I was little," Rachel told Bob. "She hates gossips." She rolled her eyes quickly, and Bob suppressed a smirk.

"After Rachel's father left, her mother needed a little help is all," the senior said.

Bob could see Rachel gently nodding in his peripheral vision. He knew that nod; it wasn't a gesture of agreement so much as irritation.

"Is that a New Jersey accent I detect?" he asked.

"It certainly is! Grew up in Camden."

"I was just near there in Philly a few months back," Bob said. "Tough town, Camden."

"You bet your sweet bippy!" Mrs. Arbogast said. "They used to say the boys from Camden could piss nails and crap glass, they was so tough."

"Yes, well... a long time ago now," Rachel said. She nodded back to the house. "We'd better go check on her, Mrs. A. You take care now, dear, okay?"

"I will! And stop by before youse leave. I just made my spice cakes that you love so much."

They walked back to the other porch. "She's right about the cakes. But as you probably guessed, her commentary on the local gossips was—"

"Lacking in self-perception?" Bob suggested.

"Exactly."

"She seems pretty spry for her age."

"You're telling me," Rachel said. "Blind as a bat without her glasses, but she ran a half-marathon a couple of years ago."

She knocked on the door again.

They waited another minute without response.

"Jeezum crow," Rachel muttered. "She's probably just sleeping still. Hold on a sec." She crouched down and lifted the corner of the front door mat. She retrieved a spare key. "She's left it there for years in case one of the locals had to help her home after a few too many at the Lions Club meetings."

She opened the door, and they entered. A small cloakroom emptied directly into the kitchen. "MOM! ARE YOU HERE?" she yelled.

They heard rustling, someone swearing under her breath. A few seconds later, Liz McGee emerged through the door at the other end of the room. She wore slippers and a dressing gown, hastily tying its waist belt.

"Lord love a duck, you don't have to yell, Rachel!" she chided, squinting against the room's perfectly normal level of light. "Thought you were the lad who delivers propane. He keeps pestering me for the right time to drop off and threatening to just pop around."

Liz looked like her daughter but with a softer, rounded face. She was a good three inches shorter, too, with dark brown eyes, apple cheekbones. *Pretty in a hungover, irritated sort of way*, Bob figured.

She nodded his way. "Who be this, then?"

"This is Bob. He's a friend of a friend. He's helping me look for Gramps."

The older woman rolled her eyes. "Land's sakes! I'm telling you, he just got wanderlust, is all. He'll either come back shortly or let us know eventually. But now you're dragging others into this."

"We have reason to believe something bad happened to your father, Dr. Peters," Bob said.

She held out a hand daintily to shake. "It's just Liz when I'm not at work. Ooh! You've got big hands, Mr..."

"Bennett. But just Bob is fine."

She was peering at him, her eyes narrowing slightly. Bob knew the look, an intensity of expression some women got when they found a guy attractive.

But it had been years. If it had happened since Maggie died, he hadn't noticed it.

The notion of ruining another important relationship – and his decade of drinking – had precluded even considering the opposite sex. He had chemistry with Dawn, but that was different, a bond of friendship and trust.

And if he was honest with himself, he hadn't even recognized that look before Maggie, and she'd had to explain it to him.

Bob felt the blood rise in his face. *Jesus H, don't blush! Don't blush just because a woman gives you a lingering glance, you idiot! Be a professional.* "Wind's blowing pretty hard out there," he said, trying to cover. He crossed his arms, self-consciously trying to look casual. "When you didn't answer the door, Rachel got worried."

"Oh, Rachel is always worried. You'll learn that about her." Liz played with a tiny silver locket around her neck. "I wasn't the best mother, as I'm sure she's made clear."

"Mom..."

"But I don't think you need to worry about her grandfather. As I told her, he's just on the road somewhere."

Bob needed her to accept reality if they were going to talk in detail. "We've seen a video that might show him dying in a car crash," he said. "I'm sorry to break that to you, but you should know."

"A video?" She stopped fiddling with the locket and mirrored him, crossing her own arms. "Of a car crash."

"It shows his station wagon being hit by another car and the body of the ejected driver. It's too far to see clearly—" Rachel began to say.

"And where did this come from, this video?" Liz asked. Her hand drifted back to the locket.

"That's not important right now," Bob said. "What is important is that a pair of men can be seen removing the driver's body from the scene in the few minutes that the police officer who attended went back to his car. If your father was driving... I hate to tell you this, Mrs. McGee, but my police friend is certain he's dead."

She was staring blankly now, as if looking past them.

"But they talked about the driver, the police. When Rachel first went in to waste their time."

"Mother... please."

"Well, that's what it probably is, more of his selfish bullshit, wasting everyone's time. Police said the car was probably stolen."

"Police haven't seen the video yet," Bob said. "There are clearly three bodies visible when it starts, two when it ends."

"Can I see it?" she asked. "The Wi-Fi's terrible here sometimes, but it's good enough."

"That's not possible," Bob interjected before Rachel could agree. "The guy who owns it won't give it up without a warrant."

Rachel turned her head for a brief second to give him a hard stare but didn't interrupt. *Great,* Bob thought. *Now I'll have to explain to her why we can't trust her mother. That's bound to go well.*

Liz nodded behind them. "Come on, let's have a seat in the living room. I'll make you both a coffee, and you can explain this nonsense to me good and proper."

"Tea?" Bob asked hopefully.

15

Liz poured Bob's tea slowly, holding a tiny silver pot above a matching serving tray. On it sat a small pot of cream, another of sugar. "You're not from Portland, I take it, Bob?"

Bob leaned forward from his sofa seat and rubbed his hands together nervously. *Get a grip on yourself, man. She's pretty. Lots of women are pretty. Nothing else is happening here.* "No, not at all."

Not at all? Like I could partially be from Portland? Good grief, you're awkward, Bobby.

"From your accent, I figured maybe Chicago, but there's something a little more... Canadian, maybe?"

"Close. Spent years in Chi Town. But I grew up in the UP. It all gets a little mixed up sometimes."

"Michigan man, then. Cream?"

"Sure, just a little."

She poured it. "The UP is pretty rugged in places." She sat down in an armchair across from them and retrieved her own cup. "Lots of outdoorsman types." She peered over the rim of the cup at him as she sipped. "You know, fellas who are good with their hands."

He nodded gently. "I've been known to chop down a tree or two when necessary."

"Well! Well, well, well." She took another sip of tea. "And what's brought you all the way out to Maine, then?"

"He fixes roofs," Rachel said bluntly. "It's not interesting."

"It's true," Bob said. "But it's rewarding knowing you're making someone's life a little easier. And it keeps me fit."

"It certainly does," Liz said. She took another long sip, her gaze narrowing again.

Bob's head felt hot.

"Oh, for cryin—" Rachel began to say. She cut herself off. "Mom, Bob has some questions about Gramps and Grammy Rose. Okay? Maybe we could just get to the point."

"Oh now, be good!" Liz told her daughter. "We don't see each other enough as it is. No need to rush things, is there, Bob?"

"Not at all." Then he glanced sideways and saw Rachel's irritated visage.

"This is serious!" Rachel said. "Mom, men shot at us last night."

"WHAT!?"

"I'm serious. We'd been asking questions about the accident scene. The next thing you know, we're walking out of a restaurant nearby and—"

"We don't know that it was connected," Bob said. "But it seems likely."

"That's..." Liz rose, an arm across her midsection. She looked anxious. "Maybe I have to rethink this." She turned back towards Bob. "Of course, anything I can do to help."

"We should clarify a few things if we can. I don't think it'll help ID the shooters, but it might help us figure out what your dad was up to. Have you ever heard the name Domas Petrauskas before?"

She looked momentarily surprised. "I certainly have, but not in a great many years. Domas was dad's cousin from Europe. Lithuania, I believe. They're the family my great-grandparents left behind when they emigrated to England. The story goes that my great-grandfather Jonas Petrauskas recognized that as monstrous as Stalin was, he wouldn't be satisfied with the territory he held and would eventually go after the Baltic states. So he sold up his shoe store and moved everyone to London. But that was a century ago, nearly."

"And Domas?"

"I didn't know him myself, but Dad said he stayed with his family here in Portland when they were young. My father said he came over and was doing odd jobs in town and on the road. Died in a car accident, I think he said."

Rachel seized on the information. "So if Gramps was carrying his ID, it could've just been as a keepsake?"

"Oh, absolutely," Liz said. "In fact, I do recall him producing something like that once, saying he wanted to hang on to his memory. Dad had spent an entire summer, two years earlier, learning Lithuanian so that he could write to family back in Vilnius, or some such place, and they'd become close friends. You know, as boys do."

"Well then, that explains that," Rachel said.

"Uh-huh," Bob said.

But it didn't. He didn't hold it against the young lawyer because they were discussing her family. But Rachel had clearly missed a few unanswered questions. He decided against raising them right then. He was pretty certain Liz was lying to them, but there was no point tipping his hand until they'd learned something new.

"Now... I sense maybe you're not buying what I'm selling, Bob," Liz said. She chewed on her lower lip slightly. She sat back down on the edge of the couch, her body language nervous, hands folded in her lap like an old Sears portrait shot.

She has a little overbite, he thought. *Cute*. "Not at all. I mean... I've got no issues," he said.

"None?" Liz nodded towards his hands. She smiled demurely. "I don't see a ring. A man with no issues, good job, fit. Is there a Mrs. Bob somewhere in town?"

Bob found himself staring at her cleavage.

The question snapped him out of it. *Good God, man. It's obviously been way too long since you've been with someone,* the little voice said.

He'd never been big on intimacy, not until Maggie. It just hadn't mattered as much to him as it seemed to to other people. The doc in Seattle had said that was part of being neurodivergent, his general stoicism about emotional things. About anything that didn't involve risk or trauma, really.

"No. Not married. Never have been." *Why? Why did you put it that way? Because you don't want to mention you were engaged. Because then you'll have to talk about Maggie.*

"Tsk! Almost seems wrong, a big, strong fella like yourself being all alone." Liz stirred her tea slowly as she said it.

"Mom!" Rachel interrupted.

"Yes, sweetie?"

"We were talking about Gramps, remember?" The younger woman didn't hide her annoyance.

Liz set her tea down on the coffee table between them. Then she leaned forward, elbows on her knees. "Whatever last night was about, I'm sure he'll turn up in a month or so, tell us he was in California selling widgets to wind farms or some such nonsense. I mean... he wasn't planning on going anywhere. He tried to borrow money from me just a few days before they found the car, to pay off his new dentures."

"He was struggling for cash?" Bob asked.

"I doubt it," Liz said. "He just figured because he was turning eighty soon, I should make his life easier whenever possible. Knowing the way he thinks, he'd probably already paid for it and was just trying to weasel the eighteen hundred bucks out of me. He didn't even need the thing."

"Then... why did he buy it?" Rachel asked.

"Because he'd set it down in the bathroom a week earlier, then not been able to find it for twenty minutes. He said if his mind went any more, he wanted to be able to chew food, even if he couldn't remember what he liked. So he bought a backup."

"He was cautious," Bob said.

"He's difficult," Liz said. "He's always been difficult. He made my mother and me miserable on a regular basis. It's why I pay him as little mind as possible."

"I get that," Bob said. "Mine was a piece of work, too."

Liz leaned in a little. "Raised you up right, though, it would seem."

He smiled a little at that. She was charming, no doubt. "Grammy Rose didn't do so badly, either," he said.

Rachel sat up straight, her expression a pained wince. "Would the two of you stop" – she gestured with both hands in a "go away" shuffle – "whatever this is. This is serious."

Liz rolled her eyes. “Oh… relax, love. I don’t get a chance to chat with too many interesting people my own age.”

Her daughter sprang to her feet. “Now’s not the time. Bob, do you need anything else?”

He got up more slowly. “I think we’re good for now. But… perhaps I could grab a number off you, Liz? You know, in case I have any other questions?” He handed her his phone.

She tapped it in. “Or even just to get together again, perhaps, when everyone’s a little more relaxed.”

ON THE PORCH, Rachel waited until the door had swung shut behind them before turning Bob’s way.

“Was that really necessary, flirting with my mother!? I mean, Jesus H, bud!? Timing, maybe?”

Bob felt another blush rising. “It wasn’t exactly intentional. She’s a charming person.”

“RACHEL! DEAR!”

They turned. Mrs. Arbogast was back on her porch, waving at them with one hand, carrying a small plate of buns in the other.

Bob was thankful for the interruption.

They wandered over.

“I promised youse spice rolls,” the senior said. “I used to make these for her when Rachel was just a teeny little thing, barely up to her mom’s waist.”

Rachel took one of the heart-shaped pastries and took a bite. Her eyes rolled up slightly from pleasure. “Ohhh, that’s heavenly,” she said.

“Bob?” Mrs. Arbogast said.

He didn’t want to offend, so he took one haltingly, along

with a proffered paper napkin, and took a sniff. It smelled of cinnamon and sugar, white flour. It probably had hundreds of empty calories to it, not to mention the carbs and cholesterol. It smelled lovely, but his brain sent him the no-go message. "I'm watching my diet," he said, wrapping it in the napkin and pocketing it. "I'll save it for later when I'm allowed a snack."

"Suit yourself, hon. But you'll want to eat it shortish, or it'll go stale." Mrs. Arbogast turned Rachel's way and lowered her voice to a conspiratorial hush. "Is your ma okay... ya know... with the..." She let the sentence tail and made the same "drinky, drinky" motion with her hand.

"She's fine," Rachel said. "She's exactly as difficult as always."

"Well, give her some credit for being the sweet soul she is!" Mrs. Arbogast chided. "She does a valuable service with her clinic, and you know how much she loves you."

"Yeah." Rachel hung her head a little once more. "Yeah, I guess I do."

"We need to get back to the city, though," Bob said, jerking his head south, trying to extract her from the awkward familiarity of the conversation. "It was nice meeting you, ma'am."

"Certainly, young man, for sure. Drop in again, okay?"

FROM THE KITCHEN WINDOW, Liz McGee watched as her daughter backed her truck up in a semicircle before heading down the gravel drive towards Seashore Avenue.

She waited until the car had disappeared completely before taking her phone out of her robe pocket.

She hesitated for a moment, her finger over the screen,

her expression doleful. But it wasn't like she had any choice. She knew that.

She never had.

She speed-dialled a number.

"Yeah. Yeah, it's me. I know, but they took longer than I expected, that's all. They're headed for the ferry terminal now."

16

The ferry ride and drive through Portland had taken place in near silence, Rachel's irritation at how Bob and her mother had gotten along obvious.

They had been back at the motel for less than five minutes when Bob knocked on Rachel's room door.

She opened it, still glaring, her mood obviously not much better than an hour earlier. He figured the conversation was going to be difficult, so it made sense to get it over with while she was still irritated. Either way, there was going to be shouting, based on their discussion at the restaurant.

"You got a minute?" he asked.

"You haven't told me what we're supposed to do next," she said. "So... sure. I'm AWOL, remember? I'm not going anywhere until we find something."

She stepped aside, and he entered the room.

Bob nodded to the breakfast table and two chairs, by the window. "Sit for a minute?"

She nodded, but sucked on her tongue a little. "Why do I

get the feeling this is going to be more that I really don't want to hear?"

"I suspect I don't mask my emotional intentions or inner feelings as well as I thought," he said. "My shrink said it's one of my neurodiversity issues."

"Ah. More information than I needed, but I guess it explains some things. Please... sit."

He took one chair, and she sat down a second later.

"Okay, spit it out."

How do I do this tactfully? As Team Seven Alpha, gaining intel had taken a variety of methods. When dealing with in-person sources, he'd generally been threatening or deceitful. Sometimes, it had been the threat of pain, other times the promise to release embarrassing information.

Neither seemed appropriate at a Motel Six in Portland at one in the afternoon with an AWOL Navy JAG lawyer.

What would Sister Eva have said? He thought about his late friend a lot. She'd had a wisdom that only came from making a lot of mistakes.

"Rachel... you know my stake in this was helping Mike. And Mike figures helping you could clear up his mess. So I've always been as straight with you about all of this as I could."

"Okay. Now you're pre-qualifying something, so I'm really expecting to be pissed."

His head slumped back slightly from exasperation. "I'm just trying to be honest even though it's often shit you don't want to hear. Can you understand the position I'm in? Even a little?"

She didn't answer immediately, instead studying him, her mouth a mirthless line. Then she pursed her lips and looked away a little, acutely aware that even though she wanted to take her anger out on him, it wasn't right. "I get that. Fine. Just... say what you need to say, Bob, okay?"

"Okay, but you need to promise to be professional about it. Because I am bound to piss you off. I piss almost everybody off."

"Except my mother," she said dryly. "She seemed positively giddy in your presence."

"Maybe." Then he regretted the line immediately. Intimating someone was lying was almost worse than just accusing them. *You knew that, but it still didn't occur to you before you said it, did it? Jackass.*

"What's that supposed to mean?" Rachel's nostrils flared a little, her jaw rigid, as if helping restrain her mounting temper. "She gave you a perfectly good explanation for the driver's license. Isn't that enough?"

Eva would've told you to let her come to the realization herself. Guide her. Help her figure it out; don't shove it down her throat.

"Think about what we know. Then think about what she said. Do it one piece at a time."

She breathed in deeply. He wasn't sure if she was girding herself for a task or just warding off the desire to hit him. Her gaze drifted to the wall as she thought back through everything they'd heard over the course of two days.

Then her chin lifted, shocked, stark realization setting in. "Shit."

Her hand came up to her mouth and covered it for just a few seconds, Rachel letting it register. Then the hand drifted back down to the table, her eyes flitting about in bewilderment at what she'd just determined.

"She lied. She lied to us. If Domas had been living with them, it wouldn't have had a Bangor address on the license." Rachel was chagrined. "Why didn't I spot that when she said it? I'm a JAG lawyer. I'm supposed to catch anything out of place, spot inconsistencies."

"Because it's family," Bob said. "Everyone has blind spots with family."

"But... why would she lie? Unless... she knew Gramps wasn't who he said he was, maybe."

Reality had begun to sink in, Bob figured. "That means the story about why your grandparents speak Lithuanian was bogus too," Bob said. "And besides... it didn't explain why your grandmother would've learned the language. Were they even married then?"

"They got married in '62, I think," she said absently, her mind elsewhere. "I... I mean, Mom's lied to me before about small things, because she's an alcoholic. And a mom. But..." She didn't finish the thought, her mouth hanging open slightly in shock. "Bob... can you give me a few minutes to process this?" she asked.

He nodded and rose. "Sure. I'll just..." He looked around the room for a safe distance and another seat.

"Alone," she said. "I need a few minutes alone." She glanced up at him sternly. "Okay?"

"I'll be next door when you're ready," he said.

Bob headed back to his room. He'd seen that look before, not too long ago, when he'd saved Marcus Pell from a private hit squad in Chicago, and Marcus had learned his parents' murder had covered up their time in the CIA.

It was a mixture of painful realities: confusion that the life she knew was a lie, a shocked sense of betrayal that someone she loved could perpetrate a hoax.

He wondered how deeply Liz was involved in her

parents' activities. Would deep-cover agents force a family member to behave as an asset? Would they share anything dangerous with them?

Rachel had stumbled on her grandmother speaking Lithuanian on the phone. Other than that, she'd had no clue. The same might well be true of her mother, he supposed.

But then why was Liz lying? Whether it was to help or to prevent her father from being hurt, she'd spun them a careful story about her Lithuanian second cousin, as if she'd been prepared that it might come up at some point.

She had to be involved, Bob knew.

He put the kettle on to make tea. He looked in the mirror above the desk and TV, the motel's cream plaster walls and oil painting reflected behind him.

Liz had been genuinely interested in him, without a doubt.

Or... she's a hell of an actress. She was lying about her father, he knew that.

Am I... getting honey trapped? He couldn't immediately recall the last time anyone had even tried it.

Then the memory flooded back.

Madagascar. The escort, the gangster's girlfriend who tried to slit my throat, a year after Maggie. The woman's timing had been fatally terrible, attempting to murderously seduce a man with nothing left to live for.

He shook his head quickly, trying to purge the notion. *Why am I even thinking about this? Liz is up to her neck in whatever's going on, even if only because she's the victim's daughter.*

Maybe that was why it had been so easy to get along with Sister Eva, with Dawn, with Sharmila in Bakersfield. *Maybe there's a part of you that misses being around women. Not even the intimacy, just the contrast.* When he'd been talking to Liz, he realized, he'd been working, actively listening. But he hadn't felt that nervous tension, that sense that the person he was talking with could blow at any second.

Maybe sometimes you just need a break from all the goddamned testosterone. You hadn't talked to Dawn in a while, or been around any women, really. And you missed it.

He rose suddenly.

Shit.

Speaking of missing things...

He'd thought critically of Rachel for missing her mother's lies. But if Liz was lying to them and had prepared that story, there was every chance she'd told someone else they were there.

And I missed that for – he checked his battered old Seiko wristwatch – *about two hours. Jesus H, Bobby. Get your head in the game.*

If whoever had shot at them at the restaurant knew when they were leaving the island, they'd also have had someone waiting at the terminal to follow them.

And they'd know where we are.

The thump and crash sounded on cue, muffled by the wall but audible from the room next door.

It sounded like a lamp hitting the ground and breaking.

That could've been an accident.

But I doubt it.

Bob headed for the door. Halfway there, he reached into the soft-sided tennis bag beside the desk, withdrawing the Colt 1911 and securing it in his waistband.

. . .

Bob opened the door to room 112 slowly, leaving just a crack. He peered into the hallway, seeing no one. He opened the door another inch and checked the circular safety mirror near the hallway exit, at the end of the corridor.

Clear.

He left the room, checking both ways quickly for movement. He took a few steps due north to Rachel's room door. He quickly moved past it, noticing it a quarter inch ajar, and flattened himself against the wall.

A second later, the door opened a few feet, and a man's crewcut head and thick neck stuck out. Bob didn't hesitate, taking one step to drive momentum through the flat-palm punch, catching the man square in temple, the zone police call a "stunner." The man's head slammed off the doorjamb, and he slumped to the ground, his pistol tumbling from his grip and onto the carpet.

Too much noise.

He hadn't had a choice, he knew. The guard would've spotted him in a split second anyway.

Keep the advantage.

He drew the Colt and pushed the door open, scraping past the barely conscious torso. The TV was on, the volume low, a noon news anchor chatting away.

He raised the pistol.

"Be cool!" The man ten feet ahead of him stood beside the first double bed, a few feet past the bathroom entrance. He was smaller and older than the guard but still athletic, an arm around Rachel's neck, a Glock 17 against her temple. The Boston Red Sox cap looked somehow out of place. "Just be cool, Mr. Singleton, and nobody gets hurt."

"BOB!" Rachel blurted. Then she frowned, as if momentarily forgetting her dire situation. "Singleton?"

"Long story," Bob said. He nodded towards the smaller man. "That's a pretty convincing accent you've got there. You know... for a Russian."

If the man was surprised at Bob's knowledge, he didn't show it. "I'm as American as you are," he said. "Only I've got fewer people pissed off at me, I figure."

Bob risked a quick glance backwards.

The man at the door was struggling to his feet.

"If you know who I am, you know the stakes. You know I'd as soon shoot you as talk to you," Bob said. "Do you really think taking an AWOL Navy lawyer hostage is going to prevent that? Because the government and I don't get along too good these days."

"Nobody has to get shot," the man said. "But if you so much as twitch, I'll put a bullet through her skull, and we can argue about your civic-mindedness after the fact."

Bob nodded to the man behind him, who was standing again. "I'd rather keep you in view than have to turn quickly and shoot you. Why don't you join your buddy, there?" He half turned, keeping the outstretched pistol trained on the hostage taker but watching the guard as he ambled past.

He was big; Bob figured maybe six four, shoulders almost as wide as the doorway. He rubbed his temple where Bob's blow had split the skin slightly. "You pay for that, my friend," he muttered.

Bob noticed the hostage taker's wedding ring. "Your wife know you're mixed up in this crap? That you're a traitor to your country?"

Again, no response. *Just a slight increase in his smirk, as if he's confident.*

He heard the shuffling feet on the carpet a split second later and dropped low without hesitation, pivoting and turning left on the ball of his foot. The other foot swung around to trip the man stepping out of the bathroom, coming up behind him.

The man crashed to the ground, a hypodermic needle flung a few feet away. He scrambled towards it. Bob rose and took a large step, his foot coming down on the man's back. "Ah, ah, ah, no, sir."

Rachel took the cue, grabbing her captor's wrist and yanking his arm from her throat, twisting it, forcing him to turn partially so that she could judo toss him over her hip. He crashed to the ground.

But he maintained his grip on the pistol, turning to train it on her from his grounded position. The door guard grabbed her arms from behind. Rachel struggled for a few seconds, but his grip was iron.

"ENOUGH!"

Everyone turned towards the door. The man entering the room was slightly older but as large as his friends, his dark beard neatly trimmed, hair just beginning to recede.

"Move again and he shoots your friend," the new arrival said. He looked at the smaller man still on the ground, keeping Rachel covered. "If she moves an inch, kill her."

He gestured at his downed colleague. "Pick it up, you idiot," he barked.

The bathroom ambusher retrieved the syringe.

"I'm guessing that's not a tetanus shot," Bob offered.

A moment later, he felt the needle slide into the side of his neck. The world became instantly softer. After a few seconds more, it was a blur, the TV in the background barely distinguishable from the wallpapered walls.

He was unconscious before he hit the carpet.

17

CHICAGO, ILLINOIS

Dawn Ellis knew she had to get moving. Worship at the Chicago Church of Christ started at ten, and it waited for no woman.

Besides... they were holding charity bingo after the service, and she had the second shift selling cards and daubers.

She jogged up the two flights of stairs to her apartment on West Monroe Street, her knees aching slightly after walking down Halsted Street to have breakfast with her friend Justine.

She looked at her dainty Timex wristwatch as she traversed the top step, then turned left down the second-floor corridor. Marcus would probably still be sleeping, she knew. He'd been out with friends at the movies the night prior.

She still had to change out of her nurse's uniform and into something casual.

Thirty-six minutes. Dang! Dang, dang, dang.

She fished her keys out of her purse while still moving,

then fumbled with the deadbolt. It slid back, and she yanked the door open, slamming it quickly behind her and throwing her purse onto the side table, by the barely used landline.

"I hope you don't have to rush out."

Dawn froze in her tracks. She glanced sideways, down the short corridor to the living room, tilting her head slightly to get a better angle.

The man sitting in the armchair was instantly familiar. But she'd hoped never to see him again.

Marcus sat on the sofa, a few feet to Eddie Stone's right, looking nervous. The CIA boss looked nonplussed, she figured, like he had better places to be.

"Mr. Stone," Dawn said calmly, "how unpleasant it is to see you." She looked over at Marcus. "You okay, sweetie?"

He nodded.

She knew she had to remain calm around Stone, in control. Bob's former boss was a ruthless man, fully capable of terrible harm in spite of his age.

"He knock? Or did he just let himself in?"

"He was here when I got back from the laundry room," Marcus said. The young man had his hands on his thighs but didn't look nervous. *Everything he's been through, guess I'm not surprised*, she thought.

"You know why I'm here," Stone said.

"I do not."

"Think real hard."

"I assume you have a gun on you, and I'm inclined to be nervous in its presence," she said. "You understand."

"I do." He leaned forward and retrieved a Walther 9mm from his waistband holster. Then he leaned further forward and placed it on the coffee table.

"There, now you can see it, and you don't have to worry."

"Uh-huh. Okay then."

"I'm looking for Bob. As tight as you three were, I'd assumed he'd left you in the dust until I got a report on that California incident." He glanced over at Marcus. "You too, right, young man?"

Dawn crossed her arms and gave him her best stern-nurse look. "And you think after that, I'd even talk to him."

Stone smiled paternally. "Miss, you can't kid a kidder. If the bond between you three – the relationship – was strong enough to survive that mess in New York State, then it's still important now. I need to find him—"

"I know. You're trying to kill him." In the event anyone was listening in and recording their conversation, Dawn figured, she might as well get it on the record.

"I'm not trying to do a damn thing."

"Please!" She flashed a finger to her pursed lips. "Do not blaspheme in our home."

Stone tilted his head back, his eyes rolling up in a moment of disdain. "Yeah, I forgot, you're a religious nut. But... I don't care. You're going to tell me where Bob is, and you're going to do it in the next minute."

"I told you—"

"Because if you don't tell me where he is in the next minute, I'm going to take this young man here out of the apartment, I'm going to have my people transport him to a facility not far from Chicago, and I'll do everything in my power to guarantee you never see him again."

Dawn felt a surge of panic. "But... he doesn't know a thing!" she exclaimed. "What good—"

"I don't care. I'll get everything he knows just so you can be sure, when I come back, that I did what I said I was going to do; so that before he disappears from your life forever, you know just how much he suffered during interrogation. So that you can live with that memory. Now... time's up." He reached forward and picked up the pistol, then aimed it at Marcus. "Where's Bob?"

"He doesn't tell me!" she blurted. Dawn's stomach was churning like a mouse wheel. The compulsion pushed her forward, a few plaintive steps taking her closer to the sofa.

"Ah! Tsk-tsk," Stone said. "You be real careful now, Ms. Ellis! This is way the fuck out of your league."

"Please don't swear," she muttered. She clasped her hands together, trying to keep calm, fear gripping her. She realized in the moment just how much she loved Marcus, more than she'd already known even. She'd already lost one son.

I can't lose another.

"Mr. Stone, I swear to God. And you know what that means to me. He didn't—" And then she caught herself, a stray memory popping into her head.

"What?" Stone demanded. "Something just occurred to you. What is it?"

If you tell him, he'll go after Bob. "Why do you want to find him?"

"That's none of your business. I've already told you what's going to happen if you don't help me, Ms. Ellis. Whether you're lying or not, the kid will pay the price."

It had been a snippet of background sound, a woman lecturing Bob about blocking the sidewalk with his toolbox. Maybe that fit in the big city, she'd lectured, but not in...

She sighed, exasperated. "He's in Portland, Maine," she said.

"How do you stay in touch?"

"Burners. He'll have tossed it already, though," she said. *Hopefully,* she added to herself.

"Give me the number. I'll give you mine. If you hear from him again, you call me. The agency doesn't want civilians dragged into our business and hurt, but we also wouldn't want to see you charged with abetting a fugitive."

"You wouldn't?" she said dryly.

"No. We'd get rid of both of you long before you saw a courtroom and started blabbing." He rose and holstered his gun. "Do we understand each other, Ms. Ellis?"

18

PEAKS ISLAND, MAINE

Liz paced her kitchen as she waited for the call to go through. It was rerouted, she knew, encryption and security causing a small delay. She peered out the kitchen window at the roiling, angry Atlantic Ocean, whitecaps smashing into the bleak crags of the dark, volcanic shoreline.

"Why are you calling me at home?" Igor Yaremchuk's voice was disguised electronically as always, a monotone clang to each sentence; but she had no doubt it was him. "You know that is not acceptable. And you were told to remain silent."

"I had to. You left me no choice. I tried to call my daughter," Liz said. "Her phone has been turned off. So has her friend's. Your men were pursuing them after they left here."

"These matters are none of your concern," he said. "Do your duty! That is all we require from you."

"This very much does concern me! She is my daughter! No matter what else I am, no matter what else we are, that is everything to me."

"We have been over this before, when she was young."

"Because of her father."

"He was a risk. The risk was mitigated. Do I have to remind you of twenty-five years? Your choice in these matters is gone; you serve at my discretion. You know this, or you would call someone other than me. If you had a choice, we would not be speaking."

"I won't let them harm her. I know where they'll have taken them."

Yaremchuk paused, letting the thought hang between them for a moment. "You know the penalty you will pay if you betray us, Mrs. McGee."

Missus. Always. Never "Doctor," she'd noticed. "I don't care! It's my daughter. I don't care how you disguise your voice or what you say, you would do the same."

Silence again. Liz wondered what he was thinking, whether he was giving her notion consideration, showing some humanity. *Or perhaps he's just figuring out the easiest way to have me killed.*

Instead, Yaremchuk said, "Okay. I will make a call, attempt to have discretion used in her case. But I promise nothing."

"That's not good enough."

"It will have to be. Do not make the mistake of considering yourself irreplaceable. Learn from your father's mistake."

The line went dead.

Liz clutched the phone and paced the kitchen. She knew she could not trust Yaremchuk. She also knew the team he'd sent would be comprised of ruthless men. *Will he even bother to call them?*

She'd meant what she said. She had no intention of

allowing them to harm a hair on Rachel's head. Her daughter was clear of all of it, an innocent, with a career and a life elsewhere.

Oh, Pa... why did you have to try to run?

He'd been old, had his time. She'd understood, even given him a friendly contact in the medical examiner's office who would sign off on his death certificate. But then he'd fled before they'd even had time to discuss it further.

She wondered if he'd finally dealt with Rose, too.

It all felt so wrong.

Lie upon lie, upon half-truth, upon a mountain of other lies. Where does it end? With all of us dead?

She took a deep breath to settle herself. Then she strode into the bedroom and reached under the bed. She withdrew the old rectangular Fender guitar case and set it on the bed. She undid the clips holding the lid closed and opened it.

The sniper's rifle was stored in perfectly shaped foam compartments. It hadn't left that spot in nearly twenty years, not since the assignment her mother had used to initiate her into the cell.

She knew exactly where they'd be taken, a property owned by a sympathetic Russian American businessman, leased through front companies.

She would be good to her word.

Nobody's going to harm a hair on her head.

Bob had been awake for twenty minutes, staring into the black. His vision was obscured, but he could feel the weight of the hood and had known instantly what was going on.

He tried to move his arms and legs, but they were secured to a chair.

The hood was removed, a naked bulb shining into his eyes from a standing spotlight just a few feet ahead.

He squeezed his eyes tight to adjust to the sudden difference, seeing spots. They faded quickly.

The man who'd removed the hood took two steps to the left, out of the glare. Bob recognized him as the self-described American in the Red Sox cap.

"You're awake. Good."

Bob looked around. It was dark, just a few emergency lights above doors providing enough illumination to gauge his surroundings. There was an empty chair next to his, also with restraints.

Steel shelves covered half the floor space of what appeared to be a half-soccer-pitch-sized warehouse. Stairs ahead of him led to a metal gangway fifteen feet above, running along three walls to offices and the main doors.

The ceiling towered overhead, maybe thirty feet up.

"Before you say anything, you need to know that we've told your companion who you really are," his captor said. "The unanswered question is what you're doing in Portland."

"Lobster fisherman," Bob said. "I'm a crewman on the Downeaster *Lucky Charms*, hunting the big surf for old, wily claws."

The man brooded on that for a second or two. "Be better for everyone if you didn't do that, deliberately behaving like you're number than a cock in a cold snap. It's wicked annoying, and my associates got bad attitudes."

It came out sounding like "yaw numbah than a cack in a cawl snap." Bob was still groggy, the effects of the drug not quite passed. But he knew enough to recognize a Maine accent when he heard one.

"That's pretty impressive. Using local lingo, local diction.

You put some practice in, didn't you, Comrade. But... why? What is there in Maine that would interest Moscow?"

The man sighed. "Believe what you want, but I've never been to Moscow in my life." He strolled over and grabbed the chair next to Bob, dragging it a foot away, turning it around and sitting so that he could lean on its tall back. "Look, Bob... I don't like this any more than you do. I guarantee you, I don't want to be here; you don't want to be here. The others? They want your head. Me? I'd as soon we all get out of here without any bloodshed. Am I right, or what?"

"Ty igrayesh' khoroshego politseyskogo. Ya ponimayu," Bob said. *I get it, you're the good cop.*

Baseball cap paused, his head jerking a tiny amount to one side in restrained surprise.

"That startled you, didn't it, Comrade?" Bob suggested. "You're definitely Russian, or you speak it. But you're not well-versed in hiding your emotions. That rules out the Foreign Intelligence Service. For you, anyhow. I'm pretty sure your friends are another story."

The man peered at him thoughtfully. "That tells me a few things, too."

"It says I'm telling the truth. I have no idea who any of you clowns are, just where you're clearly from. I'm just trying to help my friend get his job back."

The other man leaned back and crossed his arms, studying the former agent. "The policeman, Schultz. How do you know him?"

"We're in a twelve-step program together."

Ball Cap sighed. "I told you, bub, it won't go easy for you if you behave like this with the others. They aren't going to believe a CIA assassin of international renown, a man who killed dozens of their countrymen in Iraq, just happened to pick Portland—"

"Why?" Bob interrupted. "Why are you folks so interested in a tiny little city that's practically in Canada? Because that sounds a whole lot like this place is important."

The man leaned forward on the chair back once more. "Come on, Bob, you can drop the act, boy! If you talk to me now, maybe we can cut a deal, get you out of here in one piece."

Bob ignored him. "So... you're in Portland for a while, to pick up that weird mix of Mid Atlantic and Maritime Irish accents. Decades, if I'm taking a guess. I half expected you to invite me to a cellar party. Or 'cellah,' as you'd say. And you're probably close to my age, maybe even a little older if the crow's feet are any giveaway. So... you're embedded here, in deep cover. A sleeper, maybe?"

There it was, Bob thought, just the smallest twitch of irritation at the corner of his mouth. But it spoke volumes. Ball Cap tried to pretend it hadn't bothered him. "We don't have a lot of time—"

"That's it. And if there's one, there may be more of you. A cell? Rachel's grandparents? Your wife?"

Bob had caught a nerve. "She has nothing to do with any of this!" he snapped, but for just a second, switching his demeanor back to chilled out. "Look, it's up to you... I'm going to offer you a deal, Bob. Come clean now on what your people know, and I'll get them to release the girl, at least. You know they're not going to let you go. But she doesn't have to die. She's practically a kid."

"Yeah... don't tell her that," Bob said. "You remember being twenty-five and older folks still treating you like a child? Nobody wants that. Besides, she's got a temper and a critical eye for disrespect in pretty much any form. And she hits like a pro fighter."

He scowled. Bob's apparent absence of worry was getting under Ball Cap's skin. "You went to Peaks Island. Why?"

"If you know I went there, you know who we saw. You figure it out."

He got up and paced. "This... this right here is the easy part. You do get that, right? The real pisser is yet to come. I'm giving you a chance, buddy! Take the easy route, or they're going to start working on you."

"I've already told you what I know."

The lights overhead snapped on, one bank of fluorescent tubes at a time, the room suddenly fully visible.

The man who strode out of the corner, hands in his leather coat pockets, was the same one who'd arrived late at the hotel. "Enough," he said in English. "He has nothing more he'll reveal without coercion."

"Nikolai is right," Bob said. "You are wasting your time."

The new arrival stroked his beard. "You know who I am."

"Not really. I know your name is Nikolai, and the other feller who's around here somewhere is Boris, and Sascha was the dude I knocked down at the motel room door. Talking to each other openly when you think someone is unconscious is really stupid." He switched to Russian. "S'tem zhe uspekhom vy mogli by nosit' futbolku s nadpis'yu 'Fan-klub KGB.'" *You might as well be wearing a T-shirt that says 'Fan-Klub KGB.'*

"You're behind the times, my friend," Nikolai said. "We are a democratic, open nation now despite what your news tells you. But it lies. As do you, Bob Singleton."

"Whoa! Hey! Now look who's getting familiar." Bob's right index and ring fingers had found the tie to the plastic wrist restraint. But he could feel the hard ridge of the steel reinforcement strip inside the moulding. *You're not breaking that any time soon, Bobby.*

"We have told your friend Rachel the truth: that her grandfather owed my employers money for a gambling debt. That we are sent to collect it, nothing more. That we find him missing and you trying to convince her that we're spies or something ridiculous."

At the top of the steps, a wooden door opened. The second man, Boris, stepped through it, holding Rachel by the upper arm. She had a paper folder in one hand.

"We showed her your file, Bob, obtained at considerable expense, as we are in the private sector and do not have access to such things."

She can't possibly be buying this, can she? Bob wondered.

At the middle landing, she held it up. Boris let go of her arm.

"You lied to me," she said. "You told me you did security work."

"I told you what I could," Bob said.

"But that's not true, is it?" Nikolai interjected.

"You're a killer," Rachel spat. "You're not a roofer or just some guy doing a police officer a favor. You're a black ops guy, an assassin. You've killed dozens of people. They have names, locations."

"And you believe them?" *I mean, it's true. But I doubt they can prove it, and we have other priorities right now.*

"Jesus jumping Christ, I heard you! They had the sound in here piped into the room I was in, and there's a mic under your seat. That guy called you a 'CIA assassin of some renown,' and you didn't even blink. Didn't deny it. Didn't tell him he was full of shit. It all makes sense, why you hid this, why you lied about not going after my grandfather. All because... what, he got into some debt to a criminal!?"

It was clever enough, Bob figured. They hadn't claimed innocence, unbelievable in the circumstances. Instead, they'd given her something more plausible to her beliefs, a tale of Russian mob overreach gone wrong. Probably some fake paper, a promissory note from her grandfather. And the more he tried to sell who they really were, the less she was likely to believe him. Because reality was the last thing she wanted to accept.

"Ask them why they took his body," Bob said instead. *Change tack, keep her thinking.*

"They have tickets showing they arrived in town yesterday! And they say you probably work with whoever took him. That you're trying to cover their tracks by tailing me. That I'd be next." She held up the folder. "This. This says..." She glanced away, pained. "It says you once murdered a pregnant woman in Africa."

Ah, hell. "If you have a very broad definition of murder."

She was shaking her head, aghast. "I didn't want to believe it."

"First, I didn't know she was pregnant, and second, she was a killer, the girlfriend of a drug kingpin. She'd personally cut the throats of half his enemies and a government minister besides. She was in the middle of planning a bombing two doors down from a large primary school. Second, I was working for our government. You know... the one that generally does its business in English, not Russian."

"You cold-hearted, evil bastard."

Nikolai wagged his head towards the exit. "Take her back to her room. We can discuss how we can help her once we know what he knows." He gestured to Rachel. "We're going to find out what he knows, okay? Then we let you go."

Boris guided her back up the stairs. The door closed behind them.

"Oh, bravo," Bob said. "If I weren't tied at the wrists and could offer a counter-intel clap right now, it would be slow and lingering."

Nikolai ambled towards him, stopping far enough away to remain firmly out of reach. "No matter what else you tell her, she knows now who you really are: a liar, a murderer." He directed Ball Cap over to the chair, then made a "reach under" motion with his hand.

The other man reached under the chair and turned off the microphone.

"Now," Nikolai said, "Sascha will get his tools out. And then he will go to work on you. It will be simple, easy at first. Just a crude application of pain... to set the stage for how much worse it can get."

19

The biggest of them, Sascha, disappeared behind the floor-to-ceiling shelves at the other end of the warehouse. He returned seconds later pushing a table on castors.

Bob clucked his tongue. “Yah. This would be the part where he empties a pouch full of various scalpels and twisted dental implements in front of me, right?”

Nikolai peered at him quizzically. “You are a strange one, Bob. Not lifeless, like the worst of us; the glimmer is still there. But you don’t seem worried or angry.”

“I’ve been dead a few times before. You get used to it.”

“Still... Sascha will do exactly as you said. But not for show. He likes to use his tools. In Russia, he had some troubles, had to give up his job as a state interrogator. He has a sort of resentment about this.”

“Uh-huh. Neato.” The table rolled up to his left. “Already laid ’em all out, huh? Let me guess: the big, serrated blade thing is in the middle to draw the eye, right? What is that... a bone saw? I mean... really?”

Sascha leaned over Bob, his response guttural, a quiet growl. "I do not like you."

"Enough!" Nikolai declared. "To business: where is your handler, here or DC?"

Bob appreciated that. *He knows what he's doing. Asks a loaded question as if he knows whom I'm working for, uses the location to try for a backward confirmation. He knows the routine: keep it short, lead the target subject astray, let him build lies on lies until he can't remember them all.*

"Don't have one," Bob said. Then he sighed, adding, "I sense time pressure; this is going to hurt, right?"

"Right," Nikolai said. He nodded to his colleague.

The mountainous blond stepped into the punch, his brick fist smashing into Bob's rib cage, the blow catching him high, near the armpit, something cracking immediately.

"Hnnnh!" Bob grunted. He breathed in slowly through his nose, making sure the lung hadn't been punctured. *Nope. Minor miracle, given how many times I've snapped the damn things.*

"You needn't worry about your lung. Sascha is trained to hit high on the rib cage and towards the back, restrain the blow to a minor break and torn ligaments. The pain will build even if he does not strike you full force."

"Noted," Bob said. In Team Seven, they'd been trained to handle pain and interrogation drugs by being "plausibly stupid," finding a true memory that was irrelevant to the moment, blowing it into a story. Usually, the drugs just made it wilder.

Eventually, if they had enough time, they'd trip him up. It was a matter of holding out. Based on the searching first question, they thought he was still with the agency.

So... this could take a while.

Sascha turned back to the table, then faced Bob once again. He had a syringe in his right hand. He reached down to Bob's restrained wrists and injected it at the elbow.

"Why involve the girl?" Nikolai asked.

"What girl?"

The Russian sighed. "Really, Bob? Disrespect? We are both professionals! Please!"

"It's nothing personal," Bob said. "I just have bad history with your bosses in Moscow. But you knew that already."

He flexed his forearms without moving them, using them to gauge the give at his wrists. The chair was wood, the arms metal and bolted on, which made it breakable in a pinch.

But distracting them while lashed to the damn thing isn't going to be easy.

Nikolai nodded at Sascha again. The punch thundered into his upper rib cage again, the muscle compressing against broken bone. The pain stabbed through Bob's core like a spear.

He felt his heart racing. He breathed in through his nose slowly, then out through his mouth, risking yet more pain by flexing his chest and neck muscles, trying to compress the vagus nerve enough to let adrenaline kick in.

The drug was starting to take hold, his attention failing. The light in the corner of the room shone like a pale-yellow moon over the iron catwalk above them. For a moment, Bob wished he were out there, looking up at the sky, listening to the cicadas.

"What time do you next report in?" Nikolai asked.

Focus up, Bobby. Focus! Same trick, different question. "To who? My AA sponsor? He's a good guy. Works with neighborhood groups for underprivileged athletes."

“The pain will only get worse,” Nikolai said. He nodded to Sascha. “Pull out the little fingernail on his right hand.”

Sascha grinned wildly at the prospect, displaying twin rows of chiclet teeth. He reached down to the cloth and picked up pliers. He grasped Bob’s right hand. “This is the hand you shoot with, yes? I see you shoot at restaurant, remember?” He clamped the pliers onto the pinkie nail and began to pull, wrenching the tool from side to side as the nail slowly tore free of its base, flesh ripped clear of the nail bed, the pain shooting through Bob in waves.

“Gnnnnhh...” he growled through gritted teeth. The corrosive ache made his forearm muscle tremble like a drunk’s first clean day. He let out a few hot, hard breaths. His training kicked in, and he closed his mouth for a second, letting the air in through his nostrils, allowing his pulse to settle a little.

He looked over at his attacker. “Hey, Sascha...”

“Yeah?”

“Hnnnh... How’d you get so big? Your mom fuck a Skoda or something?”

The thug’s smile disappeared. He looked at Bob coldly. Then he opened the pliers and let the bloody fingernail drop to the ground. “When this is done, I ask to kill you myself,” he sneered. “And my father’s car was Skoda. Like Niki said, show some goddamn respect.”

Nikolai shook his head gently, like a disappointed parent. “You have nine more fingernails, ten fingers to break, and toes. And let’s not forget your eyes and genitals. Be wise, Bob. Answer my questions.”

“I thought I had.”

“Is your handler here or in DC?”

20

Rachel had been pacing the room since her return. The door had locked automatically behind her once they'd closed it.

The office was empty save for a desk, an empty set of bookshelves, and the sofa. They'd taken her gun and phone, stored them in a table by the guard, at the end of the hall. There was an old-fashioned intercom speaker built into the desk, and she'd been told to save it until she needed the bathroom.

She wasn't sure what to believe. She'd put on a show for Nikolai because she knew she didn't believe the Russians.

But she wasn't sure about Bob, either.

If everything in the file was fantasy, they'd gone to incredible lengths; there were case notes dating back twenty years, each outlining a political assassination or military targets. And there was more recent information, including a Russian oligarch and associate being killed in Memphis a year earlier.

Men with their throats slit, women poisoned. Democratically elected politicians blown up or shot at long range. Reading it had been like hearing a newscaster cataloguing a terrorist's notoriety, but for a man supposedly working for her country.

And there were references there to others, to a team he'd been part of. If he wasn't in Portland to take out the Russians, why was he really there?

A roofer?

It just seemed insane.

But the Russians were no more plausible. The fake contract from her grandfather's "debt" had been their biggest mistake. As secret as his life had evidently been, he'd been debt-free and addiction-free for the entirety. She didn't believe that a sober, humorless bibliophile had turned into a gambling addict at eighty.

She sat down on the sofa and tried to weigh it all.

It was hard to stay in the present; she kept thinking back to all the times Gramps or Grammy Rose had tried to hide something at the last second, or shushed someone in conversation, or changed their speech pattern on the phone, realizing she was in the room.

Bob had pegged them as spies, but not before investigation. That suggested he hadn't been expecting the Russians to show up.

And that means he might be right.

She didn't want to accept it.

Telling them she'd bought their bullshit had gotten her separated from Bob, which meant they still had a chance to escape. But she needed a plan, she knew.

It starts with getting out of here, getting my gun and phone.

She needed a weapon of some sort; the man at the end of the hall – *Boris, was it?* – was bigger than Bob. She got up and walked over to the desk, checking the drawer and hutch. *Nothing.*

The scream was piercing, loud enough to make it through the cinderblock walls. She drew in a short, sharp breath. *What are they doing to him?*

She glanced over at the empty shelves. Her eyes flitted around the room, up to the ten-foot ceiling and the upper walls. There was a vent about a foot below the join, but it was small, perhaps two feet wide. *Too narrow to fit through, I think.*

She looked down at the couch. *Standing on the back of it, I can just about reach that. Now that's... well, it's an idea.* She glanced backwards at the intercom button on the desk. *But the timing will have to be perfect.*

Boris sat at the guard post, by the door to the warehouse stairs, brooding.

Nikolai had taken the lead and gotten them all into trouble. But he knew better than to cross him, to tell Yaremchuk what had really happened.

Plus, he wanted his ten percent cut of the reward.

Now, he has me guarding a woman because he does not want me involved in interrogation, does not want me to gain any additional glory. If he were not the boss, Boris decided, he might have killed his former classmate as a matter of principle.

Boris had been playing second best for a decade. Eventually, he knew, his chance would come to turn the tables.

The old-fashioned intercom and handset on the table buzzed. He sighed. It was some relic from the eighties, like Louis DiPalma used as a dispatcher in the old episodes of *Taxi* they'd watched in cultural assimilation training.

He picked up the handset and held down the "talk" button. "What?"

"I need to go to the bathroom."

The woman was going to be an issue, he could sense it. Like so many Americans, she thought she had a say. "You have only been in there for thirty minutes."

"It's nearly my time of the month. I get a really dicey bladder."

"You can wait."

"I can... but I'll pee all over myself and your room."

Boris asked himself whether the woman was foolish enough to challenge him. It seemed unlikely. Like most women, she was probably frail and weak. That was why she'd worked with Bob, to have someone to protect her. American women thought they were different somehow, special.

But she is not stupid. The room is empty, and she is a little thing. He wondered if the order from Yaremchuk to let her live excluded hurting her a little. *But in a good way, a way she'll like if she lets me.*

It amused him, the notion. *I get my rocks off while Nikolai preens downstairs.*

"Are you coming or what? I really gotta go."

He hit the button once more. "Be quiet. I will be there momentarily."

Better safe than sorry. He rose and unholstered his Walther PPS. The timing and experience both suggested she was up to something.

Boris strode down the hall. He put his ear to the door for a moment and tried to discern any activity. Then he moved a step to his right and repeated the action against the plaster wall.

He retrieved the key from his pocket and opened the door, pushing it wide cautiously.

The room had been rearranged, the sofa pulled over to the right. Above it, near the roof line, a vent cover hung from one screw, the hole behind it open. "Chert voz'mi!" *Goddamn!*

He rushed over to the sofa and put one foot on it. He peered up at it. It was possible she would get stuck, it was so small. At best, she would not be far into the duct.

He felt a slight breeze and began to turn his head the moment before the two-by-four bookshelf slammed into the side of his face, darkness enveloping him.

RACHEL KNEW she had to hurry. She crouched beside the unconscious guard and rifled his trouser pockets, finding the key. She checked his jacket and retrieved his phone, then picked up the pistol.

She scurried out of the room and closed the door behind her, then locked it.

She had no idea how long he'd be out, but that bought her some time, she figured. *He sure as heck isn't going through that vent.*

At the desk by the door, her phone and Colt 1911 were stashed in the top drawer. She moved over to the door and peered through the block of glass. It was hard to see anything from that angle and height, but she figured Nikolai and his goons were still set up ahead of the stairs.

She glanced backwards. At the other end of the corridor was the door to the other side of the gangway. She ran down the corridor and pushed it open. She stayed low, near the wall, following it to the corner of the building.

The double front doors were just ahead and down another short hallway, based on the exit sign.

I can run. If I stay low until the hall, they won't even see me leave. But... then what?

If she tried to call the cops, they'd think she was nuts. If she tried to call her bosses at Bethesda, they'd have her arrested for being AWOL. Russian agents just didn't show up in Portland. It sounded mental.

Ahead, past the exit corridor, stairs led down to the warehouse floor. They'd place her right beside the tall shelves, she realized, able to easily get into cover. *And then what? I rush three guys with guns?*

No. But if I can distract them, maybe I can get Bob free somehow, give us a real chance.

She shuffled over to the steps.

"YEARRGGH!" Bob screamed.

Rachel glanced his way, almost regretting it. Nikolai, the bearded leader, was pacing, hands behind his back, as the giant, Sascha, crouched ahead of their captive, squeezing Bob's groin with what appeared to be a large set of tongs.

She crept down the steps, staying close to the wall, in the shadow of the tall shelves. There was a two-foot gap ahead to reach them and stay in cover.

"URGGHHH..." Bob let out a pained groan.

While they're fixated, go!

She scampered across the divide.

"Bob, I tell you, I don't like this. I do not enjoy hurting anyone. I am a peaceable man." Nikolai had resumed his pacing. "You tell us you are out, retired. And yet... we know about Memphis. We know that you killed Victor Malyuchenko, the son of Ivan Malyuchenko, a national hero. We know that you killed Alexi Pushkin, a trained former member of the Ferak Group. Forget the latter, I suppose, as he was a nobody in America. But the son of Malyuchenko? And... what, I am supposed to believe you did this for the general betterment of humanity? Come on, my guy! How am I supposed to maintain my goodwill when you give me a line of bullshit such as this?"

"He..." Bob was panting slightly, audible from Rachel's perch more than twenty feet away. "Kidnapped... a... friend of mine..."

"Yah, yah, sure. You also were just doing favor when you kill Molham Al-Maghrebi, former Egyptian security service, in New Orleans, just weeks before that? How about former South African intelligence operative Geert Van Kamp, in California? Let me guess: you were accompanying a little old lady across the road, you slipped, fell on your pistol and shot him through an open window accidentally. You see? You see how bullshit this is? You were all 'former' agents, of course. No one officially working in the United States. That could be problematic."

There was a tone to his voice he hadn't shown before, Rachel figured. It had pitched up a little, and he sounded like he was tiring. *Desperate, even. They've been working on Bob for nearly an hour, and he hasn't given them shit.*

She thought back to what he'd told her. *He didn't lie to me. He did leave a whole lot out, though.*

Stop dwelling on shit. Think. What can you do, right now? Assume you make it through this, what then?

They'd need to know who the Russians were, whether they were foreign intelligence, like Bob said, or working for a gangster. She took out her phone and used its meagre zoom function to snap grainy, close-up images of the two Russians and the man in the ball cap. She mailed them to herself,her mother, and Bob.

Behind the Russians, atop a table by the stairs, she heard his phone ping. They glanced back at it but ignored it.

"Tell us who your target is," Nikolai demanded.

"You... sound worried," Bob managed. "Like you're on the clock somehow. Your sleeper buddy here" – he said, nodding at the self-proclaimed American – "makes me think you've got a big fish locally. Now you're nervous" – he took a breather for a few beats – "and want to extract. But there's a delay, a hitch. So someone figures that's a good chance to clear up a bunch of loose ends."

Is... is he talking about Gramps!? "Extract" could only mean one thing in the context, spiriting someone back to Russia. Rachel couldn't believe it, still. Could a man who spent most of his life working on the docks or at rural fishing camps really be an important Russian spy, someone so big they'd go to so much trouble?

Snap out of it. Priorities first. Distract them; get Bob loose.

She gazed past the four men to the far side of the room. *Is there anything there...*

The fire extinguisher was attached to the wall near the back corner, beside what she assumed was a door to the loading docks or rear exit.

The bullet would reach the extinguisher before they heard the sound of the pistol's report, she knew. Hopefully, her position would be hard to determine against the nearer, split-second-later sound of the canister blowing.

Here goes nothing. She lined up the shot, using the steel shelf ahead of her as a brace.

The gun had a kick, but she kept the shot on line, the extinguisher exploding with a bellowing bass "pop," the three Russians dropping to the floor as pieces of shrapnel showered the corner of the room.

"WHAT THE FUCK!?" the man in the ball cap yelled.

Nikolai was up quickly, turning, heading towards the shredded device, a small cloud of gray smoke still in the air around it. A moment later, the other two were on their feet, drifting in the same direction.

Rachel stayed in her crouch as she rounded the shelves and scurried over to Bob. She grabbed the restraint and realized it was self-locking. "How?" she hissed.

Bob nodded past her to the cart. "Box cutters..."

She looked back and spotted them next to a bone saw. Rachel grabbed them. She snipped through the first wrist, the thin, flexible metal reinforcement taking some effort.

"One more," she whispered.

In the corner, Nikolai turned as he talked to his colleagues, noticing her. "Der'mo!" *Shit!* He drew his pistol.

Rachel fired a shot wildly at them, then another, the three men ducking behind a forklift near the wall. She turned back to the restraint and snipped it. Then she reached down towards his right ankle.

The pistol barrel was pressed against the back of her head, only for a few seconds, just long enough to know that it was there.

"Put the gun down," Boris said.

She hesitated.

"Do it," Bob said. "He looks pissed."

She laid the Colt down on the concrete floor.

The heel of his pistol came down hard across the base of her skull, Rachel slumping to the ground, unconscious.

21

They pulled the second chair up next to Bob's perch, propping Rachel up in it and securing her wrists.

"She is stupid," Nikolai said. "She could have shot one of us, given herself time to escape. Maybe even just walked out without you. Instead, she tried to rescue you."

She'd sold her earlier contempt well, Bob figured. He'd bought her outrage completely. Evidently, so had the Russians.

"Bitch hit me with a shelf," Boris groused as he tied Rachel's right arm to the chair. "I owe her for that."

Nikolai didn't want to hear it. "Do not dwell on this."

"She tricked me."

"Shocker," Bob offered dryly. "I can't imagine how she knew you were a meathead, unless you talked to her or something. Then it would've been obvious."

Boris turned his way. The slap was loud and forceful, a sonic crack that made Bob's skull rattle. "Go on," the Russian said. "Keep reminding me of how enjoyable it will be to beat you to death."

He went back to securing her left wrist. Bob's cheek burned from the slap; he noticed Boris's knuckles were bloody. "Now what could she have done to leave your mitts looking like hamburger?" he wondered aloud.

Boris excised some stress, letting go a deep lungful of air. "She locked me in the room. But the wall by the door, it is plaster and drywall, not much more than two inches thick. So I punch through it, unlatch door."

"Seelah yest' umah ni nahda," Bob offered. *When one has power, they do not need intelligence.* "That's how your boss, Vladi, sees the world, isn't it?"

Nikolai glared at him again but bit his tongue.

Boris chuckled as he tied down her right ankle. "Gol' na vydumku hitrah, eh, Nikolai?" *Poverty inspires invention.*

"Do not mistake Boris's aggression for stupidity, Bob. He is very smart," Nikolai replied.

The two Russians straightened Rachel up, her arms and legs restrained. Nikolai nodded towards Ball Cap. "Go get water; wake her."

The smaller local disappeared towards the back corner of the warehouse.

"Where'd you find him?" Bob asked. "I've mowed lawns less green. Not much fun working with sleepers, is it?" It made sense, given that Rachel's grandparents were embedded in Portland, that others might be as well. And despite excellent Russian, the man's Maine accent had been legit, unforced.

Nikolai smirked. "You! You are a clever one, Bob. In another life, maybe we would work well together. I tell you nothing about him; he says nothing. So I am supposed to assume you 'know' he is a sleeper from your comment."

"We call it a 'backward confirmation,'" Bob said.

"We? As in you and your buddies at the CIA, yes?"

"Yeah... well... former buddies. I haven't worked for them in nearly fifteen years."

Nikolai took a few steps back and studied both captives, his arms crossed. "Still you persist with this, eh?"

"Not hard to maintain as a story because it's true," Bob said. The drugs were still making his vision and thoughts cloudy, but he'd been trained to handle it, learned to push through, focus on the conversation or task at hand. "The agency... wants me dead."

"Still... even if this were true, which I do not believe for a second, you did yourself no favors by keeping your past from the girl," he said. "Now she does not trust you."

"If you had to hide, would you share with people you cared about?" Bob said. "Or would that put a target on their backs?"

"So you tried to be chivalrous, is this your new claim?"

"No, just decent. Haven't told anyone in Portland about my past life. No... no real incentive to do that."

Boris made a scoffing noise.

"Say what you mean," Nikolai insisted.

"You are wasting your breath with this one." Boris scowled. "He lies as easily as he breathes."

Sascha stepped forward and crouched ahead of Bob, so that they were almost nose to nose. "And he is rude fuck." He looked Bob in the eyes. "You say something else nasty about my mother, little man?" Without pause, he drove a meaty fist into the ball of Bob's shoulder, where the axillary nerve supplies signals to the muscle.

"Hnnnh..." Bob grunted, the icy sharpness turned to a dull ache that shot down his arm and settled in the median nerve of his elbow. It was like being stabbed in both joints at once. He gritted his teeth, offering the Russian a pained, Cheshire-cat smile.

"Now your mother is big as car!" Sascha spat.

Bob chuckled despite his pain, the line so stupid he couldn't help himself.

Red-faced, Sascha drew his arm back to hit him again, but Nikolai intervened.

"If he is unconscious, we cannot question him," he said.

Ball Cap returned with a mug of cold water. Nikolai took it from him with a sour look. "I was expecting bucket, maybe." He turned and threw the cold water in Rachel's face, the sudden temperature shift rousing her, gasping.

"Where...?" She looked around quickly, and her place in the present flooded back. "Oh. Yeah."

"It's no consolation, I know," Bob said quietly. "But you were very brave when you tried—"

"Shut up!" Boris barked.

"Or at the least," Nikolai suggested, "tell us what we need to know before I am tempted to let Sascha work on your testicles some more."

They already ached like a dozen charley horses, Bob figured. Short of rupturing the things – a fate he'd avoided by screaming early and often – they weren't going to hurt any more or less. The throbbing was agonizing, but he'd compartmentalized the pain, pushed it down so that it was in the background, always there but not commanding.

"This is foolish," Boris grunted. "He is clearly trained to withstand pain. We can drug him more, but this will take days."

"Be patient," Nikolai advised.

"No! We cannot. We do not have days. Uncle must move soon."

Well now, that's something new, Bob figured. *Who, exactly, is "Uncle"? Because when he said that name, the look his boss gave him was less than polite.*

Instead of scolding Boris in front of them, Nikolai took the other man by the upper arm and led him aside. Bob couldn't hear what he was saying, but it was whispered in Russian, the tone placating.

"Why?!" Boris replied more loudly. "We are just going to kill them in the end anyway."

"No!" Nikolai said. Then he reverted to a murmur. Nikolai glanced back at Rachel, then shook his head.

He turned back towards them. "Boris has good idea," he said. "He supposes you would not like to see the woman hurt."

"We're not friends," Rachel said bluntly.

"It's true," Bob said. "She drives me bonkers, if I'm being honest. Go ahead: do whatever you're going to do."

Nikolai crossed his arms. "I... do not believe you. It makes no sense. If she is asset and you are working a mission, you would be told to protect asset, in particular here in America. If she is not, then you are working to help person you hardly know, which is not smart, but does show you care about her for some reason."

He reached behind him and withdrew a long, curved blade from a sheath on his belt. "This is fish filleting knife. You must see, here in Portland, all the time. Super sharp, so that it does not slip when it hits bone. Instead, it cuts right through." He leaned forward and down slowly, Rachel flinching away from his hot, foul breath. "It is also most excellent at removing skin from a living person."

He placed the tip of the knife against the underside of her chin, dragging it gently downwards without the blade quite touching the skin. "Maybe... maybe we start at the top and work our way down, yes?"

ACROSS THE ROOM and on the upper gangway, Liz McGee crouched next to the rail, the Winchester Model 70 and scope balanced on one raised knee.

She'd hoped to find them captive but alone, or possibly facing a single guard.

But there was no way to go about things quietly. Igor Yaremchuk's men had thrown a spanner into the works by taking them both. Had it just been Bob, the man they claimed was CIA, she would have let it go. Instead, he'd offered a promise her daughter would not be hurt.

But Liz knew who Igor really was, how many missions he'd presided over, his years with the KGB. She knew there was a chance that even their own people would be seen as dangerous, given how long they'd all been embedded. Maybe what they really wanted to do was clean up a big mess, get their prized asset out of town while others, like Rachel and her father, were disposed of.

She raised the barrel and rested it on the rail for stability. She looked down the scope, adjusting the focal depth until she was zoomed in perfectly on the man with the knife. She didn't know him, hadn't dealt with him before. The man standing next to him, Boris Volkov, was familiar by reputation.

The shot was no more than thirty yards, no need to

account for bullet drop, no wind to skew it. But there was no percentage in killing anyone if they were true to Igor's word, if they left Rachel alone.

The man took the tip of the knife and traced a line down Rachel's throat. Liz felt a swell of panic, and it caught her by surprise. She hadn't felt that type of anxiety in years. She found herself squeezing the trigger.

Wait. Just... wait. She relaxed her finger and took it out of the rifle's trigger guard.

Sure enough, Nikolai lowered the knife. He grasped her daughter by the chin with his other hand, whispering something to her, turning her head to look at Bob. *He's asking her if this man is worth all of this. That's what I'd be doing. Letting her know she's not the threat, not the problem.*

They're not worried about Rachel. Rachel can be dealt with.

Liz felt a pang of sadness. She hadn't expected to like Bob. She'd been quite willing to play the part, to flirt with a man who could expose them, get his guard down. Instead, she'd found their toying with each other fascinating, electric.

It had been years since she'd had any interest in the opposite sex beyond the odd fantasy and self-gratification.

It had been years since her husband, Riley.

She pursed her lips at the sudden, unwelcome return to grief. Then she frowned, irritated with herself. Like much of her life, his death had been painful. Spending years less than a mile from where he was buried, all the while telling their daughter that he was alive and well but just didn't want her, had been excruciating.

Not now. Push it down; get on with things.

There was never time to grieve.

The man with the filleting knife stood up and walked around Rachel's chair. He bent at the waist and whispered something in her ear. Then he forcefully grabbed the fringe of her hair in his other hand, pulling it back and placing the blade against the top of her forehead.

Oh God...

He's going to scalp her.

Liz's finger curled around the rifle's trigger.

22

Nikolai's patience had run out. Two days of listening to Igor's orders. Two days of listening to the sleeper whine. Then having to deal with Boris's incompetence and the American spy, Singleton.

"Am I supposed to be frightened?" Rachel said.

He leaned around her from behind, the knife catching the light ahead of her face. "I could rearrange your features. Cut the end of that nose off, to start."

"Okay. Job done. I'm frightened."

He hated the pantomime. He knew they weren't supposed to kill the girl, and he also knew seriously injuring her would not make Yaremchuk happy because that was implied when they were told not to kill someone.

I should just gut the bitch. Everything that is genius is simple.

What Yaremchuk would want, though, was theater.

He grabbed her brown fringe and pulled her hair back. "Maybe I cut off just a few inches of scalp. Leave her with a ridge," he suggested.

Boris had crossed his arms and was looking worried,

probably thinking about Yaremchuk's judgment. "Too much, Nicky. Too much."

Fool. Tired, dead inside. I would gut you too if I had a chance against Sascha.

But at least he knows how to play good cop, bad cop.

"Don't maim her! I apologize for his boorish behavior, dear," Boris offered.

"You can get fucked, good cop," Rachel said.

Boris sniffed quickly but hid any anger she might have caused. "Just cut off her big toe on her left foot," he suggested. "She will never walk properly again."

"Or I could sever her Achilles." Nikolai crouched behind her and ran his left index finger up and down the bare tendon. "It would be funny to see you stumble around, try to walk with your foot flopping, like a doll's." He giggled, a high-pitched prolonged snicker like a teen boy hearing a dirty joke.

"BOB!" Rachel declared. "Ideas welcome!"

"Prosthetics are amazing these days? What do you want me to tell you? My balls are the size of an orange right about now."

"TELL THEM WHAT THEY WANT TO KNOW!"

"But... I don't know what they want. I've told them the truth; they just won't accept it."

Boris moved over, next to his associate, and crouched, his voice firm. "Bob does not care about you; I am not even sure he cares about himself. But he is a trained assassin and will say nothing without incentive."

Nikolai nodded twice. "It's true. So... maybe, because of my personal sympathy for you, we will just start with your little finger."

He grabbed her right hand in his left, taking advantage

of the restraint to pin it, using two of his fingers to spread her pinkie apart from the rest. He crouched low over it, the filleting knife held like a scalpel as he leaned in, gently resting it against the finger, just south of the big knuckle.

The next two seconds were a blur, Boris careening over sideways, pinning him down as rifle shots sounded, the thump of bullets striking Boris's torso.

Nikolai scrambled frantically, pushing his colleague's torso off him, Boris rolling over onto his back. A bullet had gone straight through the center of his chest, and he was coughing up blood.

Boris's eyes were dancing slightly, but they came to rest on Nikolai's panicked face. "I… I am okay, da?"

Nikolai snapped out of it, drawing his Walther from its speed holster. The gunshot report had reverberated off the upper warehouse walls and ceiling. His gaze traced the line of the upper concourse until he spotted the figure crouched near the main corridor exit. He fired two quick shots, the figure backing away, into cover.

He looked over at Boris. The light had gone from his eyes. Nikolai spat at the other man. "You were always a sniveling fool."

Sascha had pulled up beside him, pistol drawn, followed by the American, Chris.

The rifle barrel protruded a few inches past the rail. Sascha spotted it, lined up a shot and yanked the 9mm's trigger three times in quick succession, the shots deafening them both.

Nikolai held his head with his free hand, wincing. He glared at the big man. "WAIT!" he yelled, his hearing momentarily shot. "IF THEY HAVE OTHER TARGETS, THEY MUST EXPOSE THEMSELVES."

After a few more seconds, the rifle had not reappeared. Nikolai tapped Coach Chris on the shoulder. "YOU! GO UP THE SOUTH STAIRS. SASCHA, GO UP THE NORTH. IF THEY ARE STILL THERE, WE FLUSH THEM OUT. I COVER YOU BOTH. GO!"

He trained his pistol on the spot by the rail.

Bob recognized their advantage instantly. He began yanking at the restraint on the left; he'd been fiddling with the tie for twenty minutes, trying to loosen it.

"What are you doing?" Rachel asked.

"They're a little deaf right now from firing off pistol volleys standing next to each other. In a second, the idiot in the middle is going to figure out there are two approaches to where the sniper is located by the corridor, and he's going to send the other two up. We need to be free by then."

Bob yanked at the restraint again, the arm of the chair breaking at a weak weld, most of it coming away from the frame. He stretched to his limit, his fingertips brushing the handle of the box cutters on the rolling table.

He strained to get an extra inch, his shoulder feeling like it might separate. He felt the coldness of the metal between two fingertips.

Bingo.

He yanked the box cutters towards himself, snatching them with the same free hand as they cleared the edge of the table.

The two men were halfway up the staircases.

He snipped through the restraint on his right wrist, then reached down and loosed his feet. Bob rose to help Rachel but staggered, pain from his broken ribs and swollen testes searing through him, a sensation of persistent woe.

Block it out. Let the adrenaline take over so you can help her.

He crouched and cut Rachel's bonds. Along the concourse, the two men were converging on the tunnel. Bob searched the room, looking for…

There. On an industrial-sized toolbox by the stairs, they'd left Rachel's Colt and his Smith & Wesson .40 cal.

Bob crouched low and signalled for her to join him.

"HEY!"

Ball Cap had spotted them from the upper level. The two men rushed to the rail, Nikolai seeing their shocked faces, turning to check his six. Bob grabbed Rachel's arm and dragged her behind the staircase.

He leaned around the corner and fired two shots, the first catching Nikolai in the shoulder. The Russian staggered backwards, tripped and went down hard on his backside. The second bullet was meant for the big man, to the top right of the front hallway, but instead pinged off the opposite wall.

Bob ducked back into cover, the two men on the concourse opening fire, bullets careening off the stairs and the concrete floor behind them.

"What the hell just happened!?" Rachel asked.

"Someone shot Boris from the upper level. If I had to guess, they were aiming at his friend, and it looked like he dove ahead of him, saved him."

"Why?!" she wondered.

Bob gestured towards the back corner, past the shrapnel from the former fire extinguisher. "There's another exit out the back. We cover each other: you run, I empty a mag on them. You get to the door, find cover behind the corner and return the favor."

"Why do I have to run first?" Rachel complained. "How about I cover YOU against the two pistols who have a clear line of sight."

Bob bit his tongue. They didn't have time to fight. "FINE. On three... one... two... three!" He sprinted for the rear exit, Rachel rounding the corner, opening fire with the Colt 1911, casings plinking off the concrete floor as the two men ducked low, behind the rail.

He reached the door and put his shoulder to the latch bar, shoving the heavy exit open, realizing in that split second that it was spring-loaded and would close if he tried to find cover behind the corner.

Instead, he turned, the pistol extended. "GO!" he screamed.

Rachel sprinted towards the exit. The two gunmen popped out of cover, Bob playing the odds that the sleeper would flinch first, two bullets fired directly at his position. He swung the pistol over to Sascha just as Ball Cap ducked low into cover again. Bob emptied the mag, the shots striking the big man center mass, the Russian tumbling to the ground.

Rachel reached and passed him. Bob pulled the door closed. They ran out onto the adjacent street.

It was dark, traffic nonexistent. "Where the hell are we?"

Rachel looked at the street sign. "We're just off Terminal Street and Larrabee Road." Then a thought occurred to her. "Quick! There's an alley here leading to the train tracks. We can get lost behind the buildings."

The rear door flew open, Nikolai exiting, one hand

clutching his wounded shoulder, the other levelling a Walther 9mm in their direction.

"NO TIME FOR THAT!" Bob yelled. They sprinted across the street. Twenty yards ahead, A Dodge Dart compact sedan turned the corner of Patrick Drive, onto Terminal. Bob ran towards it, blocking the lane. He stopped just ahead of it, the pistol raised. "GET OUT OF THE CAR!" he screamed.

The middle-aged man behind the wheel and his female passenger did as ordered, both looking terrified. A second after getting out, both fled up the street.

A bullet pinged off the opposite wall, Nikolai not caring about possible collateral, his blood up.

Bob jumped into the car, threw it into drive and stepped on the gas, stopping after twenty feet to pick up Rachel. "BUCKLE UP!" he yelled.

He stepped on the gas.

"NYET!" Nikolai bellowed as the headlights disappeared down the street. "NYEEETT!"

The door opened behind him. Coach Chris poked his head through. "Did you—"

"OT'YEBIS!" *Fuck off!* Nikolai screamed just as Sascha started to rise from the floor, feeling his chest, ensuring nothing had gotten through his bulletproof vest.

A motorcycle turned out of the parking lot for an auto repair shop a half block away, heading down the street towards them. Nikolai sprinted out into the road, the pistol held high. "YOUR BIKE! GIVE IT!" he yelled.

Whether it was the helmet cutting off sound or just pure fear, the rider ignored him, instead gunning the big bike's motor, twisting the throttle as he tried to blow by the sudden danger.

Nikolai took two big steps into the road and flung out his right arm, clotheslining the rider under the chin, the man flying backwards off the bike, which crashed onto one side, a wing mirror bent.

He ran after it and tried to right the bike, but it was too heavy. "POMOGI MNE!" he yelled at Sascha. *Help me!*

The giant ran over, clutching one hand to pectoral bruises. He winced as he helped Nikolai right the bike, which had stalled. He hit the start button, praying it hadn't flooded. The bike's engine fired up again immediately.

He gripped the clutch and stepped on the gear changer, putting it into first, zipping way from his colleagues so quickly the front wheel momentarily left the ground.

The street rushed by, traffic sparse as the night settled in. He twisted the throttle, the BMW R1250 street bike hitting sixty miles per hour in under four seconds. A block later, he spotted the underpowered Dodge in the distance, turning left two blocks ahead.

The night had gone to shit, but it could still be salvaged, Nikolai thought. The bosses would accept Boris was to blame for their troubles, because Boris was dead. Dead people made convenient scapegoats.

But first, he had to catch them and kill Singleton, shut the girl up. The bike blew through a red light, Nikolai leaning left to take the corner at speed.

23

Bob glanced at the rearview mirror. He'd seen the bike take the corner at a perilous angle, suggesting it was moving quickly. It had to be one of the Russians.

"Where are we going!?" Rachel asked. "And what are you looking at?"

"Mike's place, and there's someone chasing us," Bob said.

"What?!" She turned quickly and looked through the rear window. The bike was gaining on them rapidly. "Step on it!" she bellowed.

"I am! This car wasn't designed to outrun a sport bike."

Within seconds, the bike was right behind them. Bob heard a shot. "Stay down!" he told her.

Rachel ducked low.

The rear window shattered, a second bullet passing through the windshield, ahead of where her head had just been. In his wing mirror, he caught sight of Nikolai. He had his pistol drawn but was having trouble keeping it raised.

Wound is hurting him. Good.

The sound of the next shot and the front left tire's inner tube exploding happened simultaneously, the car's traction and balance compromised, the compact swerving out of Bob's control. He yanked on the wheel, but the sudden weight shift had skewed its momentum to the left.

It slammed into a telephone pole. Bob and Rachel hurled forward, only their belts preventing impact with the dashboard.

Bob shook it off quickly. He saw the bike's image growing larger in the side mirror. "DOWN!" he yelled, leaning over to push Rachel's head down again as Nikolai passed them, emptying his magazine into the car, windows shattering.

"Out, NOW!" Bob ordered. He glanced around them quickly, the motorcycle slamming on its brakes ahead, the Russian revving the engine but holding the front wheel brake so that its back tire could spin it a hundred and eighty degrees. "DOORWAY, RIGHT!" Bob yelled. "GO!"

He bailed out of the car as Rachel sprinted for cover. His ribs were a dull, numb ache, his testicles the same, adrenaline keeping him functioning and focused. He drew the Smith & Wesson, firing two shots as the bike zoomed back towards him, the drugs skewing his focus, Nikolai wisely swerving, bullets ricocheting off the asphalt.

The gun's slide flew back, the magazine empty. Bob reached down for a replacement, then realized they were in his soft-sided bag at the motel.

Shit.

Nikolai was less than fifteen feet ahead, time slowing as he raised the pistol to Bob's chest height, the motorcycle's engine a blare of white noise as Bob anticipated the sting of the bullet... only for the Russian's trigger finger to yank back one more time, his pistol empty also. Bob recognized what was happening at the last second and threw his left shoulder at the passing attacker.

It caught Nikolai square, knocking him off the bike, the Russian's training kicking in so that he tucked into a ball, then went limp, letting flexible joints absorb some of the road shock.

Bob's adrenaline had faded somewhat, his ribs screaming with pain, his left knee swollen from slamming into the dash when they'd stopped. He headed for the prone Russian at a fast limp, flipping the gun around halfway, using the barrel as a handle, the grip as a club.

Nikolai staggered to his feet just in time, spotting Bob's streetlight shadow from the corner of his eye, able to step aside, the disabling blow whistling harmlessly by his head.

He threw his left elbow back, and Bob ducked it. As he straightened up, Bob punched the Russian in the bullet wound, the force of the punch reverberating through Bob's broken ribs, the former agent staggering and almost falling himself.

Nikolai screamed and dropped to one knee. But instead of giving in to the pain, he swung a tired leg out, tripping Bob, who crashed to the pavement next to him.

Both men struggled to their feet. A shot rang out, a bullet striking the building across the road. Bob glanced towards the apartment block; Rachel had ignored his advice and was bracing her Colt 1911 with her left hand, trying to get a bead on Nikolai from fifteen feet away. "GO! RUN, DAMN IT!" he yelled. He turned in time to realize Nikolai had struggled to his feet and had found a reserve of energy, charging him.

Bob tried to turn slightly as the Russian slammed into him, letting his momentum shift as both men went down on one side. Before Nikolai could react, he threw a left jab once, twice, a third, each snapping the prone man's head back.

Bob rolled back and away, Nikolai dazed. He rose to his feet and looked around for Rachel, realizing she was right behind him as Nikolai's hand clutched at something behind him.

Bob saw the black throwing knife at the last second, letting himself fall backward, a limbo bend at the waist, broken ribs like hot pokers through each side as the knife flew past the tip of his nose.

He crashed to the ground. The pain was agonizing, and for all his training, Bob thought he might pass out, his breathing fast and shallow.

"Unnhh."

It took a moment to realize he hadn't made the sound.

The grunt had come from behind him.

He rolled over so that he could look that way.

Rachel had fallen onto her backside, clutching at the knife, which had entered just below her sternum. She looked shocked, her mouth open, head bobbing forward in small increments. She held it with both hands, as if trying to get the strength to pull it out.

"Bob..." she cried out. "Help."

Bob felt a surge of panic, his adrenaline firing again, his own pain momentarily forgotten. He rose and staggered over to her, then flopped beside her. *Can't pull it, might do more damage, release a stemmed artery.* He reached into her coat and found her phone. He looked back, anticipating another attack.

But Nikolai was in bad shape himself and had clearly realized what had happened. He looked around for a few seconds, as if trying to find his weapon, unable to spot it. Police sirens blared, cars approaching.

He crawled, then staggered, over to the stolen car, climbing in, throwing it into reverse before the door was even closed, the front end crumpled, the engine rattling and whining as it headed back up the street.

Bob double-clicked the phone's side buttons in unison, the emergency call screen coming up. He hit the send button.

It rang once.

"911 Emergency."

"Two down, one clinging," he panted. "Knife wound to the chest is the woman, priority. Don't... don't worry about..." He felt his head spin, the combination of pain and fatigue defeating him, Bob passing out before he could finish the call.

24

Bob was dreaming. He knew it was a dream because there'd been a bunch of bad stuff happening, and it wasn't happening anymore.

He didn't know how he knew that, as he lounged on a sunbed, the ocean waves crashing against the nearby shore. He didn't remember the bad stuff specifically; that was true of most his dreams. He knew they were there but rarely remembered them.

"Have you decided?"

He looked over at Liz. She was in a director's chair a few feet away, hands on her lap as if patiently waiting for his answer. She had a bikini on and an unrealistically perfect body, which Bob again took to mean he was dreaming.

Behind her, a late afternoon sun was dropping towards the horizon, its reflection captured on the water, now inexplicably placid and perfectly still... despite the continued sound of ripples lapping at the shore.

"Hmmm? Have I decided?"

"What you want? That's what this is all supposed to be

about, right? Figuring out who you are and what you want to accomplish? A sense of purpose? A big plan for the big man?"

Bob sighed. "I thought it was just a vacation. A break from it all."

"Nope. You're always worrying about the big picture, the meaning of it all," dream Liz said. "Your purpose."

So it doesn't really matter what I say. "I just figured Maine would be nice. And that getting away from it all would be nice."

She laughed at that, a slight chortle at first, her amusement growing, the giggle growing into a full-throated laugh, at first feminine, then hard, strained, then strangled, a cackle straight out of an old fairy tale.

"Oh, Bob! You know that can't be true." She shook her head gently as she said it, like someone scolding a silly child who should know better. "You're a killer, Bob. And killers don't get to have nice things."

That doesn't sound like Liz, his dream self decided, even though some part of him understood he barely knew her. He turned her way again, coming face-to-face with a cavernous, massive mouth, a black hole just past the giant epiglottis, promising to suck him in...

Bob woke with a start, that sudden sense of displacement from re-entering reality. The room was dark. He was in bed, the sheets comfortably soft. A machine was pinging gently in the background.

EKG?

He looked around. *I'm in a hospital bed.*

He tried to sit up. The pain in his ribs was subdued, muffled by painkillers, but still sore enough to bring back his memory of the hours prior, the crash and fight.

Rachel.

A nurse wandered into the room. She took a ballpoint pen out of her breast pocket and clicked it open before reaching down and retrieving his chart. "Mr. Bennett! Good to see you awake," she said.

As she placed the chart back in the holder at the end of the bed, Bob saw a shadow drift across the door.

The nurse noticed his attention shift. "That's an officer with the Portland Police. They want to ask you some questions about the events of the evening."

Ah, hell.

She must've read his facial expression, because the nurse leaned over the end of the bed and patted him twice gently on the leg. "Not to worry, they're just trying to catch whoever attacked the two of you."

"My friend..."

"She's in intensive care. The doctor will tell you more about that."

"Please..."

"It's not my place," the nurse said. Then she saw his pained look. "I understand she's expected to recover fully. She was stabbed in the chest, but the knife didn't pierce her heart."

He let his head slump back, a wave of relief hitting him.

"In the meantime, you should relax as much as possible. We've strapped your ribs, and the swelling to your testes has gone down, but you have quite a goose egg on the back of your head, probably from when it hit the sidewalk. I imagine the pain medication is doing some good. The doctor will be around shortly."

She left the room. Bob leaned forward, trying to be sure she'd gone down the hall.

He pulled back the sheet and swung his legs off the bed. He pulled the IV out of his arm, then staunched the blood with his thumb until he spotted the roll of cotton by the bed. He wrapped it around the join and tore it off crudely before tucking the end into the makeshift bandage.

They'd left his clothing neatly folded on a chair next to his bed. He retrieved his jeans and put them on, then his golf shirt, then his socks and shoes.

His jacket was nowhere to be seen. There was nothing important in it, just a burner phone he'd been meaning to replace. But he'd found the jacket for ten bucks at a thrift shop, a collarless Club International like the one he'd had as a kid.

He winced as he peeked into the closet against the back wall of the room. It was empty save for a series of metal hangers attached permanently to a metal rack.

Not important, I guess.

Now to see about getting past the guy at the door.

He crept over and peered around the corner.

The police officer had his back to the wall and was about three feet to Bob's right. He ducked back out of sight quickly, then realized Mike Schultz was sitting in one of the metal-and-vinyl office chairs propped against the opposite wall. Bob leaned out again.

"Mike," he said. He nodded towards the constable guarding the room. "Can we...?"

"Yeah! Yeah, Const. Wiseman is a stand-up guy. Deon, can you give us a minute?"

The constable shrugged. "Whatever you need, Sarge. But I still need to get his statement."

"I'll handle it for you, okay?"

The constable peered at him warily. "Sarge..."

"Just... trust me, okay, Deon?"

He nodded twice but didn't look convinced, heading down the hall.

"He's a good cop. I've known him since he was a little kid playing tee-ball in our neighborhood."

"How...?" Bob asked.

"You made the eleven o'clock news," Mike said. "I was barely paying attention. They said it was a robbery gone wrong or something. Anyway, I glance over, and who's getting loaded into the back of the ambulance but friend Bob. What the hell happened, exactly?"

Bob filled him in on the chaotic day prior.

Mike looked aghast at the scope of it. He tapped the seat next to him. "Take a load off."

Bob slumped into it. "Yah."

"Uh-huh," Mike agreed. "Big fucking mess, Bob."

"Biiig mess."

Mike chuckled. "And all of it because you picked a town to hole up in that happened to be full of Russian spies. Heh. What are the odds?"

"Hey, man, just as long as you keep any of that espionage talk to us, okay? I don't think your colleagues would buy it. And... calamity and me are old friends at this point," Bob suggested. "You're probably lucky the whole damn state of Maine didn't drop into the ocean the day after I arrived."

"Ha! Heh heh heh." Mike laughed at that, a rich bellow from his gut. "I tend to think in your case, you're not a magnet for trouble so much as the other way around. It's bleak, my lad. But we don't give up."

"Nope. Not much point, way I figure. But I wish the rules of the game were a little clearer sometimes," Bob said. "How is she?"

"The doc who checked you in three hours ago said she'd have surgery in short order. The blade was short, only four inches, and the edge of it caught her sternum, preventing it from reaching her heart by about two millimeters."

Bob's head slumped, the breath rushing out of him, his head spinning for a second. "That's... Jesus H. Two millimeters."

"She'll be on the mend for weeks, even with a clean wound. The throwing knife was twin edged, both razor-sharp. Sliced through muscles. She'll be in some pain."

Bob sniffed and rubbed his chin stubble. "Hell. You realize I'm probably going to have to kill that guy, right?"

Mike clucked his tongue. "Uh-huh. Yeah, kind of figured. I see nothing. I hear nothing."

"They're going to be pissed at you for letting me walk out of here, too," Bob said. "If your constable friend gets in trouble, he may have to point out that you're suspended and almost certainly not supposed to be here." He winced, his ribs smarting.

"Yup. About that..." Mike reached into his coat pocket and took out a pill bottle. "A nurse I know took sympathy. Percocet. Unless you feel like flying without a plane, don't take more than one at a time." He tossed Bob the bottle.

Bob pocketed them and rose. "I need to get back to the motel, grab some stuff."

Mike reached into his other pocket and tossed Bob a set of car keys. "The Toyota's in visitor parking. You need cash?"

"I'm good."

"They'll be watching your place, I imagine."

"Maybe. They're down one already, at a warehouse near the crash site. One of the others has a bullet in his shoulder. They might be out of action until tomorrow if I'm lucky."

"If you're not?"

Bob shrugged. "No one forced them to become cultural attachés." He headed for the side exit down the hall.

"Bob!"

"Uh-huh."

"Be careful."

He pushed the side door open. "Is there any other way?"

25

His motel room door was ajar when Bob got back, just after midnight.

He backtracked down the hall, opened the glass cabinet by the emergency exit and removed the fire extinguisher. If worst came to worst, he figured, it made a decent club.

He returned to the room and pushed the door open, then paused a beat, waiting for the inevitable ambush.

"Bob!" Liz was sitting on the end of the first bed.

She got up. "You're moving badly."

"I took a few knocks. It's nothing. How did you know where we're staying?" He put the fire extinguisher down on the luggage table, near the TV.

"Rachel called me right after you guys arrived. Then I saw the eleven o'clock news. And then she wouldn't answer the phone."

"So you rushed over."

"The cleaner's from Peaks originally. I vaccinated her kid. She let me in."

Damn, this is the hard part. Now I have to tell her. "Rachel's in the hospital."

Liz's eyes widened. "What happened?"

"She'll be okay. But she was stabbed, in effect. A guy threw a knife at me, missed me and hit her. Liz... if there are things you're not telling me, now would be a good time."

She looked tense, chewing on a knuckle, her gaze miles away. Eventually, she said, "I don't think I know anything that can help you," she said. "I just... Please don't let anything happen to her."

"I'm trying. Liz... was your father a spy?"

She looked at him sharply. He couldn't tell if it was frustration or irritation. "How far, exactly, should I stick my neck out, Bob? Does what happened to Rachel actually matter to you, or are you just helping your policeman friend?"

"Look—"

"I told you if I could help more, I would," she said. "That hasn't changed."

She was being deliberately obtuse, Bob figured. He pushed past her. "I need to get my other jacket and bag."

"Please!" Liz implored. "Please listen to me. I don't know what I can tell you that would help, but I don't want either of you to get hurt. Leave this alone, Bob. Let things play out. Let Rachel go back to Baltimore and get back to work. I'm sure my father will get in touch when he can."

Bob put his leather jacket on and picked up his soft-sided bag. He pushed past her again. "You play whatever part you think you need to play, Liz. I made Mike and Rachel both a promise." He opened the room door. "I intend to keep it."

He left her behind in the room and headed for the exit. They'd paid in advance, and he'd left his key beside the bed.

He had no doubt she would call her employers as soon as he left the building. He needed to move quickly.

He had an idea about Liz and whether she was a decent shot with a long gun.

The Russians were clearly working on some sort of clock. It centered on someone code-named "Uncle." He needed to get back to his apartment, access the encrypted chat on his laptop to get hold of Adam Renton, the former NSA fixer.

He checked his soft-sided bag for the Glock 19 he'd been carrying since New York. He realized the bag also held the phone he'd used to call Dawn.

I was going to have to toss it soon anyway. He looked at the corner of the screen. *One percent battery. Great.*

He checked his text messages, but there was nothing new. He opened his email box.

There was a message from Rachel.

He opened it. Three photos were attached. They were headshots of the men at the warehouse, all but Boris.

Clever JAG. She knew we might need to ID them.

And that meant Renton would have something else to work with.

Bob dropped the Toyota off in Mike's driveway, then took a hire car back to the restaurant to retrieve his beaten-up Lincoln.

He peeked under the car. He pulled the magnetic radio tracker out and glanced at the wastebasket at the corner of the lot.

Then he glanced back at the restaurant. The same Harley-Davidson that had pulled up the other night was parked in front.

Opportunity knocks.

He kept an eye out for passing drivers paying too much attention as he walked over to it. He slapped the tracker under the teardrop tank, attaching it to the steel frame. *He'll keep them chasing shadows for a few hours.*

The Russians would realize what he'd done as soon as they got a visual. But it meant his own set of wheels was back in play.

He drove back to his apartment in a sombre mood, fully aware he could have Sascha or Nikolai waiting for him, and not really giving a damn, the constant aching in his bones wearing him down.

Rachel was hotheaded and righteous but, under her bluster, seemed a straight-up soul, a good person. More than once in the prior hour, he'd mentally pictured her in a bed with tubes running out of her nose, intubated, IVs in her arms. Then he'd pushed it away; worrying was counterproductive when he'd done all he could.

He pulled up outside the building.

Annnd... we get anomaly number one.

A rented black Chrysler 300 limousine was parked illegally at the curb, a driver behind the wheel, but no sign of him moving.

As if he's waiting for someone inside.

Or me.

Only one way to tell.

Bob got out and slipped the Glock into his jacket pocket. He closed the car door, then paused, waiting to see if the other man moved.

Didn't even turn his head. Interesting. Let's see what happens next.

Bob casually strolled across the street, in front of the

Chrysler. He looked over at the driver just before reaching the door. He'd retrieved a phone from his pocket and was talking to someone.

He glanced over at Bob, then went back to his call.

Okay, so he's waiting for someone who's waiting for me.

The Russians evidently had limited numbers. The men at the warehouse had been the same at the restaurant, barring the older one who'd gone down to the sniper.

The guy behind the wheel was a new face.

So is this them, or...?

He paused before opening the door, weighing whether to go in cautiously or make a noise. At half past midnight, waking up the neighborhood might do more to protect him than anything, Bob knew. Nobody in the business craved attention.

He sighed. The painkillers were beginning to wear off, his ribs and balls both aching.

Fuck it. I'm too tired to care at this point.

He pushed the door open. The lobby was empty, dimly lit by emergency lights. He took the stairs to the fourth floor and found 4D.

The door was open, and not accidentally. Whoever was inside had left a solid half-foot crack to announce themselves.

Bob had a sinking feeling. *It's either the cops or...*

He pushed the door open.

"Hello, Bob."

Eddie Stone was smiling smugly. The former Team Seven overseer seemed relaxed in the old green-and-wood armchair that had come with the place, a 1970s relic.

The place had already been turned over, drawers out, papers on the desk in a mess.

"We have business to discuss," Eddie said. He gestured to the sofa opposite. "Please. Sit."

"My brain's telling me I should run in the other direction, but my legs are too tired to care."

Eddie waited until he'd sat down. "Now... why don't you tell me all about Uncle and what you're doing here," he suggested.

Bob pinched the bridge of his nose with his thumb and forefinger, his anxiety level instantly cranked up. He took a deep breath and centered himself. "Gee, Edward, why don't I ask you the same question? And the reason that's relevant is that until about six hours ago, I'd never heard of Uncle as anything other than a male relative or, at a stretch, the place a man came from in an old TV show. But since you almost certainly just got here – and likely were twigged by my presence *and* have yet to try to kill me – it sort of makes me wonder what Uncle is to you."

The CIA man leaned back, stolid, his hand cradled in an arch on his lap.

"Eddie Stone, lost for words? Is that a first?"

"I'm just thinking, is all. If someone were to ask me where you rank on the list of people I'd trust with intel graded top secret, I'd have to question their sanity for even suggesting you're on it. Or that I trust anyone."

The red light flicked on the clock radio ten feet away, the alarm sounding.

The first few bars of music kicked in, instantly recognizable to a man of Eddie's vintage. He waited until it had asked whether he liked piña coladas and rain, then turned back towards Bob, peering through narrowed eyes, as if mildly confused.

"What, exactly, is wrong with you, anyway?"

"I swear to God... the damn clock radio just hates me." Bob fiddled with the remote, the power button seemingly mocking him by ignoring his first two button pushes.

"I can understand that."

"And yet here you are."

"Yeah. Because, seemingly eternal pain in my ass that you are, Bob—"

He let the thought trail off. Bob sensed he was genuinely pained by what he had to say.

"—we might be able to help each other. And if we know anything about me, it's that I'm a pragmatist."

"We do?"

"I told Kennedy two years ago that we should've just let you go live your life. But he has deeper concerns, I think, than your mere knowledge of Team Seven."

Bob peered at him. "What are you up to, Eddie? You two have been thick as thieves since 'Nam. What's changed?"

"The mission that led to the purge. Tehran. We know there was a third party supplying mission intel long before you were sabotaged on the ground."

"Okay. And your hypothesis is that it was Kennedy."

"He was friends with a Russian-American fixer, Benjamin Usmanov, who we linked to the checks that were used to pay Alan Temple."

Bob hadn't thought about his treacherous former mentor since shortly after his death. "And this has you in Portland because Uncle is..."

"A handler," Eddie said. "An embedded handler of embedded agents. Legendary in spook circles, a myth. The presumed cause of numerous leaked state secrets over the years."

"The kind of person who'd be running a sleeper cell in a small city in Maine?"

"The very same." It was Eddie's turn to be suspicious. He leaned forward and studied his former colleague. "You know who it is, don't you?"

"I have suspects, one stronger than others," Bob explained. He filled Stone in on the prior three days, leaving out the names of those involved.

Eddie crossed his arms and drank it all in. "Yeah... well, the Russians will be from the embassy crew in DC. They mobilized a few days ago but led us astray, then flew out of Baltimore while we were watching Dulles. We get the impression they're not fans of yours, Bob. But then, that's no real surprise."

"Yeah, I'm loathed by absolute douchebags coast to coast," Bob said, staring right back at him. "It's not a deliberate point of pride, but I'll take it."

Eddie squinted, his features pinched. He tilted his head, then scratched absently behind his ear. "Yeah... having a smart mouth was never going to win you friends, Bobby. The recent moralizing isn't a whole lot better."

"I never get tired of awful people trying to tell me why it's wrong to judge their awfulness, or why it's tiresome to hear about it. It means they know truth when they hear it... but they just don't want to hear it. It helps me keep a firm handle on where the moral lines are. Now... skip to the punchline. What do you want? And why should I trust you on any level?"

"Because I'm here to offer you a deal, Bob. I'm here to offer you your life back."

. . .

THEY MOVED the conversation over to the kitchen table so that Eddie could lay out the contents of a file. A series of eleven-by-seven-inch black-and-white glossy photos displayed an elderly man in an L.L.Bean hunting jacket, clearly unaware he was being photographed from a distance.

"This gentleman is Thomas Peters. His real name is Artem Lipatov. He is a Russian deep-cover agent who has been located in Portland for sixty years. Three weeks ago, he contacted our Boston field office via an anonymous drop, offering to turn over one of the most effective spy rings in US history, in exchange for amnesty and asylum."

"And? Usually that would result in the asset going into protection immediately."

"It would have... had they taken the offer seriously. In the Boston office's defense, he offered no real evidence to support the claim, and the notion that there was a sleeper cell in Maine sounded like something an old man might have seen on late night TV. So... they ignored it. They get crank calls all the time."

Bob shook his head gently. "All of this is happening because you idiots were asleep at the switch. I'd lie and claim I was shocked, but..."

"Okay, okay. It's a big job. Things get missed," Eddie said. "Anyway, he tried again a week later. This time the note was more desperate, suggesting a cleanup was underway. Then our sig ints guys picked up a voice message referencing 'family' as a possible code term for assets and mentioning your name."

"Let me guess: that's the pattern believed to have spawned 'Uncle' as a code. That's where you get involved."

"Exactly."

"And you found the location by finding me. Okay. Pretty

standard procedure for an intel hunt. So... how did you find me?"

Stone sighed. "You know, normally I'd keep you guessing, but she's bound to bitch about it eventually."

"She?" Bob realized what he meant and winced. Then he considered the possible ramifications. He fixed Stone with a cold stare. "You'd better be about to tell me that you didn't hurt her."

"I didn't. But if she hadn't—"

Bob held up a palm. "Let me stop you right there, chief. In fact, let me finish the thought for you. If you had hurt her, you'd be dead before you could think to get out of that ugly-ass armchair. And I'm sure you know that."

"Yeah, I'm fucking terrified. Anyway, Lipatov's second message made it sound like they were planning on moving Uncle soon, perhaps imminently. We had someone from Boston tail him for a day to see how legit he seemed. Lipatov's claim of a cleanup make sense; historically, the Russians have been as likely to flush an asset as try to bring them in, especially sleepers, who can be problematic. So it made sense he'd be worried. They want Uncle back, not his semi-American assets."

"So you did contact him?"

"No. The agent watching him decided he seemed like a solid citizen and therefore maybe legit. But by the time someone tried the burner he'd set up as a contact, the next day, it had gone dead. From what you've told me, the same sounds true of Lipatov."

The body at the scene. It hadn't been an attempted kidnapping, it had been Russians removing an agent-in-place they were trying to kill. "What about his wife?" Bob said. "She died more than a month ago."

"If they've been together throughout his time here, it's highly unlikely she didn't know. She may have been an operative herself."

"There's another, a local guy who also happens to speak fluent Russian." Bob took out his phone and showed him the pictures. "The three heavies I figure are your Russian embassy goons. The other guy, though, in the Red Sox cap..."

"Send it to me, and we'll run him down for you. If he's been embedded here, he shouldn't be hard to find."

Bob stepped back, both palms raised. "I said I'd look at what you have. I didn't say I agreed to this truce, or job, or whatever it's supposed to be. Can't you just flood Portland with agency people?"

"We do that and maybe Uncle bolts immediately. We don't even know yet why that hasn't happened. Plus, Kennedy gets wind that something's going on involving his friends."

"Ah. Your end of the bargain, then."

"They'll have that 'within days' timetable for a reason, and that reason probably revolves around safety, keeping everything quiet. But if we charge into town by the dozen, I imagine they'll try something more immediate and direct. Then maybe we get them, but maybe we don't."

"Whereas if I identify Uncle for you, I'm not even a new player. They're already looking to eliminate me, already expecting my presence."

"And I know you," Eddie said. "Your track record for this kind of op is exceptional."

"Plus, if they kill me, it's two birds for one Stone, right, Eddie?"

"Like I told you, Bob, I wanted to pull the plug on

chasing you months ago. Maybe it's three birds; maybe we bury Uncle, your past sins and the man who wants you dead all at once."

Bob realized he had little choice. They knew where he was, and he'd promised Mike and Rachel he'd see the matter through. But the idea that he was going to come out of it free and smelling like roses?

"Sure, Eddie. I bet that's exactly how it goes. Because this shit has always worked out so well in the past."

26

Nikolai Grusin's shoulder ached. He'd spent a mostly restless night trying not to roll over onto it on the hard hotel bed.

He'd turned down the sleeper's offer of painkillers the night prior. He wanted to maintain the appropriate level of hate for Bob Singleton, the man who'd shot him.

At the same time, he felt slightly excited; it wasn't optimism, as Nikolai never really felt anything others would perceive as "positive." It was more a sense of the possibilities, the notion that, after ninety minutes of failed interrogation, Igor would be happy to see Singleton dead.

And that would give Nikolai a hundred thousand more reasons to be satisfied.

He did not know Igor on any personal level, or any of the diplomatic staff. The only exceptions were Boris and Sascha, officially the cleaners at the New York consular offices, but on Nikolai's team from time to time. He'd known both since the academy, a strangely sympathetic relationship despite all three excelling at ruthlessness.

Nikolai had no family, his parents long dead and better forgotten. He'd listened to his father beat his mother mercilessly in childhood, night after night. She'd tried to hide it from him, to protect his feelings. But she would cry and wail clearly through the thin walls of their tiny apartment; his father would allow it, even as he forced Nikolai to take his beatings silently, like a man, or get twice as much punishment.

Eventually, he'd realized how contemptible she was, how weak. He'd known that he was stronger, that he could be the ruthless, predatory winner that his father wanted him to be. He'd come to relish the sun going down, the agonized wail of her pitiful mewling; he became buoyed by her pain, energized by her suffering, knowing he could take anything.

The FIS had bred any empathy out of him as a young man.

His only two strong emotions, in general, were anger and excitement. He enjoyed killing people. The training sessions reminded him of the visceral joy of shooting a man in the head, that sense of power. Though it was usually demanded, he did not like to kill silently and undetectably, not when a man's suffering was reduced as a consequence. It felt empty, near pointless.

Singleton's death was a quest: an assignment of true value, violent in its execution. A journey in which there was honor to be found, and scalps to be taken. Acclaim to be had, retribution, financial gain, and suffering to be meted out from upon high.

He held the phone to his ear and waited for it to connect, the exchange delayed by Igor's extensive encryption. His boss would be angry about Boris's death, forced to send up cleaners to take care of the scene.

But that was to be expected. He was probably a fool, like Boris. Most importantly, he would want Singleton finally dealt with.

"What happened?" Yaremchuk didn't introduce himself or waste time, though the two men rarely spoke.

"Yeah, boss... we had some setbacks." Nikolai tried to sound matter-of-fact.

"Setbacks!? SETBACKS!?" Yaremchuk bellowed.

The line went dead for several seconds.

"Hello? Boss?"

Eventually, Yaremchuk said, "I've heard Uncle's version. Explain. Make it good."

"Okay. You sent Boris down, and Boris was an idiot. Now he is dead. Now I handle things without him."

"And our target?"

"He is working with the granddaughter of the old man. And there is a third party, the person who shot our man and helped them escape. We were interrogating them."

"Leave that matter for now," Yaremchuk said. "I believe I know what was involved there. What did you get out of them?"

"Their man, he was difficult. He swore his presence here, his involvement, was a coincidence. I... do not see what is so special about this guy that we cannot just take him out quickly. He—"

"HE IS NOT THERE BY ACCIDENT!" Yaremchuk yowled. "We have two days to keep him away from Uncle. Yes, you kill him if you must! But not if it just makes more noise, you idiot!"

"Igor—"

The former KGB man ignored him, exasperated. "Either way, I am sending down three more men to help and leaving

Uncle in charge, via your cousin. From now on, you are just the tool they use and direct. Don't fuck this up again! We do not have unlimited personnel who can operate in America."

"Cousin" was a code name for a sleeper asset.

He was leaving the local in charge, the simpering fool in the baseball cap, Chris. He was suggesting he would take direction from Uncle, but it amounted to the same thing, as Uncle would not be with them.

Nikolai felt his blood boil.

"Boss, why!? The asset, he has been living here too long; he is next to useless."

"He will merely be Uncle's mouthpiece. I suspect he has a level of self-control and judgment that you clearly lack, and we have no other manpower options until we can arrange private operatives. I have already spoken with Sascha about what took place. He told me about your attempt to chase Singleton down. In broad daylight, on a busy public street, despite what we discussed."

"Igor—"

"More importantly, the sleeper fears for himself, so he listens. And Uncle is the wisest among us," Yaremchuk said. "Do not challenge me over this, Nikolai Ivanovich! If you ever wish to atone for your mistakes at home, I can abide no more failures!"

"I had no choice, obviously."

"You allowed him to get loose in the first place, and the girl, because you are chasing Ivan Malyuchenko's six-figure bounty. Don't!... Don't try to deny it. We will discuss appropriate discipline when you return. If I allow you to return. In the meantime, three more men will join you, freelance assets arranged through our Boston consulate."

Nikolai could not hold back his discontent. "I think this

is a mistake, boss. I cannot lie. The sleeper, he is timid. He has been here so long he no longer thinks like a Russian."

"And I shall deal with him and the others once Uncle is safely en route. For now, I want a stable hand on the tiller, not your aggression. His fear means he will listen. Are we clear?"

"Da. I mean yeah. Yeah, of course."

Yaremchuk ended the call.

Fool! He is a damned fool. If there was any justice in the world, Nikolai supposed, Yaremchuk would choke on his lunch and Moscow would appoint him to handle US domestic operations.

One day they will recognize my genius. Probably five minutes after someone shoots me.

There was a knock on the hotel room door. "Come," he barked.

The door opened, and Coach Chris entered, Sascha right behind him. Sascha's head was bowed slightly, the giant's discomfort obvious.

"Eto verno! Vam dolzhno byt' stydno!" Nikolai muttered. *That's right, you should be ashamed.*

"Ya dolzhen byl skazat' pravdu, Nicky," Sascha pleaded. *I had to tell the truth, Nicky!*

Nikolai shot a hard glance at Coach Chris. "So now the sun shines out of your arse, eh?"

"We're all just trying to do our jobs," Chris offered. "All I'm supposed to do is relay what Uncle wants."

Nikolai's temper rose again, but he managed to hold it. "Uncle," he seethed, "was the only person who knew where we would take them yesterday. Uncle clearly arranged to save the girl from harm by having a shooter there watching us. I am not even sure which side 'Uncle' is on."

"Uncle is why we're together in the first place," Chris countered. "Not the agent, not the granddaughter. They're potential problems, sure, especially the girl. This is all personal to her. But the whole point is to keep Uncle hidden and safe until the move can be made. Come Thursday, Uncle has a new identity, a diplomatic passport. By Saturday, Uncle will be on the way to Moscow, and we never have to see each other again."

He was as stupid as Boris and Igor, Nikolai decided. He crossed his arms and smirked at the smaller man. "And you think that is how this ends for you, eh? You just go back to your stupid middle-class American life with your stupid middle-class American wife, back to coaching baseball and scratching yourself? Do not kid yourself. You are not value to Moscow. I am value to Moscow. You? You are a Cold War relic, destined for disposal. They make you feel like boss, but next week, or the week after, or a month after, they call on someone like me to make you vanish."

"Nicky..." Sascha began to intercede.

"No, he is a big boy; he can take it." Nikolai took a few steps forward so that he could tower over the baseball coach. "He sees the reality."

The baseball coach ignored his attempt at intimidation. "We have two full days left. I've spoken with Uncle. He wants us to lie low and stay close in case Singleton tries anything else. Uncle thinks it's possible Singleton was telling the truth, that his involvement was accidental because of his police friend. Uncle believes that if we offer him nothing more to pursue, the clock will run out on his efforts and the girl's. Are we clear? Unless he offers himself up on a platter, nobody kills anyone or otherwise makes a spectacle of themselves." Then he lifted his head and stared

Nikolai in the eye from inches away. "Do we understand each other?"

Nikolai gritted his teeth, tried to regulate his breathing, suppress his rage. He wanted to throttle the little man, a gnawing compulsion. *But that will have to wait.* "We are clear," he managed.

THE CONVERSATION WAS STILL WEIGHING on Coach Chris two hours later, as he stood in his modest home's kitchen and dolloped sugar into his coffee.

The day prior had gone about as badly as possible. They'd lost an agent, the targets had escaped, and Nikolai's murderous temper seemed likely to boil over. And he wasn't entirely sure the thug was lying about his future. What if they only cared about Uncle? What if this had all come about because Artem Lipatov had realized, as Nikolai had threatened, that they were all expendable?

"Well, hey there! And who might you be?" Coach Chris's wife, Carly, threw her arms around him.

She kissed his ear. "You got in so late last night, and that call about missing dinner was hurried. You okay?"

"Yeah. Yeah... fine. Tony issues."

"How was he?"

He hated lying to her. It came as naturally and easily as breathing because he'd had a lot of practice. But it sucked.

Like most of his life choices, Chris figured, it was out of his hands. "Worst he's been in years. Full-on relapse."

"Ah, geez." She turned to lean against the counter. "You think he needs clinical care maybe? I know you'll help as much as you can, but..."

He shook his head. *Don't oversell it, idiot.* "Nah. He

already seemed two hundred percent better by last night. He's been clean a few days now. I'll still have to check on him occasionally."

"Are you going to miss this afternoon's game? If so, you need to call John or one of the other coaches."

"No, I'm good," he said. "Can't skip the important stuff, right?"

She was quiet for a moment, and as he turned and took a sip of coffee, Chris got the sense she was studying him.

"What?"

"We've been married twenty years, hon. I can tell when you're trying to keep me happy. But something's really eating at you, has been for days."

He wanted to tell her. He'd always wanted to tell her. But telling her could be a death sentence. *And she'd pack a bag and be out the door anyway, even if they didn't make the call.* She might even turn him in, he knew. Carly was a patriot, a believer in the American dream.

He needed his family. Coach Chris figured it was really all he had left.

27

Bob sat on the top row of steel bleachers, behind home plate and the protective cage that separated the crowd from the Little League ball players, preventing injuries from stray foul balls.

"STRIKE TWO!" The young player at the plate had taken a huge cut at a curveball, bat passing the plate just as the ball dipped into the dirt, smothered by the catcher.

He stepped away from the plate and tugged at his belt, knocked the dirt off his cleats with his bat, then took a few practice swings.

It felt odd, being surrounded by so much normalcy. Bob had sunglasses on and a new ball cap, a Boston Red Sox number in dark blue and red. The Detroit Tigers hat he'd had since Miami a year earlier had finally been lost during the fight with Nikolai.

The good mood was the Percocet doing its job, he knew, everything seeming a little more pleasant, the dull ache in his ribs out of mind.

Most of the crowd wore Portland Privateers caps, and a

few had shirts, too, which seemed excessive for a Little League game. *They sell merch at these things now?*

Bob's own Little League career had lasted for two games at age fourteen. It had been glorious, in a confusing, sudden sort of way. They'd lived in the woods of Michigan's Upper Peninsula, and his mother had home-schooled him at his father's insistence.

Her attempt to socialize him had been to enter him into Little League, assuming maybe sports were something her retired drill instructor husband would accept. He'd never even played the game before, but his preternatural co-ordination and reaction times had proven an unfair advantage, going eight-for-eight at the plate and hitting five home runs.

Scouts had been after him and his mother after the second game. He remembered the anger on his father's face, pulling up in his massive old International Harvester Scout utility vehicle, getting out seething, seeing them being pursued by strange men asking questions.

Back home, they'd both taken a beating for that adventure.

He'd finished the day as confused as when it had started. He didn't know if he liked baseball; the other kids had treated him like he was a weird curiosity because he was home-schooled. All he'd been sure of was that he wanted to avoid another beating.

It seemed so long ago but still so familiar.

His gaze flitted to the home team dugout, down the third-base line. Chris Jefferson had one foot raised, on the steps up to the field, and was leaning on that knee, trying to gauge how they should signal the runner on third.

It was strange seeing him a day later, pretending to be a civilian.

It had taken Eddie Stone's people less than two hours to identify the sleeper from Rachel's photo. They would already be building profiles of every aspect of his life, based on what Eddie had said, finding the local links, the patterns of movement, the habits and tendencies that would betray anyone with whom he worked.

They would have a tap on his phone by now, intercepts on all his internet communication. Jefferson didn't know it yet, but his life as a sleeper agent was already over.

The same NSA analysis group that had identified him had also said he appeared to have been embedded since childhood, based on his official documents. They speculated that like most long sleepers encountered, he would have become tied down, developed roots, a love of his existing life that could be used against him.

They had leverage, and Chris Jefferson was a useful tool. If he had contact with "Uncle" directly, it could possibly be backtracked, traced. If he didn't, he had enough involvement in the matter at hand to draw the others out.

Twenty feet from the ball coach, a woman got up from the bleacher seats and walked over to the dugout. She leaned over the rail and said something. Jefferson turned and moved over to her. They talked, and then she gave him a kiss on the head.

That would be his wife.

A kid on the bench got up and jogged over, a boy of maybe twelve or thirteen, earnest, with red hair and freckles. She leaned over the fence rail and kissed the boy on the top of the head. A moment later, Jefferson put his arm around the kid's shoulders.

A kid. He has a kid.

The boy turned slightly, so that Bob could see his face.

He had a prominent scar on his upper lip. Other than that, he looked like any young teen, a little restless, a goofy smile on his face.

The NSA group clearly hadn't gotten that far in their research. And there's the rest of your leverage right there.

It was one thing to fall in love with a place, Bob figured.

It was quite another to have a wife and kid.

His background, his time in cover, none of it suggested Jefferson was the kind of killer he'd been palling around with a day earlier. He would have emotional vulnerabilities, people he wanted to protect more than himself.

Coach Chris's back was aching as he pushed the lawn mower out of the shed and into the family's modest backyard.

He'd cleaned up after the game, including collecting the bases and helping his assistant, John, roll the infield dirt flat again. The team had lost, so the planned celebratory pizza dinner was off.

He'd gone home and eaten a quiet dinner with Carly, his son, Max, chatting throughout about Pokemon and *Fortnite* and things he'd seen on TikTok. He'd smiled and tried to listen, his mind on the mess they'd left in their wake over the prior two days.

Then he'd gone out to do yard work, to try to take his mind off it all.

He pulled on the lawn mower's cord starter. For everything else going on, it seemed surreal to have to still do the chores. But the grass wasn't going to cut itself.

The mower coughed once but didn't turn over.

"You're going to have to tell them eventually, you know."

He wheeled around.

Bob Singleton was sitting on the picnic table by their back fence, using the tabletop as his seat, feet on the bench.

Chris panicked, his eyes flitting across the yard and back to the shed for a weapon.

"Just... relax. We're not doing that here," Bob said. "Not with civilians ten yards away, even if they are indoors. They might come out here, and then what happens?"

He'd seen Singleton's file, seen how much pain he could take during Sascha's interrogation, heard how nonplussed and unfazed the man had been by all of it. The girl? She'd been nervous, maybe even frightened. The girl was nothing to worry about.

But Singleton scared him.

He began to creep sideways, one slow step at a time, trying to get himself between the door and Bob. "I won't let you hurt them," he said.

Bob rolled his eyes and appeared mildly insulted. "Jesus H, Coach. You sure picked the wrong team, didn't you? You think I'm anything like your friends Nikolai and Sascha? Or the late Boris, for that matter?"

"I know exactly who and what you are," he said. "And I didn't pick anything."

Bob nodded towards the other side of the bench. "Sit. We need to talk. And there's no avoiding it, not now."

Sascha had shown a moment of compassion earlier in the day, after the debrief. He'd told Chris to carry a piece because he'd never know when someone was coming for him. That was the business they were in.

He'd taken it politely and ignored it. He hadn't regularly carried a gun in four decades undercover, and there seemed little point in altering that policy. A day earlier, at the warehouse, he'd deliberately aimed well wide of both Singleton and the woman, unable to take the idea of murdering a man in cold blood, even with everything he'd seen.

He walked to the back of the yard and sat down. "What are you going to do to me?"

Bob ignored the question. "I wasn't lying when I said I don't work for the government anymore. But I can still call in favors. They had a workup on you in fairly short order. They know you've been here since you were a child."

"For me, it's like I was never anywhere else."

"A training village?" Bob questioned.

The coach nodded. "In the Amur Oblast. It was just like here, down to the parking meters needing quarters and the cops ticketing jaywalkers. The only thing that never made sense was the church. It was always locked, and I've often wondered why they bothered to build it."

"Your parents didn't tell you what the town really was?"

"Not until I was nearly thirteen, long after we had moved. I asked my mother questions about my friend Andy, who we'd left behind, about where the town was. About why we never visited or stayed in touch with other residents. She was afraid one day they would be asked to silence me, or someone would take me away. She wanted me to know that what we were doing was noble, a fight for the soul of the common man against the evil forces of capitalist repression."

"But over time..." Bob prompted.

"Over time, it all seemed like a distant dream. Or nightmare, maybe. My mother convinced my father that my training should continue. I... think they loved each other. Hard saying, not knowing."

"And they were active?"

He nodded. "But for my safety, they kept the details to themselves. They only involved me once, for a dead-letter drop, just before my father passed." Chris's eyes flitted to the back door of the house. "She might notice the mower's not going."

"If she comes out, we're just old friends having a chat. Right?"

He nodded again.

"Who is Uncle?"

The coach's head dipped. "So there it is. The real reason you're involved in all this. Nikolai was right."

"It's not why I got involved. It's the price for getting help from my former colleagues. I need a name."

"Even if I had one, I would not give it to you. The government will do what they want with me. I know that. But my wife and child have nothing to do with this. The FIS will not care. If they think I've betrayed Russia, their lives will be forfeit as mere punishment."

"So you'd rather be arrested, humiliated as a traitor, have them humiliated—"

"Than risk their deaths? Yes. Every day." Chris's head sank into his hands. "I didn't ask for any of this. I was forced into this world, can't you see that? Until Artem Lipatov disappeared, I had nothing to do with anything. All I did was coach ball."

"But I take it they paid you?"

A single nod, reluctant.

"Artem Lipatov?" Bob hadn't heard that name before.

"The man you know as Thomas Peters. You do realize—"

"Pretty quickly. It's why I'm tied up in the mess to begin with."

"Because the first time Boris and Sascha came down here, it was to silence him."

"They carted his body away from the accident scene," Bob suggested.

"And buried it with lye a few miles out of town, as far as I could tell. What are you going to do with me? You must know already. I could've shot you at the warehouse, you realize."

But his eyes flitted sideways as he said it, like he didn't even believe it himself.

Bob felt a swell of pity for the man. Yes, he'd taken dirty money, probably for years. But like most sleepers, his role had been minimal, his actions forced on him by his parents. What could he have done? If he'd come clean, told the truth, he would have had no bargaining chip, no intel he could share that would help America, no reason for them to not jail him or, worse, stick him on a plane back to Moscow in the next prisoner exchange.

And then he'd have lost his wife and son.

What would Dawn do? She'd have Jefferson be honest, Bob knew, turn himself in. But she'd try to smooth the path first.

That's about the best I can offer.

"What I'm going to do is get whatever contact number you have for Uncle—"

"It's encrypted, bounced off satellites to hide the location. By the time anyone cracks it, he'll be long gone. I can't even tell you what he really looks or sounds like; the call is always disguised electronically."

"Nevertheless, they'll want to try. You, in the meantime, I will offer this deal, and it's the best I can do: help me set up your friends Nikolai and Sascha, get them out of the way, and I will talk to my CIA contact about them going easy on you."

"Really?"

"It won't be good, whatever they offer. You're going to jail, barring us somehow coming up with a better reason not to put you away. But if they think you can help, if they understand the circumstances and I let them know you're a helpful fella – my guy on the inside – maybe it's a minimum-security country club, with visiting. And maybe it's not for the rest of your life."

Through the kitchen window, they saw Carly waving. Chris held up his hand to signal five minutes. She nodded and went back to polishing a dish.

"I don't want to lose them," the coach said.

"And I'm your one shot at preventing that," Bob said, rising. "You have a place where we can talk more, go over what you know, get that number?"

The coach got up. "My study."

"Then let's go. We have plans to make."

THE PASSENGER SEAT of the beaten-up Lincoln was occupied when he got back to the car.

He climbed behind the wheel and looked over at his uninvited guest, the smoke from Eddie Stone's cigarette curling around the septuagenarian's head, bouncing off the roof vinyl.

"Really? You just light up in someone else's car?"

"We don't like each other, remember. If I can annoy you while getting this job done, it's just a bonus."

"Well, put it out, or I'll rearrange your face using the dash as a scalpel."

Eddie chuckled, but clearly didn't want to push the issue. He rolled the window down a crack and tossed the cigarette out. "So?"

"He's in."

"The deal?"

"You'll help minimize what happens to him."

"Like fuck I will! He's a dirty traitor. What he deserves is a bullet behind the ear and an anonymous hole somewhere."

Bob turned his head and registered his annoyance with a dead stare. "Have you ever considered, Eddie, that maybe when it comes to reading people, you're not the genius you seem to be? Me, Edson Krug, Mikey Smalls – the list of your 'disappointments' suggests maybe your original assessments were less than accurate."

"Your point?"

"He's not a KGB wet-work specialist, he's a baseball coach from Maine. And he was a true sleeper, untouched and unused for all but one day of his forty-odd years under cover. He didn't even know what his parents were until he was in his teens."

"How is this my problem?"

"I'm doing a job for you under truce. It would make my life infinitely less stressful, I suspect, if I killed you and dumped you in a hole somewhere. You know why I don't?" Bob asked.

"Because you'd have the entire agency on your ass."

"I already have the entire agency on my ass, and a few others besides. The reason I don't, Eddie, is that 'convenience' isn't a good enough reason to kill someone."

"And yet you've killed *lots* of people, a whole lot of whom you barely knew."

"Because they were a threat to others. That's it. That's all. This guy is a threat to no one. If you kill him, you'll deprive an innocent teenage boy of his father and make a widow of his equally innocent wife. If, on the other hand, you want me to keep trying to find Uncle for you, then you need to do what I want. And I want you to cut him a break."

It was Eddie's turn to offer a quick head turn, followed by a piercing stare. "You know, I've wondered in the last year if Krug wasn't right about you, Bobby."

"Krug was never right about anything."

"Yeah, but he had you pegged from the start. He said before the Tehran debacle that you were a bleeding heart. One day, he figured, you'll hesitate, feel sorry for the wrong person. And that's the day your head gets blown clean off."

"It'll still be my call to make, though. Not yours. Just remember this: if you don't stick to your side of this bargain, the next time we see each other, I'll be looking for payback on his behalf. Am I entirely fucking clear, Eddie?"

"Crystal. What about the arrangements?"

"We've agreed a meeting location, a church they've used before, and my backstory. He'll tell them I've offered Uncle safe passage for a million dollars, and to bring the money in cash. His associates will come loaded for bear to eliminate me. Uncle won't show, of course."

"Of course," Eddie said. "But we know they have limited numbers and won't expect you to have support. As long as we leave one alive, they'll likely scurry back to whatever rathole they're living in, maybe right to Uncle himself."

"Then we're good to go," Bob said. "How much support are we talking, by the way?"

"This whole deal is unofficial. I can't risk word getting back to Kennedy, so it's just me and my driver, Agent Karl

Hayes; but he'll be staying in town, to pick up the pieces in the event we fuck this up. Is manpower likely to be an issue?"

"No. Like you said, they're running out of bodies. I'd assume Uncle has called in at least two or three reinforcements, but any more than that and they risk followers or ongoing surveillance tracking them here from DC. It's probably going to be Nikolai, Sascha, and whoever they can rustle up."

"Huh. Sounds like a fair fight," Eddie said. "Not ideal. Never is."

"We have the advantage of surprise," Bob said. "They'll know it's a trap. But they'll figure it's their trap."

Eddie looked at his watch. "We have work to do. You're going out there tonight, I take it?"

"Once you and I are done."

"Then I'll go with you," the spymaster said. "We need to know the scene cold, and we need to be set up long before Jefferson tells them where and when."

"Sure." But Bob knew preparation tended to count for little when the bullets began to fly.

28

MOSHE CORNER, MAINE

Letting the Russians pick the location assured they would pick somewhere familiar, somewhere used before.

Somewhere they believed would be safe ground.

Bob pulled the Lincoln onto the shoulder of State Route 237, just north of Mosher Corner, west of the city.

It was a village, not much more, a handful of houses, a church, and a correctional center about a mile up the road.

The church was a little white dot with a tiny bell tower, a few hundred yards down Old Canal Way, a near-deserted road winding through the fir and spruce trees, the right turn just yards away. "That's it," Bob said, pointing it out to his passenger.

Ahead of the little white building, a sign near the turnoff read "St. Sergius Roman Catholic Church."

Eddie seemed unimpressed. "It's tiny."

"I did a little research after I talked to our new friend. Turns out it closed more than a decade ago after years of declining congregation," Bob said. "Russian migrants kept it alive for years. People supported it during the Soviet era because it was seen as a statement against the regimes of Stalin and Khruschev. But it was strict; its resident priest was a hard-ass. They lost their sense of community, and people defected to the larger Russian Baptist congregation up the road."

"It doesn't look shuttered."

"It was bought by a numbered company about a year after it closed and has been rented out occasionally since then. Same numbered company owns that warehouse you described."

Eddie turned his head side to side, checking out everything around them. "You have to hand it to them, they know how to avoid attention. There's sweet diddly fuck out here. Someone hears a gunshot, they probably just assume it's hunters."

The light was beginning to get low, the sun skirting the horizon. They got out of the car and walked the last forty yards. Bob kept his head on a swivel, but there were no signs of other cars.

They crossed the gravel parking lot. They circled the building perimeter. The only door aside from the double main entrance was along the right side, near the back of the building. "Probably leads to the vestry," Bob guessed.

They kept going, moving behind the white clapboard building. There were two windows along the back wall. Bob got close to the wall and peered at them on an angle. "Contact strips and sensors, so pretty basic security. Be your basic forty-five-second window to shut it down, then an audible alarm, which isn't much good if there's no one around to hear it. Be nice if we had a master pass, but I can clip the box if necessary."

Most commercial security systems came with a master code that could reset the system in case a user got locked out and forgot it. Stone leaned in. Then he stepped back, took out his phone and dialled a number.

“Yeah, it’s me,” he told the other end. “Look, I need a bypass on a security system, but we’re on a time crunch, trying to keep things quiet. Can you get ready for a rapid search? We’ll need a return in pretty short order, probably less than thirty seconds.” He nodded. “Uh-huh. Perfect. Stand by.”

He looked over at Bob. “Okay, crack the door and find the panel, but toute suite, Bobby. We don’t want half of rural Maine showing up uninvited.”

They moved back to the side door. Bob put his shoulder to it once, then again with more force, the wood around the lock hasp splintering. He stepped inside, eyes trying to adjust to the half-light of the surrounding tall windows. He looked up and saw the contact strip at the top corner of the door, then followed its wiring along the wall, through a back curtain, into the priest’s changing area, or vestry.

“Got it!” he called out. “It’s an old Tandy Radio Shack Model 1100 from the eighties. Serial is...0881-ff-4422-00-4455.”

Bob watched the second hand on his Seiko. He figured they had about fifteen more.

Fourteen...

Thirteen...

Twelve...

Eleven...

“Try 01020399,” Stone called out.

Eight...

Seven...

Six...

Five...

Bob hit the enter button.

The lights on the panel turned from red to green, and a beep sounded.

His watched ticked by forty-five seconds, Bob holding his breath for a moment, worried they'd missed something.

Silence. "WE'RE GOOD," he yelled out.

Eddie joined him inside. Bob walked out of the vestry to find him surveying the pews. "This place is small for an ambush," his former boss said. "If you walk in through the front doors, they can stick a guy behind the altar, another behind a few pews, I guess. Have someone come out of the back, via the curtain, one in the upper gallery."

Bob motioned to the other side of the room. "They still have the old confessional booths."

Eddie looked on approvingly. "Yeah, that'll be it, then. They'll have someone in the other booth. Either he'll try to hit you there, or they'll converge on it while you're room blind."

"You brought the cameras?" Bob asked.

"I did. I'll have eyes on the vestry entrance and rear door, as well as the main hall. Nobody's going to come in or out without us knowing where they're positioned. I'll either use the side entrance if we need the more direct approach or the back window if we want to be quiet."

Bob nodded his approval. Then he glanced over at the older man. He had a smug look on his face, that sense of confidence. "Admit it: you've spent the last two years chasing my ass around the map. But you'd rather be doing the job. Look how friggin' happy you are right now."

Eddie eyed him warily. "Am I smiling?"

"Well... no. But you never smile. You're definitely happy, though."

"Don't assume this is going to change anything. I told you, if we get Uncle, I'll try. But you know damn well that it's not up to me."

"I do."

"And, Bob..."

"Yeah, Eddie."

"I still don't like you."

"And I still think you're a crooked bastard who would sell his own grandmother for an ice-cream cone."

"Yeah, maybe," Stone said. "I mean, she's been dead since '57. She's not much good to anyone these days. But... that right there, that judgmental, condescending shit, like you're better than the rest of us. That. That's why I don't like you."

"Another day or two, this'll all be dealt with, and I'll either be free or dead already, or you can go right back to trying." Bob headed for the door. "I'll wait in the car while you finish setting up eyes."

He opened it and was about to take a step out when Eddie called back to him, "Hey, Bob."

"What?"

"You figure if it was me coming after you instead of the guys Kennedy has hired, you'd have made it this far?"

"Eddie, you're seventy-one. We're lucky you made it from the car to here. If you decide to come after me on your own?" Bob looked around the church again. "Prayer might not be a bad idea."

Bob parked the car outside his building. Eddie had called his driver ahead to tell him they'd be back soon.

"Tomorrow, then," Eddie said, his hand grasping the car door handle.

"Yeah. Hey... Eddie."

"What?"

"You ever feel bad for the team? The ones who made it back only to be betrayed by their own department? Because we've known each other a long time, and every so often, I get a whiff of conscience and human decency out of you."

Eddie's head dipped. "I feel bad about every soldier we ever lost. In 'Nam or from the agency. And Team Seven." He looked up, his expression serious, unemotional. "Are you asking me if I blame myself or feel guilty? No. I didn't make those calls."

"But you did execute the order. And probably more than a few of the people."

He could see the older man's tension, his discomfort at discussing his craft. "What do you want me to tell you, Bob? I'm a soldier. It's a tough job. There's no 'but' there; it's what I was made to do, I guess. You think I liked it when a harmless dweeb like Mikey Smalls got his brains beaten in? Or when Krug decided to go off-mission in Africa, molesting local women and shooting civilians?"

"You know that's not what I mean. You still choose to—"

"Because I'm still needed. And it feels good to be needed," Eddie said. "I have to work under an exemption because of my age. I should be retired. But they value me when the world goes to absolute shit and official channels don't work. I'm the guy who decides how we set it straight through unofficial channels. Do I like it? No, I fucking love it. And if the price I pay is some black nights and a dead wife, then I'll live with it."

“Charming,” Bob said. “You’re just a sweetheart, aren’t ya?”

“What else should I do? Swallow whatever delusion you’ve bought into, self-righteousness about precisely who you kill, even as you continue to do basically the same shit out there that you did for us? I know your body count in the last eighteen months. If you think any of that’ll ever wash that guilt away, end those black nights, you’re only kidding yourself.”

Eddie got out of the car.

“Well... great talking to you, I guess,” Bob said dryly.

Eddie started walking. “Yeah, fuck you, too,” he muttered, without looking back.

Bob watched him disappear around the corner.

The driver, Agent Hayes, had been watching his building since they left, so there would be no surprises waiting upstairs. But hanging around didn’t make a lot of sense, from a risk perspective.

There was a rooming house down near the docks that had lockers and cots. It wasn’t much, but it was anonymous.

29

His phone's buzz woke Bob from his slumber just after six the next morning.

He checked the screen.

Liz.

He was certain she'd lied the day prior, that she knew more than she let on. She had to, based on the pre-prepared statement about her "cousin" Domas Petrauskas. She'd been given a script and had delivered it.

Not helping her cause was the fact that until the very last, Nikolai and his goons had avoided hurting Rachel, when they had no such compunction towards Bob himself.

He hit the green button. "Liz."

"I just got a call from Rachel's doctor. She's going to be able to see visitors at nine this morning. I thought you might want to see how she's doing."

"I take it you'll be there."

"At some point."

"Liz... Look, I don't know how deep you're in, but there are alternatives—"

"We've been over this. I can't help you."

"I know you're worried about Rachel, but—"

"But nothing. She was two millimeters away, Bob. Two millimeters from me losing her forever."

"She's safe now. And we can get you—"

"They killed my husband. They killed Riley. He didn't abandon us. He's not off living his life somewhere else, any more than my grandfather's on the road, selling Bibles. We buried him in the marsh on Peaks less than a half mile from his home and his seven-year-old daughter."

"Liz—"

"So do you see, Bob? Nobody doing this has a choice, not really. Not me, not you. You know what's driving me, and I have to guess there's something driving you: duty, honor, guilt, shame. Whatever it is... please, try to understand."

"They'll never let go. They'll kill you first. Liz, please just listen—"

"I... I have to go."

She ended the call abruptly.

Once they knew Liz had a daughter, they had all the leverage, Bob knew.

But... maybe you just like her. Maybe she's been up to her neck in the family business for a long time.

RACHEL WAS SITTING up in her bed, reading a battered old copy of *People* magazine. It had been pored over so many times the cover was starting to come off at the staples, the pages mottled and creased.

"Well, you look a whole lot healthier," Bob said.

She looked up and smiled. It disappeared quickly, and she proffered the magazine. "I don't get out for another week, at the minimum, so they can monitor things. But they don't allow phones, and all they have to read are" – she checked the date on the cover – "thirteen-year-old copies of *People* and *Us Weekly*."

He recognized what she was doing, lowering the immediate pressure in the room created by his appearance.

"I'm sorry. That knife was meant for me," Bob suggested.

"True, but not the point," she said. "I've had a lot of time to think in the last two days... a lot of time to think about the first twenty-five years of my life. The little weird things about my grandparents, their aggression towards one another, Grammy Rose spending all her time in the capital."

Rachel hung her head, and Bob could see the depreciated love, the burgeoning shame of realizing her life was a lie, and her family liars.

"I don't want to be patronizingly simplistic or anything," he said. "But you know none of this is your fault. You were a kid. The fact that your mother managed to keep it from you from so long, to protect you in that way, is kind of a miracle. She's a shit spy, but a much better mother than maybe you realize."

"I... get all that. It doesn't feel that easily defined. But that's not the point I wanted to make. What I wanted you to know is that I should be apologizing to you. I know I can be hotheaded sometimes, but the truth is neither of us is responsible for any of this. We're both side players dragged into it by caring about other people. So I know what happened to me isn't on you, okay, bub? And I mean that; I'm so grateful for what you've tried to do for me."

Bob felt the flush of embarrassment again, the mortified discomfort of praise. He swallowed hard and crossed his arms. "Yeah. Yeah, yeah." He rocked on his heels nervously.

"Wasn't expecting that. Real nice of you to say and everything."

She smiled, her eyes lighting up a little. "Bob! Are you blushing?"

He grimaced at the notion. "What!? No! No, it's... it's all good." *Gahd, why doesn't this get any easier!?* "Anyway, all that stuff aside—"

"Hah!" She chewed on her lower lip, and he had the uncertain sense she was restraining herself from laughing further. "All aside, huh? Just like that!" Rachel snapped her fingers.

"I was *going* to say that the reason I actually came over was to update you. I think this is all going to be over pretty soon. Things are coming to a head."

"How so?"

"The Russians are on the clock, somehow. The less you know about the specifics right now, the better. But a government associate of mine thinks it could be a matter of a day or two before they pull out."

Her good humor disappeared. "What are you going to do?"

"Stop them."

THE DONUT SHOP on Valley Street was a popular takeout place, a steady stream of customers lining up for glazed treats and high-octane coffee. But in typical Portland style, Bob figured, they hadn't taken advantage by putting in a drive-through.

For such a busy town, it tried awfully hard to seem laid-back.

He waited in line and bought a tea, then made his way to the first booth by the doors.

He sat patiently, sipping his drink, eyes on the doors for a further five minutes until Chris Jefferson arrived.

The coach took a seat across from him. "Why here?" he asked.

"Active-duty agents, the type involved in black ops or wet work, keep fit. They don't eat shitty, sugar-based diets. It also means they tend not to wander into donut shops."

Jefferson scoffed a little at that. "Is there anything you do that isn't measured and careful?"

"Sometimes when it does me the least good," Bob said. "Everybody makes mistakes, bud. It's sort of what I wanted to talk to you about."

Chris stared forlornly at the vinyl tabletop. "Is this the part where you give me a line of shit about how you're going to help me get out of all of this because you need my help tonight?"

"Nope, although the sentiment is understandable. No, like I told you, I don't work for the CIA anymore. Even if I did, I couldn't promise that. But I do have an agreement that they'll try to work with you, go light on you. They'll debrief you, probably for weeks. And they'll try to scare you into being as honest as possible. Given how little you know, you might even have been looking at a noncustodial sentence. Except..."

The coach's head sank. He knew where the problem lay. "Except I took their money. Does it help if they know I had to?"

"Why? Teachers make a living wage in most states."

"Yeah, but they don't necessarily have a son with chronic

health problems. Max was born with a deforming orofacial cleft."

The kid's scar. "He needed surgery?"

"Yeah… I mean… when I say deforming, it was so bad the other kids from about age three started picking on him, calling him a monster. I'd been leaving all the FIS money in a separate account up until then. But the surgeries required to fix it… our insurance didn't cover it. It ended up costing nearly three hundred grand."

"They were paying you well."

"Not really, not in American terms. But they started when I was eighteen, and it accumulated for twenty years. There's another two hundred thousand still in the account."

Bob weighed it. He took a sip of tea. The store was busy all day, apparently, the line stretching to the door. "I don't know. They're not sentimental people, and they'll want as little of it public as possible. Maybe if I pitch it as 'he let them pay for his kid's surgeries but otherwise didn't spend it'? Maybe. Maybe that'll work for you. Either way, it beats the alternative."

"What do you think Nikolai plans to do to me?"

"Based on other sleeper cells or rings that have collapsed or been pulled? We don't have a whole lot of examples this big to choose from, but chances are good they planned to visit you once Uncle was gone. They'd probably stage it to look like a murder-suicide with your family. Fits with the anti-firearms narrative out there generally, and they like an easily accepted story."

Coach Chris's mouth hung open slightly. "I hadn't considered—"

"That they'd kill your wife and kid? Pretty much a given. They'll worry about pillow talk, about what you might have shared. From your interactions, their goon squad doesn't exactly trust you."

The coach leaned in conspiratorially. "No, but their boss does. Igor Yaremchuk, the 'cultural attaché' at the DC embassy. He's lost faith in Nikolai and has me in charge tonight. He also says they're moving Uncle tomorrow night, just before midnight."

"From?"

"That's what I've got, bub, and that's all."

Bob studied him. He seemed to be sincere, but a man protecting his family could go to great lengths and wasn't immune to trusting the wrong people. "Coach, do you know what your Russian birth name was?"

Chris nodded. "It was Roman. Roman Ratachkov. But... it's so alien to me it might as well belong to someone else."

"Okay. I guess I can understand that, the depth they went to assimilate you," Bob said.

He'd wanted to see if the man paused, pretended to not remember it or that it was offensive to him. Any sign that he was putting on a performance about his dislike for his countrymen. But he'd played it straight.

"Tonight, what can we expect?"

"Well, they bought that you might be in this for a payday. It fit with their prior intelligence, that you were out of the agency years ago, and with why you might have been tied up with Victor Malyuchenko, a gangster."

"But they'll still suspect a trap."

"Having me demand we pick the location seems to have worked. They've brought in five more men. Two are assigned to protect Uncle; three are joining Nikolai and Sascha at the church. Yaremchuk considers it a priority that you be taken out. They anticipate you having support; if it's considered overwhelming, more than one or two people, he wants me to blow the building once you're inside. They're out there this morning, setting remote charges. But I'm the one who's supposed to push the button."

"I should feel flattered."

"They'll assume you're going in blind because you're only supposed to have the location an hour in advance."

"Then we're not going to get a better chance," Bob said. "They'll want a close-range hit and have a field of fire set up to ensure I can't escape. We just have to let one of them run. Right back to Uncle."

Chris had stopped looking around the donut shop and was gazing at the tabletop in brooding fashion.

"I'm not going to pretend I can't see your predicament," Bob said.

"It's not loyalty," he replied.

"I know. I get what this is to you, an imposition on the reality you'd made for yourself and your family."

Chris sighed. "I was just thinking about how disappointed my father would be in me, for wanting to be American. I have a lot of fond memories of my father, you know, even though he was dedicated to his role, to spying on us. But I think my favorite was of one of my visits to him in hospital, when the cancer was killing him. He was always in good spirits, all things considered, more cheerful than he'd been for much of my life."

"Cheerful with cancer?"

"Surprisingly so. Most of the time he was serious and focused. He'd tried to accept my love of baseball by framing it in those terms. 'It's a good cover,' he'd say, 'very American.' And I'd say 'it's more than that. It's effort paid back one thrill at a time.'"

"He wasn't wrong. That's pretty damn American," Bob said.

"Right at the end, I showed up at the hospital one day to find him watching the Sox beat the Jays in extra innings. And he beamed a smile at me and said, 'I finally get it. It's like summer to a young man: one thrill at a time.'"

A happy moment with his father? Even in his forties, Bob felt a mild pang of jealousy.

"It was good to see him happy in the one moment where we'd never been closer to understanding each other," the coach continued. "Because the rest of the time, it feels like he was the man who ruined my life."

Bob nodded. That part, he got. "You think I wound up in the trade because my old man was stable and loving? The man could frighten a grenade. But I guess there's folks who had it worse. My old man didn't let me into Little League… but he didn't indoctrinate me into the KGB, either."

The coach was silent for a moment. "Thank you for trying to be understanding."

"Understood," Bob said. "Just don't fuck this up, or I'm as likely as anyone to kill you. And that'd be a damn shame."

30

BOSTON, MASSACHUSETTS

The store looked all wrong, which was worrisome. It had taken Bob nearly two hours in traffic to get to Boston, then another twenty minutes navigating the congestion around Fenway Park.

He stood in the parking lot and looked up at the sign reading "Wizard's Den Comics and Games." Then he re-examined the address he'd jotted down on a slip of paper.

Right place, allegedly.

He opened the glass front door, a bell chiming. As advertised, the walls were lined with comic books in Mylar bags, splashes of color, covers like a thousand small posters of Marvel and DC heroes battling their nemeses.

The rest of the store was crammed with shelves loaded with games, as well as row on row of floor-standing racks full of even more carefully preserved titles. At the back of the shop, a long glass cabinet filled with model miniatures from *Wizardry*, *Warcraft* and Dungeons & Dragons also doubled as a main counter.

The twenty-something guy behind the register was

engrossed in a graphic novel, propped up on a stool and chewing on the end of his pinkie like a smoker missing his oral fix.

"I feel like I'm in the wrong place," Bob said as he approached.

The clerk put the graphic novel facedown on the counter. "What do you need?"

"I'm supposed to tell you I'm a close personal friend of the family," Bob said.

The kid sniffed. Then he reached under the counter. A second later, Bob heard the deadbolt turn and latch on the front door. "PA!" the kid yelled towards the back shop.

A few seconds later, the beaded curtain dividing the two areas was spread apart, and an older version of the clerk, complete with a gray beard and long gray hair in a ponytail, emerged holding a cup of coffee in one hand.

"One second," he said, strolling past Bob before he could interject. At the front door, he flipped the open sign over to display the "back in twenty minutes" sign.

He returned, stopped next to Bob and took a sip of coffee. Then he sniffed a little. "What can I do you for, friend?"

"I'm a friend of John Butcher," Bob said.

The old guy nodded towards the beaded curtain. "Okay, that'll do. Follow me, man."

He led Bob into the back room, then took a hard left towards a safe vault door set into that wall. "What would've happened," Bob said, "if I hadn't known both passwords."

The old guy shrugged. "You wouldn't know it to look at him, but Junior is a hell of a shot. And I guarantee you, when whatever he's reading goes down on the counter, that free hand goes under it to the sawed-off double-barrel Beretta shotgun. At the range you were standing? I'd say getting it wrong could be fatal."

He spun the dials on the safe's old-fashioned combination lock, then repeated the action with the rotary control. He leaned back to pull the door open, using his body weight to account for its substantial mass.

Bob looked inside.

The collection of weapons lined two sets of shelves on either side of the vault. It wasn't much compared to other places on John Butcher's national list. But it was the closest under-the-table supplier to Maine, so it was going to have to suffice.

The weapons had sticker prices on them, another first. He picked up a pump-action Remington TAC-14 20-gauge, the barrel reduced, the stock shortened to a pistol grip.

"You've got a good eye there, dude," the old guy said. "The barrel's only fourteen inches, so she's not street legal to anyone but the fuzz, but she's highly concealable. She's got an M-Lok for attaching a sight or light, weighs in at a spec over five-point-five pounds, five-shell capacity on a three-inch chamber. You'll obviously want to be close for maximum effect, but any way you slice it, she's a devastating piece of personal-protection engineering."

Bob looked at the sticker, then back at the old guy. "A thousand dollars? Are you kidding? For a grand, it'd better be more than devastating. It should drive me to the store and back."

The old guy shrugged, exposing his dog tags. "What can I say, brother? That's the going rate when it's under the table. You dig?"

Bob nodded at his necklace. "'Nam?"

"Yup, twenty-third infantry. You serve?"

"Iraq and Afghanistan, a few other places. So... I don't get the brothers-in-arms rate or nothing?"

The old guy stared down his nose warily. "Brother, you get the 'comic books aren't selling like they used to' discount, which is to say the same price anyone pays. I've got overhead, bills. And most people buying this stuff are somewhere on the road to self-enrichment, if you get my drift."

"So there's no 'I'm not a criminal, I'm just helping good people' discount?"

The dude smiled and crossed his arms. "Well, think of it this way: by paying twice what it normally costs without all that annoying paperwork, you're helping out this good person." He poked a thumb towards himself.

Bob looked at the sticker again. His bankroll was dwindling as it was, the roofing jobs just covering his bills. "Do you do buybacks?"

"With what this gear generally gets used for? No. No, holding on to material evidence of someone else's crimes is not, generally, a good practise even when the product is under the table."

"Of course not," Bob said. "But like I said—"

"Look, buddy. I know John well enough, and if you're okay with him, you're okay with me. But the price is the price."

Bob felt dejected. "Okay. Got any GPS trackers?"

"I do indeed," the gray-haired veteran said. "But they ain't cheap."

PORTLAND, Maine

Bob seethed about the price of the weaponry all the way back to Portland.

By the time he got there, it was past two in the afternoon. He stopped at a Vietnamese restaurant on the south side, ordered lemongrass chicken for lunch, and called Dawn while he waited.

"Bob!" She picked up on the second ring, which was rare.

"What, are you watching the burner or something? That was awful quick."

"I had a visitor." She filled him in on Eddie Stone's visit. "I'm really sorry. I tried to throw him off, but he threatened us."

"Not your fault," Bob said. "I was sloppy, talking to you on a busy street where you could get audible clues."

"Are they there?" She sounded worried.

"They are. He is, anyway. He's leveraging my help on something."

"Leveraging?"

He wanted to tell her about the deal offered, that it might all be over soon. But history suggested prudence, waiting until the CIA boss actually came through.

What you should do is tell her to never call you again, that it's too dangerous. What you should do is let her and Marcus live a peaceful life without you in it to ruin everything. He hated the idea of her being under threat. But she was the closest he'd had to family since his mother's death. And he hated the idea of losing what they had even more.

"Yeah. A temporary truce, I figure. We'll see."

"That sounds... optimistic?"

He couldn't help but wonder if the querying tone was due to how vague he was being or just her surprise at him finding an upside. "It's Eddie Stone. I wouldn't assume anything," he said instead.

"Do I need to move now? Would that even matter?"

"Nope. As long as you're a legit ratepaying citizen, he can find you damn near instantly. But that's also your protection. Unless they saw you as an imminent threat, the potential heat from going after a civilian would be way too high. He might try to intimidate you, but Eddie's been around long enough to know there's no such thing as a successful conspiracy. Eventually, if more than one person knows something, someone talks. They'll leave you alone unless you start talking publicly about me, about the Team. I take it this is being monitored?"

"It is."

"I'm going to send you an app, okay? It's a peer-to-peer chat system, with no recording or tracking. Chat is wiped within minutes of it occurring. You'll need to install it on a new burner, but once you do that, I can contact you with new details to reach me if you need to, okay?"

"They won't like that much, I expect."

"I won't give much of a shit—"

"Bob! Please! Language!"

"Sorry. You know I don't mean nothing by it."

"I do. But please try, at least with me."

"I will. And please don't ever worry about calling me."

"I didn't know what else to do," she said.

"It won't be a problem again, I promise," Bob said.

There was another reason it wouldn't happen again, he vowed. *If Eddie Stone touches a hair on either of their heads, he's a dead man.*

31

MOSHER CORNER, MAINE

Bob lay on the tarp and watched the church through Eddie's night-vision spyglass. It was a half hour before the meet, and there was still no sign of the Russians.

To his left, his former boss sat up, secure that they couldn't be seen through the heavy bushes. He took out a cigarette and lit it.

Bob heard the "thwik" of the lighter flint. He turned the other man's way. "Really?"

"We're not snipers, and nobody's looking for flashes of light," Stone said. "So just relax, will you? Jeez! You used to be the coolest customer I knew. Now, every goddamn thing has you on edge."

Bob lowered the spyglass completely and just stared at him, peeved. "Really? That's a *surprise* to you? After you sent hit squads and freelance mercs after me for *two years*, trying to blow my head off? You're surprised I'm a bit tense? Asshole." He went back to the glass.

Eddie blew out a cloud of smoke. "When did everything get so goddamned personal with you, anyway?"

Bob shot him another contemptuous stare. "I warned you, Eddie. I fucking warned you before Tehran that everything was going to shit. That the targets were increasingly political, that we knew we had a leak months before we went over. And when it went to shit, you hung me out to dry. You hung us all out."

The older man seemed nonplussed, blowing a series of perfect, tight smoke rings, each dissipating a moment later in the light wind. "Somebody had to pay, Bobby. American bodies being paraded on CNN. It wasn't going to be Kennedy going down. And it was ultimately his call; I made your pitch to him." He turned Bob's way and leaned down, pointedly. "I didn't hang you out to dry; I just followed orders."

"I'm glad that level of restraint remains so important to you," Bob muttered sarcastically. "It's not to me. And if you ever go near Dawn and Marcus again, the next time we see each other will be the last. I could've killed you in New York, but I didn't. I regret that too much, sometimes."

"Too much?"

"Believe it or not, Eddie, despite your self-delusion to the contrary, we're *not* the same. I *do* feel bad when I kill someone. 'It's just business' is never enough of an answer. Most of this world's problems, the way I see it, are based in the need of shallow men to seek out power. You keep talking about 'people like us,' but I'm not like that. You are."

Eddie butted out the cigarette. "The fact that you felt better or worse about some deaths than others is your problem, not mine. Hang on... cars approaching."

He ducked low again, so that both men were lying prone. "Pass me the glass," Eddie said.

Bob did so. Eddie kept it on both SUVs until they'd parked outside the building. "Now, we get to find out how accurate your new friend was. I count... well, so far, so bad."

"What's wrong?"

"He said three guys plus himself. I count five." Eddie passed him the glass.

Bob focused in. As Coach Chris got out of the lead Range Rover, he glanced casually in their general direction and slightly shrugged his shoulders. "I could be wrong," Bob said. "But I think he just gave me the 'what can I do about it?' shrug."

Two men got out of the second car, three from the first. He recognized Nikolai and Sascha.

Bob passed him back the glass. "The two big fellas with Ratachkov... we've already tangled. You know the other two?"

Eddie looked long and hard, then shook his head gently. "Nah. I'm guessing from general appearances that they're mercs. Heavy footwear, enough bulk under the jackets to be wearing vests. One of them's going around to the back of the Mercedes. Hold on... Yeah, he's got the hatch open. He's handing rifles to the others. Looks like MP5s and a couple of longer assault rifles, maybe..."

"KP-9s. They have a thing for Kalashnikovs for some reason," Bob said dryly.

"American-made Kalashnikovs, though." He checked his watch. "T-minus ten minutes. Get your head wherever it has to be."

Eddie crouched on his haunches and opened the soft-sided kit bag to his left. He took out a seven-inch OLED tablet and booted it up. A few moments later, he was staring at a split screen provided by the four cameras, two in the front of the church, two in the vestry and rear office area.

"Your boy looks on the money. The giant is going into the priest's side of the old confessional. We've got one more behind the pulpit, and your friend Nikolai crouching between the front two rows of pews. There's another guy in the balcony. That leaves the fifth man, who I'm guessing has gone into the back, to cover the rear exit." Stone looked up from the screen, beaming. "See? I told you."

"Just wait until I've given confession, okay?" Bob said.

"Bless me, father, for I have sinned," Eddie intoned sarcastically. "I'm a miserable middle-aged fucker who's lucky to still be alive."

"Yeah... no thanks to you," Bob said as he got up. "Time for me to load up."

NIKOLAI SAT in the second row of pews and watched Coach Chris give instructions to the two mercs Yaremchuk had procured in Boston. They were both former soldiers, both with heavy criminal records for armed robbery. They'd shown a willingness in the past to do the necessary, and they didn't care who paid them.

They did not worry him.

The sleeper did. *He is shaky.*

He hides it. But he is frightened.

He gestured for Chris to join him.

"We good?" Chris asked.

"You will have eyes on the doors, yes? If he brings backup of any sort, we need to know. If he comes with a team, you wait for me to bolt through the back before you blow the charges, yes?"

"Of course, yeah."

Nikolai looked around. The other men looked relaxed, even Sascha. *They feel strong because he is one man. But that assumes he comes alone.* "My gut tells me something is not right." He glared at the baseball coach. "Do I have anything to worry about, little man?"

Chris shook his head.

"Good. Because know this: I have strong connections in our trade, with our people. If anything happens to me tonight, they will find you. Got it?"

Another nod.

"Then go, get ready. Let us know when he's arrived."

Chris headed towards the double front doors.

Nikolai supposed he'd enjoy killing the sleeper. He was an annoyance, a second-guesser, clearly no longer Russian at heart. He would die badly, Nikolai supposed, begging for his life. It held a certain appeal.

But that was for later.

Bob had parked the car fifty yards back down Olde Canal Way, at the only other business on the street, a lawn care operation. He drove it to the church and parked at the top of the driveway.

The building's lights barely illuminated the parking area. He got out and opened the Lincoln's trunk, removing the long "duster"-style overcoat and his kit bag. He opened the bag and took out the Glock 19, then took off his jacket and put it in the trunk.

He picked up the body armor lying in the trunk and stared at it for a moment. Bringing it along had been on Eddie's orders; he'd always preferred freedom of movement without the extra bulk. But if one of them went down, Eddie had stressed, the other had to survive to follow the Russians back to their boss.

Bob put on the vest, then the duster. He pocketed the pistol and four extra magazines.

He retrieved the Remington and opened the left side of the long coat. A pair of metal clips had been stitched into the fabric. They held the shotgun suspended, the pistol grip resting at the base of the left-hand pocket, which in turn had been sliced open so that he could reach the weapon directly.

He did up one button on the jacket and closed the trunk. Twenty yards nearer the church, he could see Coach Chris sitting in a Mercedes SUV, face lit slightly by the glow from a small video screen.

The sleeper agent noticed movement and looked up briefly, making a split second of eye contact before his attention returned to the screen.

Good so far. No head shake means no exterior ambush.

It had occurred to Bob that, were their roles reversed and he in the Russians' shoes, he'd have set up the ambush outside the front doors. Twin snipers with tripods, hidden in the woods on either side of the parking lot, could have cut his opponent down before he stepped inside.

But the Russians had limitations in both people and planning. It was clear Nikolai, the one who'd chased them, saw himself in charge. There was no way Coach Chris had planned the attempted hit at the restaurant. It was too musclebound, too direct.

Clearly from his behavior at the warehouse, Nikolai had a short fuse. That could be useful, Bob figured.

He mounted the three wide steps and took a deep breath,

awaiting the shot he wouldn't even hear coming with the same perfunctory acceptance as a dozen times before.

His hand rested on the door. He glanced back at the Lincoln in time to see Eddie Stone scurry into cover behind it. They'd timed the walk from the doors to the confessional booth at fourteen seconds.

Now you just have to trust Eddie.

Faaantastic.

He pushed the double doors open. Past a pair of decorative stone columns, the nave was brightly lit from chandeliers high above. Their glow reflected softly off the polished stone floor aisle running between the pews.

Sell it, Bobby. You're not supposed to know anyone's here. He looked around, turning as he walked as if cautiously eyeing every corner.

He approached the confessional, which he figured was mistake number two. *Get me in there, then riddle the thing with bullets.*

Instead, Nikolai had decided to be clever.

The confirmation code was supposed to be a request to be blessed, followed by an admonishment from the "priest" that "only God's children pass to the kingdom beyond."

Bob pulled back the beaded curtain and stepped inside. He did not sit down.

"Bless me, father, for I have sinned," Bob said, undoing the coat. "It has been too long since my last confession."

On the other side of the screen partition, a bulky shadow shifted in place. "Only God's..." the figure managed to say before Bob levelled the shotgun and opened fire, the big barrel and .20-gauge shells going off with a bass-heavy boom, a half-foot hole blown through the wall, the other man knocked off his feet.

Bob worked the pump and then dropped low, rolling out of the confessional and coming up in a crouch. He saw Nikolai rise from the pews on the other side of the room, another figure popping up from behind the pulpit.

To his right, Sascha had collapsed out of the other confessional box, one hand affixed to a gaping neck wound. He was bleeding badly, his free hand searching for the pistol he'd dropped. Bob shot him from close range, aiming high at the prone figure, the shell shearing off part of the man's skull.

The two other men opened fire, and Bob rolled behind the end of the oak pews. They were thick, but not enough to stop bullets. The MP5's 9mm slugs chewed up the wooden benches, automatic weapons fire echoing around the room.

Bob tossed the shotgun aside, the other men across the room, out of its ideal range. He drew the Colt 1911 and chanced a glance, a man stepping out from behind the curtain to the vestry. As he strode into the room, Kalashnikov leveled, Eddie Stone pushed open the front doors and opened fire, gunning the third man down before taking cover behind one of the stone columns.

Nikolai pivoted his way and sprayed the column with bullets, flattened ammo rattling off the floor like dice.

Bob tried to line him up, but the big Russian ducked low into cover again. The man behind the pulpit popped out of cover for a split second. Bob wheeled that way, turning and firing in one smooth motion, the second bullet hitting the man between the eyes. He stumbled backwards, bracing himself against the rear wall, before sliding to a sitting position, immobile, a smear of blood tracking his path.

From the corner of his eye, he scoped movement, Nikolai getting a bead on him. Bob tried to turn and throw himself clear, the Russian's MP5 spitting fire. He felt a sickening punch to his chest, then another to his shoulder, his momentum arrested as he crashed to the stone floor.

He felt his wind knocked out, but the vest had done its job.

He wheezed, struggling to find air.

He rolled onto his back.

The merc from the balcony had crept down to the nave. The man's shadow fell over Bob.

Bob peered through one eye, squinting against the bruising pain. The man was pointing the MP5 at his face from less than three feet away.

And that, as they say, is that, Bob figured. *Adios, it's been—*

Eddie popped out of cover, his pistol braced as he emptied three shots into the merc from thirty feet away, the third striking his target in the back of the head.

The merc staggered forward, confused, the shots not registering. He turned to figure out what had happened, then collapsed, his brain no longer properly signalling his legs.

Bob rolled over and looked back. *Stone. But he's exposed to—*

Nikolai's machine gun fired off a quick burst, and Eddie dropped next to the column.

Shit.

FROM THE SAFETY of the Mercedes SUV, the man once known as Roman Ratachkov watched the gun battle erupt in his undersized monitor.

This is insane. All of it feels absolutely mental.

A week ago, I was wondering if I was going to get a chance to coach Single-A ball. Now I'm in a parking lot, in the country, waiting for two groups of lunatics to kill each other.

So much of his childhood had really been to prepare him for such moments. The hours spent at the gun range, the martial arts training, the language skills and articles about military and political tactics. It had been decades since he was at peak fitness, but he'd once been able to do fifty one-armed push-ups, his back as straight as a board.

But it had seemed an illusion, the notion of ever actually being a spy. He'd gone to the same high school at which he now coached; he'd married a Vermont girl, a minor sin for competitive reasons only. He'd raised Max to be as patriotic as he was, to love his country.

But not to sell it out.

He stared at the remote detonator on the passenger seat. He picked it up. It was heavier than it looked, a metal box the size of a cigarette pack. It featured an on-off switch to arm it, and one red button.

He thought about what would happen if he just pressed it immediately.

Maybe Bob was telling the truth; maybe he had stumbled into it all. Maybe his friend had reasons for not bringing more support. But if those things were true and he blew up the church, Chris thought, there might not be anyone left who could identify him.

But then he thought of Igor Yaremchuk and Uncle, of the other two men sent from DC, sent to guard the handler. They would not let him go. They would simply find other gunmen to accomplish the same task.

It had gone exactly as Bob predicted, but the numbers were not working in their favor. They'd taken out three mercs and Sascha, but Bob's friend was seemingly out of the fight and out of camera shot, Bob pinned down by Nikolai.

If he loses, they'll kill me anyway.

They'll clean up the town and anyone left in it, just as they did with Thomas and Rose Peters.

And then maybe they'll kill my family.

Even jail was better than that.

He unbuckled his belt. He reached over to the glove box and opened it, taking out the Sig Sauer P226 and speed holster. He got out of the SUV, clipping the holster to his belt and drawing the nine-millimeter.

Coach Chris headed towards the church doors.

32

Bob tried to crawl away, his wind slowly coming back. He shuffled between the pews on his stomach. *Just need enough time to recover.*

He crawled towards the shotgun.

A foot came down on his left hand, breaking small bones.

Nikolai kicked the shotgun away. "Turn over," he commanded.

Bob did as requested.

Nikolai did not even bother to raise the MP5. From that close, Bob knew, aim wasn't going to matter.

The front doors to the church flew open.

Both men's attentions were drawn that way, to the sight of Coach Chris entering, pistol drawn. He fired off two shots, neither hitting home. Nikolai turned and let off a single burst, a bullet catching the sleeper in his left arm.

"Aiiehhh!" Chris yelped. He dropped his gun and fell to his backside, instinct kicking in, prompting him to shuffle behind the column.

Bob used the distraction, rolling over again and swinging his leg out, his foot slamming into Nikolai's ankle, the bulkier man going down hard.

The MP5 slid under the row of pews.

The Russian followed the momentum of his fall, tucking himself into a ball and rolling into a crouch. He pulled an eight-inch blade from the sheath at his waist.

It took all Bob's strength to push himself up from the ground. He felt a stabbing pain near his left armpit. *Ribs again, damn it.*

Nikolai was on him in an instant, charging forward, taking big swipes with the knife. Bob ducked backwards, an electric jolt of pain from fractured ribs coursing through him. He felt his head swim but managed to step to one side, the Russian's stabbing motion finding only air.

Bob was running on instinct, leaning in as the knife flashed by, trying to lock the man's arm up, smash a forearm against his knee to drive the blade from Nikolai's grasp.

The Russian half-turned and headbutted him, Bob looking away at the last second, Nikolai's forehead slamming into the back of Bob's skull. Both men staggered away.

Bob shook his head forcefully, tried to focus, turning back towards his opponent.

He saw the glint of light on stainless steel at the last second, years of training prompting him to go limp, the knife flashing by him from Nikolai's locked-wrist toss. He fell back, letting his palms arrest his fall, pushing off and turning in one motion to come back onto his feet.

The pain was nearly unbearable, like someone had driven javelins through his broken hand and rib cage. Both men were panting, squaring off like boxers, shuffling in a circle, each looking for an opening.

A split second of worry flashed through Bob's mind, the memory of a blade striking Rachel. He glanced behind him to see the knife buried in the side of the confessionals. He looked back at Nikolai, noticing the blood pooling near the Russian's armpit, the gunshot wound from two days earlier having opened up.

"That's... That's got to hurt," Bob managed.

"You do not look so good yourself. Maybe you just give up, go quick and painless, yes?"

He swung the blade again, but Bob was quicker, high-stepping forward to kick it from the other man's hand. He came down in a partial crouch and spun on the spot, leaping up, his other leg coming around in a spinning high kick.

But his foot found only air, the move slowed by his injuries, the Russian recovering quickly, dropping low and driving a hard punch into Bob's already bruised groin.

He went over sideways, the pain overwhelming, his senses tricking his immune system into emptying his stomach, bile rising up from his stomach, a mouthful spewed onto the stone floor.

Nikolai lumbered over to Bob's shotgun and retrieved it from under the pew. He pumped the breach with one hand and chambered a shell.

He raised the gun and pointed it at Bob's prone figure. "Now, finally, you die. No last-second saves, no bullshit. No witnesses. And I will make a lot of money from this, courtesy of Ivan Malyuchenko. I am supposed to tell you that, to know he is why you are dying today."

The oligarch. Father of the late Victor, ex of Memphis, Bob thought. *There's the past doing its catch-up thing again. Nothing comes without a bill attached.*

"Just do it already and quit yapping," Bob demanded.

Nikolai ignored the request. "The truth is I would do this for free. Goodbye, you despicable American pig." Nikolai levelled the shotgun. "I hope you burn in—"

The bullet slammed into the Russian's leg, the gunshot sounding from near the doors. He went over sideways and slammed into the ground; the shotgun spilled. Bob watched through the haze of pain as Nikolai tried to right himself, grabbing at the thigh wound.

The Russian shot a look towards the right-hand concrete column. Coach Chris was leaning against it, seated, legs outstretched, the bullet hole in his left arm seeping, the pistol in his right hand still smoking. The arm was wavering, his strength diminished by blood loss.

"Chertov predatel!" Nikolai spat. *Fucking traitor!*

The coach dropped the gun, letting his arm slump to his side. Bob could see Nikolai trying to figure out what to do next. He looked over at the shotgun. Then he looked towards the double doors.

Bob managed to push himself to a crouch, pushing down the pain, trying to ignore it.

Nikolai began to limp towards the doors, dragging his wounded leg behind him.

Is he... fleeing?

The idea had been to let Sascha live because he seemed the dimmest of them. That option had been taken away. Bob knew it wouldn't matter as long as the coach had tagged both vehicles with the GPS trackers.

With no other local support, Nikolai will run to Uncle.

"The bomb!" Coach Chris managed. "He's going for the switch!"

Nikolai pushed open the doors and went outside.

Bob did the mental math. Nikolai hadn't put the sleeper in charge, that had been Yaremchuk, Coach Chris had said.

He wants me dead, most of all. He accomplishes everything if he just—

Oh shit.

Bob got to his feet and staggered towards the door, the pain driving up his adrenaline, his shuffle becoming a fast walk.

He stopped at the coach and crouched, putting the other man's arm around his neck. "Hold on tight!" he barked as he stood, raising them both up. Tears pooled in his eyes from the agony of supporting the other man's weight against broken ribs.

The two staggered towards the doors. "EDDIE, GET OUT!" Bob screamed.

Eddie looked dazed, leaning against the second pillar, a gaping bullet wound high on his chest, near his right arm. He pushed himself to his feet.

Bob put his shoulder down, shoving the doors open and spilling out onto the church's front steps. Nikolai was already at the Mercedes, leaning in through the open window. Bob pushed ahead, the two men staggering down the steps. He could hear Eddie's panting not far behind them.

He threw the two of them forward as well as he could, Nikolai's finger surely reaching the button.

But nothing happened.

Bob looked up, puzzled. He saw Nikolai climb into the vehicle, its lights suddenly glaring through the dark.

He helped the coach up again, Eddie already past them, raising his pistol with his weaker hand and firing haphazardly at the Mercedes as it backed up slightly, then pulled towards the road.

"There's a safety switch," Coach Chris said.

The gunfire from three feet away had temporarily killed his right-ear hearing again. "WHAT?!" Bob asked.

"THERE'S A—"

If they'd had any hearing left, the deafening explosion reduced it to a hum, the dull boom followed by a sonic wave of heat and expelled air pressure that blew them both face-down to the ground again. Wood siding and shattered glass were flung across the parking lot, moving at hundreds of meters per second as St. Sergius Roman Catholic Church disintegrated in a tornado of flame.

Bob covered the top and back of his head with his hands, waiting as debris rained down around them. Each ear offered just a high-pitched, continual whine, as if a dead patient's heart monitor had gone up an octave.

He felt a hand on his shoulder. He turned to find Chris trying to get his attention, also deaf. "I KNOW!" he yelled. He pointed at the other man. "You have...?" He made a phone-to-ear motion.

Chris nodded.

Bob tapped himself on the chest, then waved after the fleeing Mercedes. "GOT IT?"

Chris nodded.

Bob ignored his discomfort and pushed on towards the Lincoln, the smell of burning timber stinging his nose, the stagger once more quickly becoming a walk, then a jog.

33

Nikolai felt the car's tires bite into the tackier asphalt of Route 237.

The pain in his leg was numbed by the painkillers he was already on for the chest wound a day earlier. But he knew he needed to get to safe harbor.

He needed to get to Uncle.

There was a chance he'd taken out Singleton with the blast. But at least one of the men had run for a moment longer than the others, framed in the car's rearview mirror.

He'd weighed stopping, going back to make sure. But there were three of them now, the odds against him if they'd avoided the brunt of the blast.

He felt the buzz of his phone in his jacket pocket. Nikolai took out his phone.

"Yeah?"

"What happened?" Yaremchuk had been expecting a call several minutes ago.

"It was a trap. He flipped the sleeper and had support."

"How many?"

"Everyone except me."

"Bozhe moy…" Yaremchuk muttered. "You are okay?"

"I have a gunshot wound to my left thigh. I need to come in, Igor, get help from Uncle."

"Out of the question."

Nikolai slammed his palm against the steering wheel in frustration. "Igor, I am a good soldier! I never do you no wrong, never. So why cannot I just go to the island, get—"

"I said no, and I meant it! Uncle is too important. You cannot draw attention."

Nikolai swerved to avoid the slow driver ahead of him, the boxy SUV sliding a little as it pulled back into the right lane.

"I can still be important! I can still help—"

"Shush! Of course you can, Nikolai Ivanovich. You cannot go to Uncle because you might be followed. But you can still help keep him safe. You can eliminate another target for us."

Bob got into the Lincoln and pulled out his phone, opening the tracking app.

The Mercedes was already a mile ahead, maybe more.

But I'm pretty damn sure I know where he's going.

He slipped the car into drive and stood on the gas, the back end sliding out on the gravel as it reached the road, even the slight bump of hitting a solid surface causing agonizing pain.

Then he hit the brakes, stopping for just long enough to take the pill container from his pocket.

He popped the cap and swallowed another Percocet. He

knew it would sap his energy, make him drowsy when he needed to be alert. But the pain was intolerable without it.

A moment later, the car was on Route 237, heading back towards Portland, its four-point-six-liter engine growling as Bob punched the gas.

Now, we see if he runs right back to Uncle.

The Russians were leaving in a day. Assuming he'd even realized they were out of the church, Nikolai wouldn't have liked the remaining odds, three on one with him wounded, Bob figured. So he was heading towards numerical superiority. Though he'd be exposing his boss, he seemed the kind of man who would value his own safety over a common goal.

Bob breathed in short, even gasps, trying to prevent his ribs from moving as much as possible. He glanced down at the satnav tracking screen. The Mercedes was inside the city, heading up Brighton Avenue. He did a quick mental calculation. *He can be at the dock in under ten minutes.*

He checked the clock on the dash, pulling the car around a slower vehicle, ignoring the solid center line.

It was just after nine o'clock, the ferry to Peaks Island still running for nearly three more hours.

He glanced at the satnav again, just in time to see the tiny car icon take the traffic circle right onto Deering Avenue. But instead of continuing towards the water, it turned right at Park Avenue.

Bob frowned; the route didn't make sense. *Why would he head towards West End if he wanted to reach the docks more quickly?*

The car hit a pothole, and his hand twitched on the wheel, almost swerving into the other lane, the stabbing pain utterly distracting.

Just hold it together. Focus.

What had he said at the church? His orders were to leave no witnesses. *So perhaps he thinks we were still in the church, or near enough.* It could be an edge, Bob knew, a false confidence that no one—

Then he held the thought, realizing where the Mercedes was going.

He's headed for the hospital.

He's not trying to reach the ferry.

He's going after Rachel.

Bob's foot slammed down on the gas, adrenaline kicking in again, helping him guide the big vehicle around traffic. Nikolai was at least two minutes ahead, maybe three.

He wouldn't just barge into the hospital, guns blazing, Bob knew. He still had to keep a low profile until Uncle was out of town. He'd have to bind his wound, then find a secondary way into the ward where she was resting.

And that's his three minutes eaten up, right there.

It took just a few minutes to reach Congress Street, Maine Medical Center's five stories towering over its neighbors. He abandoned the Lincoln in front of the multistory parking lot.

The Percocet was beginning to kick in, the worst pain in his ribs and from his chest bruises beginning to subside. He ran as best he could, sprinting inside and across the car park's lower level to the stairs.

Move it, move it, fucking move it, Bobby! If he gets too far ahead, she'll be dead before you even have a chance to stop him.

At the second floor, he ran across the tunnel to the hospital's main building, shoving other visitors aside, barreling through the double doors.

The sudden silence of the hospital's interior, its whitewashed walls and tube lights, grounded him. Bob slowed down. An orderly stared at him and began to speed up his pace, keeping his eyes on Bob even as he scurried in the opposite direction, towards the elevators.

I must look dandy, sweating like a horse, two obvious bullet holes in my shirt, a vest clear underneath.

He nodded at the man and smiled but kept walking.

He reoriented himself. Rachel's room was in the East Tower. Bob headed south, crossing another concourse, two more large buildings between there and his position, two hundred feet of corridors. He'd hoped for some obvious sign Nikolai was ahead of him: a trail of blood from his wound, staff or security cast aside. But there had been nothing.

The elevator to the East Tower's second floor was just ahead. Bob rounded a corner and saw the doors closing, Nikolai's gaze full of alarm at the sight of his pursuer.

The stairs.

He can't take the stairs because of his leg.

The Russian had obviously stopped to bind or tourniquet the wound. It had cost him precious minutes. Bob burst through the emergency door to the stairwell. He clambered up the stairs two at a time, using his left hand on the rail for balance, each heavy breath providing a jab of pain.

At the corridor to her room, Bob spotted him. He had his pistol in hand, the remains of a white shirt tied around his thigh. He was limping as fast as he could. Bob drew the Colt 1911 just as the Russian looked back over his shoulder and spotted him.

A nurse stepped out of the room to Nikolai's left. He saw his opportunity, grabbing her and wrapping a burly forearm around her neck, the gun pointed to her temple. "You follow, she dies!" he spat.

The nurse looked terrified. "Please!" she blurted. Nikolai

began walking backwards, dragging her along with him, his limp slowing them.

Bob followed cautiously. They rounded a corner, taking them down Rachel's wing. Bob saw the blur of dark blue ahead of her room, the police officer rising quickly, his hand going to his service weapon.

"DON'T!" Nikolai barked. "You draw that gun, she is a dead woman."

Bob kept moving forward, slowing his pace to an idle walk. "You're done," he said. "No way you get out of here. No way the cops allow it. No way I allow it."

"GUNS DOWN!" Nikolai barked again. He stopped ahead of Rachel's room, turning so that his back was to the wall, the woman in front of him, close enough to dissuade action but leaving him a view of both his opponents.

"Sir, lower your weapon; you are under arrest!" the cop ordered.

"GUNS DOWN, OR SHE DIES!" Nikolai screamed, the nurse's eyes wide with fear.

The police officer began to lower his gun.

Bob did not.

"Sir," the police officer said, "I'd advise—"

"Nah. I got this," Bob said.

He aimed at Nikolai carefully, gun at eye height, the adjustable rear sight groove perfectly framing the front sight. His grip was firm but not too tight, his forearm muscles relaxed but holding the weapon perfectly level.

Nikolai began to turn his way, the pistol barrel leaving her temple for the barest of moments. He turned his head quickly to look back towards the cop. "I SAID—"

Bob squeezed the trigger without hesitation, the bullet striking Nikolai at the base of the skull, where the basal ganglia tie the brain to the spine; motor functions instantly paralyzed.

He collapsed to the ground, blood spewing from the wound, a puddle forming around his head, the terrified nurse left standing in place.

She began to scream.

IT TOOK Mike Schultz fifteen minutes to get there. When he arrived, Bob was seated outside the room, the young police officer beside him, another officer further down the hall ensuring the scene wasn't disturbed.

"Thanks for waiting, Ted," Mike said.

"I'm supposed to remind you, you still owe a statement from the other day," the young man said, holding his peaked cap hat to his chest. He nodded towards Bob. "Shall I give you his version before homicide gets here, or...?"

He let the thought trail. Bob knew why; the officer wanted to know if Schultz would request Bob repeat his version, to see if it stayed consistent.

"Let me hear it from him," Mike said. Bob watched him study the scene. They'd cordoned off the portion of the hall where Nikolai had gone down, using yellow tape. His body still lay in the pool of blood.

Next to the single shell casing ejected by Bob's pistol, an orange evidence flag stood on a strand of wire and a small plastic base. Blood spatter ran across the wall where the Russian had been standing.

"Mr. Bennett, I take it this is the same man who stabbed her?"

"It is," Bob said. "I came by to visit and spotted him getting into the elevator."

Mike made a performance of it. He glanced at his watch. "Visitation has been over for hours."

"I did mention to you the other day that I'd been working late. I thought they wouldn't mind."

"Fortuitous," Mike said.

The officer crossed his arms and looked unhappy.

"You have something to add, Officer Davies?"

"The vic had a hostage at gunpoint. I'm glad he made the shot and all, because it was a hell of a shot and probably saved that nurse's life. But he endangered her by taking it, and that's the version I'm telling homicide."

Mike looked back at Bob. "Is that true?"

"I was a sniper in the military," Bob said. "I knew I had the shot, and he looked ready to snap. I figure he came back to kill Rachel because she could identify him in court."

Mike looked past him to his colleague. "Any ID?"

"I already called it in. It's fake," the young officer said. "Belongs to some guy in Stowe, Vermont, but has this dude's picture on it."

Mike turned back to Bob. "You're going to have to talk to the boys from homicide about this tonight. Are you otherwise okay?"

"Not the best day for this to happen," Bob said. "I fell off a roof earlier and cracked a rib. It's brutal. Other than that, I'm good."

Mike nodded to the younger cop. "Why aren't they here yet?"

"Not sure. There was something big out in the country about an hour ago. We had guys out helping the county mounties with a building fire and homicide. Something like that; I heard the call."

"Well then, Mr. Bennett, it appears that, risk

notwithstanding, your friend is very lucky that you and Officer Davies were both here at the right moment in time. But you're in for a very long evening."

Bob looked over at the officer, then back at Mike. "Can we talk with some privacy?" He looked back at Davies. "We go back a ways."

"Ted... can you give us a minute?"

The young man deferred to rank. "I'll be chatting with Officer Newman if you need me."

He headed down the hall to the other guard's position.

"Bobby, this is a mess," Mike said. "Homicide's going to spend as long as they can wringing every detail out of you. I know you said you've got stuff in your past. How much of an issue is this going to be for you?"

"My past and my current identity aren't really linked," Bob said.

"Your 'current' identity?"

"I told you I used to work for the government. It wasn't pretty. It required a new life, a new background."

"So they're not going to find anything incriminating."

"Nah. They'll get the same story Davies got, and if they're like most police officers I've known – and no offense at the presumption – I figure they'll just be happy I was carrying."

"And the piece?"

"Registered to Rachel, I think," Bob said.

"Tidy. Where do we stand on the rest of... you know, my stuff."

Bob had to be honest. "It's not good. This guy, he's a Russian hitter named Nikolai, regardless of what his ID said. Your missing body was Rachel's grandfather, and he was also a spy, a deep-cover operative here for decades."

"Jeezum crow," Mike muttered.

"I have pressure on me from my former employers. They want to bring down the spy ring her gramps belonged to, and I have less than a day to do it. How long do you figure they're going to hold me?"

"It'll be hours. But... they have an eyewitness that you weren't the aggressor, that this guy took a hostage, that he's the same guy who stabbed Ms. McGee in the first place." He looked at his wristwatch. "It's... nine forty. They'll spend at least an hour or two here on the scene. If past examples are anything to go by, you're not getting out of police HQ until solidly six o'clock tomorrow morning."

Bob tipped his head back and prayed to the ceiling tile for some relief. "Cutting things real fine on this one." He still had to find Uncle, although Bob was pretty sure he knew where to look.

Mike nodded towards Rachel's room. "Does she know?"

Bob shook his head. "She's still on partial sedation for the pain. Didn't even wake up to the gunshot."

At the end of the hall, two men in dark suits were making their way past the checkpoint, along with another man in civilian clothes.

"That'll be the detectives and the photographer," Mike said. "I take it from your demeanor that when you get out, you're going right back after these assholes, then?"

"That would be a solid bet."

"You need a hand?"

"You're in enough trouble already," Bob said.

"And you aren't!?"

"Yeah. But what else is new?"

34

Mike hadn't understated the zeal of the two homicide detectives. They interviewed Bob separately first, then together, for nearly four hours.

Bob had been trained in holding a story together under duress, but he was also drugged and exhausted. Rachel's partial sedation had helped his cause; they still hadn't interviewed her at length and only had his version to go by.

He'd walked out of the station just before five in the morning, after surrendering Rachel's pistol and promising to stay available. If they thought his story of them being "mugged" and then the mugger coming back to kill a witness had sounded far-fetched, they hadn't let on. The younger detective had let on at one point that Nikolai had stolen a motorcycle as well, injuring its rider.

Bob checked his phone. There were fifteen calls with no messages left.

A black Chrysler 300 pulled up at the curb.

That'd be Eddie, then.

. . .

THE BACK WINDOW slid down with a whir. "About fucking time," Eddie Stone said. "Get in."

The door swung open.

Bob got in and slammed the door. Eddie had a sling on his right arm. He was wearing sweatpants, the outline of a large, thick bandage on his right thigh obvious through the material.

"Well?" he said. The car pulled away from the curb, the street empty so early in the morning, the limo's ride velvet smooth.

"He didn't go back to Uncle. He went after Rachel McGee. I shot him at the hospital." Bob frowned. "Wait a second: how did you know where I was? I thought DC was out of the loop on this."

"They are."

Bob scowled at him. He took the burner out of his pocket. "You're tracking me, right?"

Eddie shrugged. "We have plenty of history. It seemed wise. And we have less than a day to resolve this. I want you on a short leash. Chances are good whoever's accompanying Uncle is a face we haven't seen before. That's the real reason Igor Yaremchuk sent two more agents down here: whether Nikolai was successful or not, he couldn't lead us back to someone he's never met."

"And that means," Bob said, "they can just go to the airport, fly out of here as unknowns. Can't stop every flight, check every face. Even if you had the manpower or the airport security cams did stellar work, by the time you had the results back, you'd both have alerted Kennedy of what you're up to, and they'd be gone anyway."

"One thing in particular has me stumped," Eddie said. He winced. "Damn it. Nothing worse than getting shot."

"I mean… there is," Bob said.

"So I'm supposed to be grateful? Jesus H, Bobby, you're an asshole sometimes." He sighed, resigned to it. "Anyway, it's been bugging me since Jefferson/Ratachkov told us they were moving out at midnight: why? Why that time of day rather than during the day itself? The number of available flights will be minimal compared to business hours."

"Unless you were right the first time. Maybe they're hitting the open road," Bob said.

"Either way, we've got roughly seventeen hours," Eddie said. "Then we work this backwards. If we can't get someone to lead us to Uncle, we figure out who our most likely suspect is. Theories. Give 'em."

"My first thought was that Uncle has to be someone everyone involved dealt with. But initially the only name that came to mind was Yaremchuk himself. But he's been in DC the entire time, right?"

"As far as we can tell, yeah."

"That led me to Gramps, Thomas Peters," Bob said. "I figured maybe what we had was two factions, one trying to get him out, the other trying to take him out. He tries to run and go to ground but, instead, gets himself killed in a car accident, and one side picks up the body. So what they're trying to get out isn't Uncle himself but maybe his collected intelligence, his data. Something physical."

Eddie shook his head. "Don't buy it. Too much effort's being taken to eliminate you and Rachel. If he's already dead, what's the percentage in shutting down prying eyes? All they had to do was go to ground until the deadline was up. But they were worried, which means they thought you were after something – or someone – specific."

"I didn't buy it either," Bob said. "Like I said, it was an idea. And that leaves us with…"

"Liz McGee." Eddie looked self-satisfied. "Maybe Gramps WAS Uncle at one point, but he passed the mantle on to his daughter."

"It would explain a lot," Bob said. "Like someone saving us – or, more accurately, saving Rachel – at the warehouse."

"She plays you off against the Russians, but then her daughter goes AWOL and wades into her mess. But she knows the Foreign Intelligence Service doesn't give a damn about her personal problems."

"They'd already killed her husband, years earlier, for threatening their ring. So Liz figures they'll have no issue with killing Rachel, as well. So she shows up at the warehouse and protects her, then disappears again, not realizing Nikolai has made it out." Bob turned and studied the older man for a moment. "You realize you can't leave DC out of this any longer, right? Let's say I go over to Peaks Island, I confront her. If she doesn't go quietly or I'm overpowered, she's going to flee to the mainland. Someone has to be at the ferry terminal to take them down."

Eddie made a scoffing sound. "Sure, when it's my political ass on the line, suddenly Bob Singleton acknowledges that sometimes he needs help."

"But…?"

Eddie looked exasperated, which Bob figured was probably the nearest he came to empathy. "But you're not wrong. We have a shot at Uncle; we can't fuck it up."

"You could always go through the Boston Field Office. By

the time word gets back to DC, Kennedy probably won't be able to intervene."

"Twice the reason for him to hang my ass after though, right, Bob?"

"Or maybe Uncle gives us what you want, says Kennedy took part in the Tehran debacle, and you wind up in his job."

"Jesus tapdancing Christ, you're an optimist all of a sudden? Problematically, even if Boston agrees, by the time they've made it official, it'll be this afternoon, maybe early evening. I can't chance her splitting early."

"I'll head over to the island as soon as the ferries start launching, in about thirty minutes," Bob suggested.

Eddie fixed him with a cold stare. "No, you mental patient! What you'll do, after we drop you at your apartment, is get cleaned up. You look like eight bags of shit in a hot car."

"Charming."

"Uh-huh. Don't scare the locals, Bob. It's not conducive to a quiet approach."

"Oh... okay. So you're going to call them and explain that the church fire they spent all night battling was a CIA gig, then?"

"Ha ha. Very funny." The car pulled over at the curb outside Bob's building. "Get showered and changed, get something to eat. I need to make calls. We'll shoot for the 8:30 a.m. ferry," Stone said. "Maybe we get lucky, get the Boston boys here, wrap this up by lunch. Then I can get the fuck out of this two-horse town."

Bob opened the car door. "Boy, I'd just bet they'd prefer you stick around, what with your sunny disposition and all."

"Eight thirty," Stone grunted. He slammed the car door. The Chrysler pulled away from the curb.

35

But they were too late, Bob immediately realized.

The ferry ride over had been uneventful, with no sign of anyone who might've been a threat. Eddie's driver had fetched the Lincoln for Bob from city impound, and the drive from the ferry terminal to Liz McGee's house had been unchallenged and brief.

Her car was nowhere to be seen, the house unlocked. A cursory look suggested hastily removed clothing items, with closet hangers left empty and some on the floor, a gap in the hall closet items where suitcases might've been.

There was a note on the kitchen table marked "Rachel." Bob opened it.

"I'm sorry. I'll contact you when I can. Mom."

Bob searched the house methodically, looking for any sign of where she might have gone. Her computer was password protected; he made a mental note to tell Eddie it needed to be cracked.

In the bedroom, under the bed, he found a long,

rectangular hard-shell case. He slid it out and set it on the mattress, then clicked the latches.

The rifle was familiar, an old military standby. *Winchester Model 70 and a high-power scope. Good gear.*

It meant that wherever she was, she was likely armed. She hadn't felt the need to take it, which meant she had an alternative.

But chances are, she's a hundred miles from here already.

He continued searching, rifling through the desk in her small office. He found the box of bills and letters Rachel had dropped off. He went through the dozen or so pieces of paper: her grandfather's orthodontic bill, a handful of notices for that month's unpaid utilities.

He took out his phone and speed-dialled Eddie Stone.

The older man didn't stand on ceremony. "Well?"

"She's gone. Coffee pot's cold; no sign she's been here this morning. She either left late last night or very early today. There's a space in the hall closet that could've been for suit-cases, and there's clothing missing. Her car's nowhere in sight."

"FUCK!" Eddie barked. "If you'd confronted her about Uncle days ago, this wouldn't be happening right now."

"Yeah, sure, because that's a fair assessment on the info I had."

"I DON'T GIVE A FUCK ABOUT YOUR FAIRNESS!" he bellowed. "We had a line on the single most important Russian asset operating on these shores since Aldrich Ames, and you let her go!"

"I'm guessing this means we're back to where we were," Bob said.

"The deal is off, if that's what you're asking. No Uncle, no removing Kennedy from the board. And if Kennedy's still around, you go back to being his public enemy number one. You feel me, Bobby? You fucked up again."

"Hey, you could've called for help any time you liked! You could've brought in a team, snagged everyone involved in this, grilled them for days. But you didn't want your boss to know you're trying to depose him, so you played it quiet and paid the price. How the fuck is any of that my fault?" Bob demanded.

He clearly wasn't listening. "And of course, I've just gotten Boston to agree to send a team down. They're probably fifteen minutes out at this point. And I get to call their boss and tell him to call them home. Do you have any idea how embarrassing that is?"

"Eddie—"

"Don't fucking 'Eddie' me, Bob. We're not friends. I saved your fucking life last night at that church—"

"Which you sent me to in the first place."

"—and this is the fucking thanks I get?"

There was no reasoning with him when his temper was firing, Bob knew. "Maybe the baseball coach knows something useful," he suggested instead.

"He doesn't know shit! He knows less than shit! He's been here so goddamned long, inactive, he's about as Russian as a fucking Hershey bar! And you can forget any deal for him, any kid gloves. He's going down hard. Fuck his wife and kid!"

Bob let the call go silent for a minute, then added, "You done?"

He could hear his ex-boss's heavy breathing through the line. His back was clearly up. "I'm half-tempted to tell Boston to keep coming, make any excuse so they're here waiting for you when you get back."

He was beginning to get under Bob's skin. "That's an

option," Bob said. "It's better, say, than you waiting at the docks alone. Because if you try to take me alone, Eddie, I'll kill you. I mean... if you try with a handful of dogs from the Boston field office, I'll still kill you, but it'll be messier."

He ended the call.

Shit.

Everything's gone balls up.

He glanced back at the kitchen, the dishes still in the draining rack, the cold coffee pot still one-third full. His mind drifted back to the first time he'd met Liz, the obvious chemistry between them. He hadn't felt that strange comfort, that good-humored familiarity, in a very long time.

It seemed a damned shame, all of it.

And he knew he had to tell Rachel her mother was gone and was a Russian asset, that her life was as much a lie as she was beginning to suspect. That they'd murdered her father, buried him on the island.

This shit never gets any easier, does it?

RACHEL WAS SITTING UP, reading another ancient magazine, when Bob arrived.

She looked up brightly, happy to see him. Her expression shifted when she saw the look on his face.

"This isn't good news, is it?"

He shook his head. "No, no, it's not."

He told her what he'd found, their suspicions, and about Nikolai's death. By the end, her mouth hung open slightly.

But then her expression shifted, her surprise giving way to a furrowed brow. "I don't believe it," she said. "I mean... I guess that's the normal reaction when someone's mother is accused of something, but..."

"Unless it's someone we just haven't encountered, someone who knew everyone involved but was so careful they never entered the conversation. But in all likelihood, your mother is Uncle," Bob said.

"And she just... ran? That's so unlike her, to run from trouble. She didn't have it easy, being a single mom. She had all sorts of problems with her clinic over the years; she didn't run from those."

"Those situations weren't likely to end in her being whisked off to Moscow," Bob said. "This one was. This only was going to end one of two ways for her: either she was Uncle, and they'd take her, or she wasn't, and they'd kill her. They're winding up an old operation here."

He filled her in on Chris Jefferson/Roman Ratachkov, as well as the coach's explanation of the intelligence-gathering ring based in the capital, Augusta, and at the luxury fishing and hunting lodges.

"All of this is due to obsolescence." Her voice sounded weak, shattered by the sudden stress. "All the lies. All the stress over Gramps and Grammy Rose."

You could tell her about her father now.

Or you could leave that alone, let her have something, a dream that someone important to her is still out there.

But he knew he couldn't lie, not now, not while her life was unravelling. "They also murdered your father. He didn't abandon you. You deserve to know that, that he cared. He started digging, suspected your grandparents. So someone, probably Yaremchuk, had him shot and buried on the island."

Her mouth dropped open again, her gaze distant, as if searching for a memory she could believe in, something to cling to. "Oh... Oh God," she managed.

Bob's heart was breaking for her. Five minutes earlier, she'd looked optimistic. Now her life was being destroyed, torn apart like a small boat in a big storm.

C'mon, Bobby, give the woman something better than that to believe in. Anything.

"I think it's why your mother went along with all of it," he said. "She knew what could happen to you if she fought back or tried to run. The only reason she's gone now is that she knew they were coming for her next. Probably Ratachkov and his family, too."

"I... need some time to process all of this," Rachel said. Then she looked up suddenly. "This means your friend Mike is probably in the shit, doesn't it?"

Even facing the dissolution of everything she believed in, she was thinking of someone other than herself, Bob realized. For all Liz's faults as a human, she'd raised a good person. "It does. But at least he'll have the accident vid, proof he wasn't lying. From my observation, when you're a fifty-something man and a boss is gunning for you, it's generally the end of the line, career-wise. So maybe that would've happened anyway. But... yeah. I guess I failed him, too."

"Eh?" That didn't sit well with the young lawyer. "Bob... look, he's lucky you were there to fight for him in the first place. So am I. None of this is on you. You're just the dude who tried to help everyone involved."

"That's nice of you to say, but—"

"But nothing. It's true. I was horrible to you because your past made me assume you were lying to me, and because I didn't want to accept truths that were staring me in the face. And I'm sorry for that. Don't... Don't let yourself think anything different. Okay?"

"Sure," Bob said, trying to sound sincere. The facts

suggested he'd made a mess of everything, but the sentiment was appreciated. "I'm going to meet with Mike, fill him in. Give him the bad news."

"And then?"

"Then... I'll have to hit the road. There are people in DC who want my head, old political bullshit."

"Just like that? You just have to run?"

"That's all I ever do, it seems."

HE LEFT Rachel to process everything, getting a suspicious glance from the officer stationed outside her room. He headed down the hall, towards the elevator and the tunnel to the parking lot.

A nurse looked up as she was about to pass him. "Mr. Bennett?"

"Yeah." He didn't recognize her, his hackles up immediately.

"We met the other day, but you were sedated. Your ribs," she said, tactfully not mentioning how they'd been broken in the first place.

"Ah. Yeah... I don't remember much about that night, to tell you true."

Her eyes widened knowingly, and she raised an index finger. "Your jacket."

"My jacket? Oh... my jacket. Yeah."

"You left it behind the other day when you left prematurely. The doctor was rather upset, given that you might have had a concussion."

"It was unavoidable," he said. "My jacket wasn't with my other clothes."

"They took it off as soon as you arrived, to treat your

injuries. It was in the closet at the end of the ward, but you snuck out." She gestured with her head in his direction and turned to lead him down the hall.

At the nurses' station, she retrieved his jacket from a functional steel rack against the wall, the other hangers all empty. "Here you go," she said.

"Thank you," Bob said. "It's a favorite."

"You take care of yourself, okay, Mr. Bennett?" She headed back down the hall.

Bob folded the jacket over his arm. He headed towards the double doors to the elevator waiting area.

Something bumped against his forearm. There was something in the coat pocket, he realized.

Too small to be a piece, thankfully. That could've caused problems.

He reached into the pocket and pulled out a heart-shaped pastry dotted with raisins.

You're kidding. He'd forgotten the gift from Liz's neighbor. He pushed open the doors and looked for a garbage can. There was one near the elevator doors.

He walked over. The doors opened, another nurse stepping out just as he was chucking it into a bin.

Her hand came up to her chest dramatically, as if shocked. "Please! Please tell me I did not see you just throw away a perfectly good cinnamon-raisin plushki?"

"A what now?"

"A plushki. That's the name of the little piece of heaven you just binned."

"It was four days old," he said. "It was probably stale."

"Ah," she said knowingly. "Darn shame. My babushka used to make them for us when we were little."

"Uh-huh. Sorry. If I'd have known, I'd have given it to you," Bob said.

She sighed again and went on her way.

The elevator door opened, and he got inside. It was time to go talk to Mike, then see if he could even get into his apartment, or whether Eddie was angry enough to be true to his word.

The week had been a disaster, he figured. *And that's how it always goes; like Eddie said, even when I try to do right, everything goes wrong.*

MIKE SCHULTZ HAD TAKEN the news well, all things considered.

He'd spent the early afternoon in an internal affairs interview, not free to talk until after 3 p.m.

He'd treated Bob's call as good news. The video was something, more than he'd had before. At least he had some ammunition, some clear sign that he'd been telling the truth.

As he drove back downtown, Bob hoped it was enough. Maybe they'd consider their initial approach too mistaken; maybe the police union would go to bat for him, keep the higher-ups off Mike's back.

Sure. Keep those optimistic thoughts coming, Bobby, and maybe you can convince yourself you didn't fail him, too.

He stopped at the public library. After ninety minutes on the free-use PCs, he had a list of potential places to move next. If he was certain of one thing, it was that an angry Eddie Stone was likely to be a problem. The greater the distance he could put between himself and Portland, the better.

But first, he had to go home. There was almost nothing in the apartment that couldn't be replaced, he'd realized. Nothing but a laptop, clothing, a second pistol, some cash.

And Eva's locket.

Traffic was heavy in the late afternoon, people leaving work for the day. He parked across the street from his apartment building.

There were no obvious signs of anyone waiting for him. But to be sure, he got out of the car, walked to the next corner and crossed. Then he found the end of the alley running behind the block and peeked around the corner.

The black Cadillac Escalade's windows were entirely tinted, too dark to be street legal in Maine. The plate said Massachusetts, in any case.

That sonuvabitch actually did it.

He called Boston back, just to get me.

The little gold locket was the only thing he had left to help remember his friend in Tucson, who'd died heroically protecting a mutual friend from gangsters.

That's why, Bobby. That's why you aren't allowed keepsakes. Because shit like this happens.

The locket wouldn't lead them anywhere. But he couldn't abide the idea of leaving it behind, having to let go like that. To let her down one more time.

He tilted his head and studied the car for a second. How many CIA assets *can* you fit in a Cadillac? It sounded like a bad joke setup line, but it was relevant.

I'm guessing no more than five.

He had nothing else keeping him in Portland, nothing but some decent memories and one good friend.

Maybe two, now.

But Bob knew he damn sure wasn't leaving without that locket.

36

Bob kept his steps light, avoiding debris as he made his way up the alley. The Cadillac was parked ahead of the apartment block's rear doors, which were set back, under the second-floor balconies.

A figure stepped out from the door area, a man in a black suit. Bob flattened himself against the near wall and remained still, trying to avoid the kind of small movements a man might see from the corner of his eye.

The guard walked past the back doors of the SUV and looked down the alley in the other direction.

No time like the present. Bob moved quickly and deliberately, creeping up behind the man, his foot kicking a pebble at the last second.

The man began to turn out of curiosity.

Bob grabbed him by the side of his skull, fingers spread so that he could drive the man's head into the frame of the car.

The guard dropped to all fours, stunned. Bob crouched and threw a hard right cross, connecting with the mental nerve near the tip of the man's chin. He crumpled to the ground, unconscious.

Bob searched his pockets and retrieved a set of wrist restraints. He bound the man's hands behind him, then took off his tie, balled it up, and stuffed it into his mouth just as the man started to come around.

"Mnnnh!" The agent writhed in place on the ground like a fish, trying to find his footing.

No time for this, Bob figured. He leaned over the prone finger and stomped down with all his weight on the man's left ankle, the snap audible, the guard's bellow muffled by the cloth filling his mouth.

"Quit wriggling, or you'll make it hurt worse," Bob said. He reached inside the man's jacket and confiscated a Glock 19 pistol from a shoulder holster. Then he took out the man's earpiece and inserted it into his own right ear.

He opened the back door to the building cautiously, avoiding its hinge squeaking by keeping the gap narrow. He looked up the stairwell, between levels, waiting for thirty seconds, until...

There. Hand on the rail.

Taking out the guard by the door to his hallway would require patience, he knew. He crept up the stairs to the third floor, peeking out to ensure the hand was still visible, just twelve feet above him.

Eventually, Bob knew, he'd get tired of standing in that one spot, waiting for the others to finish searching. He kept his eyes on the hand for a minute, then five, then ten.

Come on, come on! Move already, you weirdo! Who doesn't move from one spot for ten straight minutes!?

As if on cue, the hand disappeared. Bob leaned out and took the first two steps so that he could see a little of the floor above. The guard had wandered over to the window on the opposite wall. Bob knew if he waited until he turned around, the man would have a better view of the stairwell.

So no time like the present.

He jogged up the first half flight to the landing, his steps light and silent. At the bottom of the last flight, he moved into a sprint, flying up them. The guard heard him immediately and began to turn his way. Bob tossed the Smith & Wesson overhand, end over end. The pistol smacked the guard between the eyes even as he reached for his gun, the man stumbling two steps backwards as Bob flew up the last eight steps.

The guard shot out a front kick, instinct telling him to protect himself rather than call for help, the wiser move. Bob blocked the kick with a two-hand downward shove, pushing it aside. He pivoted so that he was side on, lowering his target profile and throwing a vicious elbow to his right. It caught the guard flush, his nose breaking, the man staggering, falling onto his backside.

Bob's side kick was well timed, his heel driving through the man's forehead, knocking his head into the wall at blinding speed.

Bob stayed put for a moment in a fighting stance, waiting to see if the man immediately recovered. But he wasn't moving.

He'd just finished restraining the guard when the earpiece crackled to life.

"Everything okay out there?" a voice asked.

He ignored it, pulling open the door to the fourth-floor hallway. They'd be along momentarily, he knew.

He looked down the hall. His apartment was twenty-five

feet away, halfway along. He broke into a jog, the door opening before he'd taken two steps.

He began to run.

The figure didn't hesitate, turning out of the apartment and into his path, pistol already levelled. Bob zigzagged, the shot wild, the boom of firing pin meeting black powder accentuated in the confined space. He threw himself at the gunman, knocking them both down, Bob scrambling over the man to get his knees into position, pinning the agent's arms to the ground. He threw another hard right cross, the man's eyes lolling back in his head as he slipped into darkness.

Bob heard the creak of the floorboard ahead as the man's partner stepped into the apartment's front hall.

The remaining agent had him dead to rights, the shot from no more than ten feet away guaranteed to punch his ticket.

And Bob knew they weren't there to arrest him.

Fuck.

His only thought in the moment was what Dawn would think, whether she'd ever know what had happened to him.

The agent smiled, aware that he had his target at his mercy.

Somewhere behind him, a song began to blare on a tinny clock radio, Rupert Holmes asking about piña coladas one more time.

The agent was caught off guard, looking back quickly for the source of the sound. Bob timed his rush perfectly, lowering his head and driving it through the man's midsection like a linebacker taking down a quarterback.

The man's pistol flew from his hand and bounced a few

feet away on the carpet. Bob scrambled over him, using both hands to slam the man's head into the hardwood floor. He reached the pistol, his left hand finding the grip.

He rolled over to face the door, the second agent retrieving a nine-millimeter from a speed holster. Bob fired twice, both bullets striking the man center mass, his target going down. The third man tried to rise, stunned. Bob was up more quickly, covering the distance between them, hammering the agent's chin with the butt of the pistol.

The fourth man hit the floor, out cold.

Bob's ribs were screaming in pain again, sweat building on his brow, breath coming hard and fast. He allowed himself the luxury of five seconds' recovery, then searched for the man's wrist restraints.

Never figured I'd be grateful for that goddamned song.

IT TOOK him less than five minutes to get his things together. The locket was where he'd left it, in the top drawer of the desk by the front window.

He slipped it into the back pocket of his wallet. *You're not going anywhere, Eva.*

He threw his clothes into his soft-sided travel bag, along with the fourth agent's Glock 19 and the two spare magazines he'd retrieved at the same time. He took his Bob Bennett papers – a driver's license, social security card and passport – and used his trusty Bic lighter to burn them in the sink, flushing the remains down the toilet.

In the background, he could hear the men writhing on the floor, one of them protesting or trying to talk through his gag, without success. The third man's vest seemed to have taken the brunt of the two shots he'd fired, though he was in obvious pain from the deep bruising.

He was halfway out the door when the men's phones began to ring in sequence.

After a third went unanswered, the landline by the door jingled.

Bob picked it up. "Hello?"

"Did you kill our guys?" Eddie Stone asked.

"Sending them here was really stupid, Eddie. Sending anyone after me is generally a really bad idea. I figured you'd know that by now."

"I asked you a question."

"The answer is I don't know. Three I took out without fireworks. A fourth took two in the right upper pectoral. I don't think I hit him in the heart, and he's not coughing up blood, so his lungs are intact. He's wearing a vest, so he should be okay. But if I were you, I'd get off this call and ring the guy an ambulance."

Stone paused a beat, then said, "Eventually, your time is going to be up, Bobby. You could save us both a lot of effort..."

"If I go, I'll take you with me," Bob said.

"The Boston guys... they're all young, green," Stone said. "That guy's got a family. You're always giving me the moral gears, pretending you're better than all this—"

But Bob had stopped listening. He hung up the phone gently, a thought occurring, twigged by Stone's statement.

That guy's got a family.

He thought back to the events of the day, the conversations in the hospital, the trip over, going through the box of bills.

Now, wait just a second...

Things were clicking into place.

He took the bottle of Percocet out of his jacket pocket and popped another pill.

37

Rachel was asleep again when Bob got back to her room. He checked his watch. It was nearly six in the evening, visiting hours about to end. He looked over at her guard cautiously, wondering if anyone had been alerted, called to grab him if he reappeared.

The cop outside the door folded his arms with a sullen expression as he entered.

Bob gave her a gentle shoulder shake. "Rachel!"

"Hmmm?" She opened her eyes. "Achh... I was out, sleeping! What!?" Then she realized who it was. "Bob... what's up?"

"Don't ask me to explain; I don't know how much time we have. If your grandfather wanted to hide somewhere, do you have any idea where he might go?"

"Bob... we already know he's dead... I don't—"

"Please... just trust me. On the island, specifically. Is there anywhere he could go where people just wouldn't normally think to look? Somewhere only family would consider?"

She looked puzzled. "Not... really. The clinic? I mean, it's a day clinic. There are no beds, just exam tables. I guess he could've hidden there, but it's very public, surrounded by other homes and businesses. I'm sure someone would've seen something, even if they were careful."

"Anywhere else?"

She shook her head again. "No. There's nothing in the last..." Then she paused. "Wait a second." She looked up at him. "Yeah. Yeah, there is one place."

FLORIDA AVENUE RAN across the middle of the Peaks Island, a river of asphalt that saw little traffic after dark.

Bob's car was about to pass the community dump entrance when he spotted Liz's tiny electric Nissan parked twenty feet past the gate.

He pulled over to the verge of the windy road. He got out of the car, turning off the engine and headlights, and walked over to the gate.

The dog's growl came from about ten feet past the entrance. Bob glanced in that direction, the parking lot well lit, in time to see a muscular four-legged torso hurling itself against the door of an oversized cage.

It barked with a baritone authority, growling and snapping at the wire door, rattling its metal hinges.

He walked past the cage slowly and cautiously, the door to the snub-nosed mutt's hut padlocked. He glanced through the side windows of Liz's car, but it was empty.

He turned slowly, glancing around the wide-open yard. There were large dumpsters lining the back corner of the property, a couple of small buildings. But there was no sign of any other movement.

It was nearly seven thirty.

Bob walked back to the Lincoln, the dog still snarling and barking as he pulled away.

He'd read up on Rachel's proposed hidey-hole while taking the ferry over. Battery Steele was a gigantic twin-gunned artillery bunker built into the Atlantic side of the island. It had been built in 1942 to protect the US east coast from a Nazi invasion. The artillery guns were long gone, the bunker now just a pair of lengthy corridors, crossing each other, mostly darkened. The top of the structure, a Maps search showed, was overgrown with moss and vegetation.

A minute later, the car reached the point where Florida Avenue ran above the old bunker, amidst the marshy interior on Peaks Island.

Battery Steele was striking, the size of a small factory, half-circles of concrete at each end acting as protective overhangs for what had once been massive artillery guns, each sixty-eight feet long, firing sixteen-inch-diameter shells.

Standing ahead of its front entrance, it was clear people came over to take a look pretty frequently. It was covered in graffiti, giant name tags in yellow, pink and white, a snake swallowing its tail, a giant owl.

Rachel said it had been open for decades, abandoned but a historical curiosity. The corridor running due north from the entrance wasn't long enough to fall into complete darkness, with the other end also completely open, the late sun nearing the horizon, casting long shadows down it. But most of its hundred-foot interior corridor was shrouded, inscrutable.

The room he needed was two-thirds of the way along. Most people were unaware that the battery also contained a basement. It was accessible through a rusty old hatch, held shut with an industrial-strength padlock.

The place was musty, dank and damp. Bob had been in worse bunkers in the field, but the passage of time had not been kind, and he could feel its ghosts, its tense history.

There seemed to be no one else around. He checked the hall both ways again before entering the dark room, his penlight letting him see the floor. It traced a path across the cement, the brightness startling a trio of rats, which promptly scurried past him and out the door.

There. The hatch was where she'd described, in the room's bottom left corner. Her grandfather had taken her there when she was little. He'd had a key to the padlock, and it had taken Rachel years to figure out that he'd simply cut off the one that was there and replaced it with one of his own.

Bob didn't have time for that, or a metal saw.

Instead, he'd brought a half-sized crowbar. He placed an angle end under the thick, rusty metal hasp attached to the door, then pushed down hard on it. The metal squealed from fatigue, screws popping out their housings.

He pulled the rest of the hasp away. If the basement was small and occupied, the noise would've been noticed, he knew.

Bob tried the hatch cover. It rose about an inch before something arrested its progress.

There's another lock, on the inside.

It was probably another padlock, Bob figured, something easy and quick to install. But the hatch looked rusty, the metal worn by decades of sea air. He placed the pry bar under the lip and leaned on the bar with all of his weight. It creaked, the groan growing louder until the internal screws gave out, torn from the rusty metal by the pressure.

The hatch popped halfway open, its weight causing it to slam shut again a moment later. He reached down, stretching with his arm and standing back as he pulled the trapdoor open.

Nothing. If someone was planning to open fire, they were waiting for a proper target.

Bob walked back to the door to the tunnel and made sure it was still deserted. Then he went back to the hatch and took a knee. "MR. PETERS!" he bellowed. "IF YOU CAN HEAR ME, I'M A FRIEND OF LIZ."

It had been the bill for new dentures that had gotten him thinking. His daughter was certain Peters didn't need them. And it had been just weeks before he'd apparently fled.

It was abnormal behavior, to spend so much on a "backup" dental plate, something he'd never heard of before.

Unless he'd had another use for them.

"MR. PETERS, I'M COMING DOWN. PLEASE DON'T SHOOT ME," Bob yelled.

He was taking a hell of a risk, he knew. Liz wasn't down there with him, or the hatch's outer padlock wouldn't have been secured. No one else would know they were there and be able to lock it behind them.

Assuming his theory was right, that meant the allegedly late Thomas Peters was alone.

He checked the stability of the iron ladder attached to the wall, then began to climb down it. He wasn't quite all the way down when he was forced to squint, the sudden glare from an oil lamp overwhelming.

As he reached the bottom, a voice said, "That's about far enough. Hands! Let me see them."

Bob put his hands up. He turned his head, his eyes adjusting to the low light.

Tom Peters was as old as he'd expected, a wrinkled octogenarian with some of his daughter's appearance. He was scowling. Under a loose T-shirt, Bob could make out the padding from a large bandage running down one side of his torso.

The room was nearly empty save for a cot in one corner, a pair of oil lamps, a wood table with two stools, and a radio. There were two suitcases along one wall, a sign Liz had been there recently.

"You're Bob, I take it. The man who claims to no longer be a spy."

"Never really was."

"An agency dog, then, one of their killers. Either way, I should shoot you just for the danger you caused my granddaughter."

"Sure," Bob said, gesturing at their surroundings. "This... this is all my fault."

Tom's head dipped a little, his eyes downcast for a split second. "I'm fully aware that this is my responsibility, young man."

"Because when they came for you – as I'm guessing they had for your wife – you used Liz's coroner connection to get hold of a corpse. You smashed its face in, replaced its teeth with your dentures."

Peters sighed. "He was an old John Doe, not as old as me, but close enough. A bum nobody was going to miss. I was going to set the car on fire. I'd taken about ten steps away from it, just surveying the scene to make sure it looked realistic. I'd figured the angles out a day earlier, that if I hit the concrete median about ten degrees off straight-on, it would do convincing damage, and the cushion I'd brought would protect my sternum from hitting the steering wheel."

"Because the old Pontiac didn't have an airbag, which served your purposes. You swapped places with the body, which is why the video showed someone in the back seat. You had to slide it over from the passenger position, easier done from the back seat. Then you had to rub that damaged face into the wheel, leave enough tissue and blood behind in case it survived the blaze. What happened?"

"I knew they'd placed a tracker on the car and were watching the house, keeping tabs on me until they could send someone. They were using two men, alternating every few hours. But I'd also seen them take breaks to use the washroom at the corner store up the street."

"So you waited until you had a window," Bob reasoned.

"I figured that would give me at least five minutes' head start, maybe ten. I hadn't counted on a drunk driver coming the other way, not paying attention to the temporary median."

"The second car hits yours, ruining your carefully plotted scene. The 'driver' of your car is partially ejected, the two occupants of the other car fully thrown through their windshield."

"It was horrific." He gestured to the stools. "Please, sit."

They made their way over to the table and sat down. Tom retrieved a thermos. "I have coffee, if you'd like."

"Sure."

The older man poured them each a plastic cup. It was lukewarm, but the man clearly wanted to talk. And they couldn't go anywhere immediately anyway, Bob knew. Not without Liz. And she couldn't be far off, he knew, not without her car.

"I knew I didn't have enough time to torch it all, and even if I did, I would have to move the John Doe back into the vehicle. All of it would leave more evidence of tampering, more to cast doubt. I watched for maybe twenty, thirty seconds, then saw headlights approaching from the south."

"My friend Sergeant Mike Schultz," Bob said. "Unlucky enough to be nearby when someone spotted the second car hitting yours from the cross street. It was called in, and he was there two minutes later."

Tom still had the pistol in his hand, although it was now resting on the table. "So I had to run. I was a half mile away, heading back toward the docks, when the adrenaline began to fade, and I realized a piece of the front windshield strut was embedded in my shoulder. I'd thought the pain was from the impact with the wheel, but felt wetness, then considerably more pain. It was all I could do to huddle under a cargo bay for the rest of the night. I couldn't go to a hospital, but the wound was deep and painful. I knew Liz could patch me up. Fortunately, that put me a few blocks from the house."

"So you grabbed your other car, which is why your Subaru was missing, and you went back to Peaks Island and her clinic."

Behind them, the ladder creaked. Both men turned. A second later, a pair of feet in flats appeared.

Liz had a panicked expression on her face as she peered into the room, trying to ensure her father was still there.

She saw Bob, and it turned into a frown. "Shit," she said.

"He knows," Tom said. "He knows everything."

"Then—"

Bob interrupted her, reaching across the table, snatching

the pistol from the old man's grip before he could react. "Go ahead and finish that sentence."

She sighed, resigned, and tilted her head back. "You should have shot him as soon as you saw his feet on the ladder." Then she glared at Bob. "Well… I'm sorry, but family is family. I've already lost my husband and mother to these men. I didn't want to lose my father as well."

Bob handed the gun back to Tom. "Just making the point. Where were you? I tried calling."

"I left the house this morning, and we were waiting here. But I had to retrieve my documents and some cash from a drop box, in the woods by the dump. What are you going to do with us?"

Bob glared at Liz. "Your daughter doesn't seem to get it yet, but I'm on your side. I figured, given your age, that you might've been injured in the crash, tried to reach her clinic. But I didn't put the dental plate together with the corpse until I'd given up on the idea that you were Uncle."

"Uncle? Me?" Peters looked bemused. "In a sense, I'm flattered. But—"

"What now?" Liz interrupted.

"That's up to you," Bob said. "You were clearly planning on running, based on the missing suitcases." He nodded to the two big Samsonites against the wall.

"I've arranged a float plane pickup for tomorrow morning," Liz said. "I have no illusions about whether they'll let me live. I know far too much; if not for the police attention it would've drawn so soon after my father's disappearance, they'd have done it before now, I suspect."

"She has no choice," Thomas interjected.

"It cost everything I had, and I had to work with the

pilot's window. He's flying without a registered flight plan, without his locator beacon on."

"Canada?" Bob suggested.

She nodded. "I knew Rachel would worry, but I figured I'd be able to let her know where we were eventually. There's a fishing camp in the Miramichi area of New Brunswick, owned by an old political friend of my mother's. We were going to be dropped off along the Nova Scotia shoreline, then make our way across by land from there."

"Float plane can stay low, below radar, set down if necessary to avoid attention," Bob said. "Dangerous as hell, but doable. There's only one problem: you don't have another night."

"What's happened?" Liz asked.

Bob filled her in on the church fire, Yaremchuk ordering help in from Boston. "There are at least two men on the island already, to protect Uncle, possibly more. You can bet they're also tasked with eliminating you because you could still alert the authorities before Uncle is spirited out of the country. I don't think they realize your father is still alive. They buried the stolen body in a lye-filled grave out in the country."

"Then they'll be hunting for me," Liz said.

"They'll have left eyes on the ferry terminal to make sure you don't get past them and back to the mainland," Bob suggested. "Maybe a boat patrolling the shore, too? Something they could rent easily enough like a ski boat or pontoon?"

"Unlikely tonight," Liz said. "The ocean is roiling."

"So?"

Tom shook his head. "The waves and chop would be brutal

on any small craft they could rent," he explained. "And on this side of the island, where the rocks extend far out from shore, bad weather is a death trap to anyone but an experienced pilot. And they know Liz isn't one. She's been watched near constantly until the last few days. No, they know we're stuck here without the ferry or a pickup by air, so they're not out braving the waves."

Bob rubbed his chin stubble and considered the logistics. "I figure that puts us up against three guns, minimum. Uncle didn't last this long by leaving loose ends behind."

Liz looked around at their confines. "Then we stay here for the night."

"Dangerous," Bob said. "There aren't many places on the island to hide. Once they realized you weren't home, they'll have begun scouring the place. And it's tiny, four miles around and only one across. Once they're done talking to your neighbors, the clinic's neighbors, the local businesses? They'll start combing the woods and find this place. Or just come right here. It's sort of prominent, judging by all the graffiti."

"Then we have to go immediately," Liz said. "My car is not far away."

"Okay," Bob said.

She looked unsure. "Just like that? I figured you'd cut some sort of deal with your former employers to take Uncle in. Otherwise, all of this was just about Sergeant Mike Schultz's career."

"All of this *was* about Mike's career, originally," Bob said. "Then my former employers, as you put it, got wind your handler might be here. So... yeah, I cut a deal. My slate wiped clean if I brought their prize in."

"And you're just giving that up to save us?"

"I'm giving it up because I promised Rachel I'd help her

figure out what happened to her grandfather. And a promise is a promise. Plus, way I figure, if you two don't get the hell out of here now, you'll probably be dead by morning. Priorities and all. Besides, if I'm right, Uncle will be leaving via Boston sometime after midnight, and we still have hours before that happens."

She stared at him intensely, aware he was risking his prize to help her escape. Bob had felt that chemistry again, the sense she saw more in him.

"You know," Liz said softly, "if things had been different..."

"Yeah. Maybe. But..." Bob left it at that.

Tom stood up, wincing. "He's right. We cannot wait until morning. They will find us before then. We must go, take our chances via the mainland."

"You're still in pain."

"I ran out of pills," he said.

Liz frowned. "Why didn't you tell me? I could've arranged something."

"Not without more questions," Tom said. "Not with them watching you near constantly. That you even made it here to visit me and bring supplies without being seen was fortunate."

"Good point," Bob said, taking out the bottle of Percocet and handing it to the man once known as Artem Lipatov. "Just one. They're strong as hell." He turned back to Liz. "I saw your car parked at the dump."

"It's off the road, at least," she said. "I walked... wait a second: where did *you* park?"

"They don't know what I'm driving, if they're just in from Boston," Bob reasoned. "They won't recognize the Lincoln."

"No, they won't," Liz said. "But Uncle will."

Her father glared at him. “You cannot be serious!? You parked in plain sight?!”

Bob glared right back. “It’s been a long fucking week trying to save your family from being murdered, okay? Cut me some slack.”

Liz moved over to the wall and grabbed one suitcase. “You go up first, and I’ll pass them up to you, okay? Then we can help Father up.”

Bob nodded. He took out the Glock 19 and checked the load. Then he noticed Tom staring at it. “Just being cautious, is all,” he said.

He began to climb the ladder. Liz had pulled the hatch ajar. It clunked loudly against the concrete floor as he pushed it open fully. Bob climbed out of the tunnel.

A pair of flashlight beams trained on him, and he felt the pressure of a pistol barrel against the back of his head.

“Good evening, Mr. Singleton. Sure led us on a merry damned chase, didn’tcha? Goddamn!”

The New Jersey accent was unmistakable. He held up a hand to ward off the glare so that he could make her out.

“Good evening, Mrs. Arbogast,” Bob said. “Or do you prefer Uncle?”

38

"Your dime, sweetie," Arbogast said. "Now, let's retrieve Liz and figure out what we're going to do with you."

"You're not curious how I knew?" Bob asked.

The sprightly senior shrugged. "I figured it was the gun pointed at your head and my mere presence."

"Nah. Until a few hours ago, we'd all guessed it had to be Liz, taking over the reins from Tom."

"But?"

"But the Russians seemed to be working under the impression Uncle was the same person all along, for nearly sixty years. That meant someone older. And New Jersey homemakers aren't in the habit of baking plushki."

She closed one eye in an embarrassed half-squint. "Ah hell. As long as I've been doing this, and even I still make mistakes."

"It was a small one. What did you call them? Spice rolls, I think. If I didn't keep a strict diet, I'd have eaten it, and it wouldn't have still been in my pocket when a nurse handed me my jacket. One of her colleagues spotted it, said her 'babushka' used to make them."

"Her grandmother," Arbogast said before slipping into Russian. "I ya unichtozhen staroy stranoy." *And I am undone, by the old country.* "Now there's some irony for youse."

"I'm curious: why Jersey?"

Arbogast shrugged. "I tried to learn the Maine accent but never could get a handle on it. Is it Boston, is it Vermont upper crust? I never could figure out what these jerkwads were talking about half the time. By contrast, New Jersey was a piece of cake." She nodded towards the hatch. "Tell her to make her way up. I figure she's carrying, right?" She reached over to a concrete ledge on the wall and placed the flashlight there, beam up, then turned a setting on its outer edge, a broader beam providing a makeshift lamp, the room gloomy but visible.

"Yeah. I have to admit," Bob said, "your cover is perfect. If I didn't know better..."

"It's been a long time," Arbogast said. "Tell her we have a grenade we can chuck down there if all else fails."

No mention of the old man, Bob thought. *They really don't know. That's something.*

He leaned over the hatch. "LIZ! They know you're down there. She has three guns. You can't fight that alone. There's three of them, so we're outnumbered."

"I CAN TRY," Liz yelled back.

"They have a grenade. If you don't come up, toss out the pistol and surrender, they'll toss it down there and close the hatch. You don't want that, believe me."

There was a pause, silence. Then, "OKAY! I'M COMING UP."

They could hear her feet on the iron ladder. A pistol popped out of the hole and landed beside it.

A moment later, Liz appeared.

"So now you understand," she said as she clambered to her feet.

"Uncle was right next door the whole time," Bob said. "Keeping an eye on her prized assets."

"I didn't want the kid hurt," Arbogast said to Liz. "But if you'd brought her into the fold like you were supposed to..." She let the thought hang there, horrifically. "She's a hothead, but a smart kid. She'd have been a hell of an asset, working for the Navy JAG office. Probably hears all sorts of interesting things." She nodded to one of the two goons accompanying her. "Restrain them. We don't want any more surprises."

"What now?" Liz said.

Arbogast tilted her head slightly, like someone studying a child. "Ah... come on, sweetie pie. You know what comes next."

"But not here, at the tourist attraction?" the younger woman asked. "No one else around at this time of night. Nothing to see when it's dark."

Arbogast's eyes flitted around their perimeter. "Big empty structure like this, the shots would echo all the way to Boston. No, we'll take you off to the woods, try to put you in the ground near Riley. I can do that for you, anyhow."

Bob studied Liz's face in the dim glow. She looked distant in the moment, trapped in a bad memory.

"She shot him in the back of the head while we were eating supper," Liz said, her tone bleak and empty. "Just let him bleed out on the kitchen table while I screamed."

"You should have known better than to defy me. I told you too many times—"

"When we defy you, we defy Moscow," Liz intoned coldly.

"That's about the face of it, sweetie pie. You can't say you weren't warned." Then Arbogast frowned and looked around. "But… why come hide here? You got an evac pickup figured out or something? We got nothing off your phone tap."

"I just wanted to see it again before I left," Liz said. "Bob saw me pull my car off the road at the dump, parked a ways up Florida Avenue. Put two and two together."

The old lady's eyes narrowed. "Why don't I believe you?"

"Because you're a professional, and professionals are always careful," Bob said. *I need to get us moving, now, before she digs any deeper and finds Tom.* "But she's not lying."

Arbogast smiled, a sort of half-grimace, the contempt obvious. "Yeah. Smooth move there, Ex-Lax, parking by the road and all. That Lincoln could be seen from space."

Bob kept his mouth shut. He looked over at Liz without turning his head. She was glaring at him, but also not saying another word. *She gets it.*

One of Arbogast's men moved behind them, restraining each at the wrists.

Arbogast waved her pistol towards the door. "Let's get this over with."

THE WOODS RAN RIGHT UP to the old gun battery. Within a few paces, Liz and Bob found themselves on a dirt trail winding between the thick stands of birch, spruce and conifer trees, their captors just a few feet behind them.

It had begun to lightly rain, droplets pattering the wind-rustled leaves and foliage. Arbogast shone a light on the path ahead of them. “Keep moving,” she cautioned as Liz slowed. “It’s not far.”

They exited the trees and crossed Florida Avenue. Bob stopped for a moment and turned, trying to gauge whether he could make it to the car and his backup piece before one of them was shot.

Not likely. Arbogast was careful, staying just out of Liz’s reach but close enough that the outcome of crossing her would be in no doubt.

“Isn’t there another way we can work this out?” he asked.

Tom was elderly, albeit fit, still recovering from his shrapnel wound. They needed to delay the march as much as possible.

“Now what could you possibly offer?” Arbogast said. “You’re a repeat problem for my employers, Mr. Singleton. They’re going to be ecstatic that I managed to throw you in for good measure. Might even give me a reward.” She nodded to the man right behind him. “Yuri...”

Yuri pushed Bob ahead with his free hand. “Get moving,” he grunted.

They entered the thicket of trees on the other side of the road. Liz stopped, crouching.

The two thugs moved towards her.

“JUST... take it easy,” Liz said, a palm held up to halt them. “I’m just trying to tie my darn shoelace.”

Arbogast sighed and tutted. “With your hands behind your back? No, you’re trying to delay. Such a good soldier, for so long. And now this. I’m very disappointed in you, Elizabeth.”

"At least being a traitor caused her guilt," Bob muttered. "You don't seem fazed at all."

"Because I have nothing to be guilty about," Arbogast said. "This nation is decadent, foolish and complacent, full of fat, stupid people and fat, stupid ideas. There are still places on this earth, like Russia, where old standards are respected. Where men are expected to be providers, where weaklings and degenerates are not tolerated."

Liz stood up. "And yet during all the decades you've lived next door, I don't think I was ever at your house once without the TV being on. You sure love your decadent *Family Feud* and *Wheel of Fortune*, don't you, Sybil? Your soap operas and your tabloid news. And you always liked to talk when you got back from Portland about how you got a chance to grab a big ol' degenerate Big Mac and an equally sinful chocolate shake."

"She's a hypocrite?" Bob mocked. "Shocked! Shocked, I am."

Arbogast clearly didn't like the tone, but a counterargument wasn't springing to mind. Instead, she gestured with the snub-nosed .38 towards the woods ahead. "Just get moving."

Bob knew their biggest problem was numbers. There were branches near the path, potential weapons he could bend and spring to distract them. But even if he could get his hands ahead of him, take one guard down quickly, they had the advantage of numbers.

They marched another hundred feet, the path disappearing entirely, Liz and Bob forced to push through overgrowth.

In the middle of the woods was a tiny clearing where

someone had chopped down a handful of trees, leaving stumps covered in moss.

"Right here," Arbogast said. She smiled and gestured to the larger stump. "Riley's by that one. It was a shame about him. I always liked him, even if he was a jabrone."

"When you murdered him, you didn't even say you were sorry," Liz muttered.

"Because I wasn't. I was working. Now, down on your knees, okay?"

The pair knelt. If Tom was planning to intervene, Bob figured, he was taking his damn sweet time.

"You may not realize it, Mr. Singleton, but in my country, you're considered an enemy of the state," Arbogast said. "Even before you murdered Victor Malyuchenko, you had a price on your head from the war in Iraq. For all the brave Russian boys you killed in the field."

"Brave? They were mercs!" Bob scoffed. "Fighting a proxy war they had no business being near, to make money for oligarchs in Moscow, the kind of men who would spit you out like a bad piece of shellfish."

Arbogast chuckled. "I'd expect you to say that, my dear. I know all about you, Mr. Singleton. I know enough to have Yuri and Ion stand back a ways. I know you never go down without a fight. But guess what? Your time is up." She nodded to the two men. "Kill them."

The shot rang out a split second later, from somewhere behind them, the man she'd identified as Ion stumbling forward, then to one side, his two companions puzzled, not realizing he'd been struck in the head and chest by bullets because his brain hadn't registered it yet, and they couldn't see the wounds in the dark.

Ion staggered three paces sideways, a hand going up to his neck. He drew the hand away and stared at it, puzzled by the slick, wet blood. Then blood loss kicked in, his heart going into arrhythmia, consciousness beginning to escape him.

The big man crashed to the ground just as another shot rang out.

Arbogast registered the direction immediately, stepping sideways into cover behind a thicket of tall, thin fir trees. Ten feet away, Yuri followed suit, both peering in the darkness of the forest behind them, looking for their attacker.

Arbogast signalled to Yuri to round their attacker and get behind him. "Go!" she ordered. Yuri plunged into the woods, heading back the way they'd come.

Bob hissed at Liz, "Now, run!"

They both rose and broke into a sprint. Arbogast turned and fired, but they were already into the trees, barely visible in the gathering darkness except as moving shapes.

Bob figured the dump and Liz's car couldn't have been more than a hundred feet ahead. But they were slowed by the terrain, the sprint immediately turning into a slog, the ground marshy, reeds and knotweed grasping at their ankles, old fallen tree limbs and the narrow trunks of long-dead poplar and birch tripping every other step.

The rain had picked up, obscuring the already dark path ahead. A root caught Liz's toes, and she smashed into the forest floor, face-first. Bob skittered to a halt. He crouched next to her. "Quickly! To your knees first, then use my body for balance." She fumbled herself to a leaning position, then used him to balance herself as she found her feet.

They took off running again.

He glanced back in time to see the muzzle flare from two pistol shots, about fifty feet behind them.

Liz heard them and stopped. "Dad!"

She was about to run back, but Bob blocked her path. "We can't help him!" he barked. "He's given us a head start, just..." He stopped, putting a hand on her shoulder to make sure she stayed put. "Shhh."

To their left, Bob could see a figure moving swiftly through chaotic clumps of dead trees, twisted limbs, saplings and overgrowth, just fifteen or twenty feet away. Whoever it was, they were big and quick. That ruled out either of the senior citizens.

"Go slowly," Bob whispered, angling them slightly southwest, away from the other man's path. "Yuri's trying to cut us off. But if I've got the angles right..." He didn't get to finish the thought, the treeline coming up quickly.

Just past it was a small, rounded field of open grass, the community dump on the other side, the fading light of the evening giving way to tall light standards that bathed the property in a gossamer glow.

There was no avoiding it, Bob realized: when they ran out of the trees, they would have no cover.

"We're going to make a run for it," he said. "When we get to the other side of the field, use the parked vehicles and trucks for cover. Stay low; don't give him a target."

Liz looked back over her shoulder. "Where's Mrs. A?"

"She's eighty years old. Distance runner or not, she's probably unable to keep up," Bob said. "Ready?"

Liz nodded.

"Go!"

They took off, sprinting, Bob deliberately angling his run slightly to the northwest so that Yuri would target him as the nearer opportunity.

A shot rang out, then another.

He ignored them, chancing a glance to his left, seeing Liz settling behind an old green pickup truck. It looked like it had been parked for decades.

A bullet pinged off construction debris at the back of the property. Bob clambered over it and crouched low. He ducked behind a pair of tall, rusty dumpsters, then moved to their south corner, looking for movement.

The numbers were still against them, he knew, as long as Arbogast was unaccounted for and they were unarmed and constrained.

The facility was scrupulously clean compared to most of the tips Bob had seen, people using the dumpsters spread liberally around to toss away their bags of trash. The smell wasn't much better, though, a mix of decaying food and stale milk.

It was also small enough that if either of them broke towards Liz's car, parked behind the main building, they would be in the open for several dozen feet. And even if they could get there, their hands were still tied.

He looked left. Liz was peeking out from behind the green pickup. Bob shook his head violently, making it clear she should stay put.

He turned and crept along the back side of the rectangular, rusted bins. At the back of the lot was a narrow utility shed, the only real cover away from the main buildings and dump trucks. Bob watched it patiently for close to thirty seconds before the barrel of a pistol protruded ever so slightly around its far corner.

There he is.

Two piles of dirt and construction debris sat twenty feet wide of the shed, to its right. Bob figured Yuri had to be staring back at the main buildings, at her car, waiting for someone to step into the open.

Instead, Bob went east, between the two mounds, crouching low. He circled the smaller building to its back wall.

Behind the building, a dirty, off-white wood table sat against the rear wall. A handful of common tools littered its surface, including a crowbar, a lug wrench, and a level.

A battery-powered reciprocating saw.

Bob glanced heavenward. *We don't have much of a working relationship, but if you're up there, thank you.*

He turned his back to the table, reached down, and picked up the saw by looking over his shoulder to judge the distance. He knelt down, then slowly flopped onto his backside. He lowered the saw gently behind him, so that it sat on its square, fat end; the plastic bounced slightly on the hard-packed dirt, but the tool remained upright.

Step one.

He shuffled forward, then used his left foot to take off his right shoe. Then he reversed the process. He stood up, then crouched low at the knees and rolled onto his side.

Bob strained with all his might, pushing down and back at the shoulders while bending tightly at the waist, trying to force his hands under his feet. His shoulder sockets screamed in pain, for a moment feeling like they might dislocate.

He grunted hard as he pushed one more time, shoulder ligaments strained, damaged ribs throbbing with pain. He paused to contain his accelerating breathing, keeping it even.

One more firm push and the loop popped up over his toes, his hands now ahead of him. He closed his eyes for a moment and held his breath, then released it, accepting the stabbing soreness in his muscles.

To his right, perhaps fifteen feet away, he heard a noise, a slight shuffling sound.

Shit.

He turned and rolled up onto his knees ahead of the saw.

He'd realized immediately he wouldn't be able to depress the saw's trigger with his wrists tied, not while also sawing off the reinforced restraint. He glanced around the side of the shed, seeing no one.

Did he hear me?

Bob knew he didn't have long. He fell back onto his buttocks again. Then he placed his left foot behind the drill to act as a counterweight, looping his right big toe through the trigger guard. He leaned over as far as he could, shoulder and back muscles already straining to hold the tie against the thin, serrated blade.

As soon as he triggered the saw, he knew Yuri would be alerted.

Please have some juice in the battery. Please.

He heard footsteps.

Bob pushed down on the trigger. The saw fired up to a buzzing whine, the blade splitting the wrist tie instantly.

The footsteps became a run.

Bob popped to his feet, reaching down towards the old worktable. He grabbed the lug wrench, pivoted on his right foot as the figure came around the corner, swinging the lug wrench and tossing it, full force, into Yuri's face as he rounded the corner.

The tool clunked off the man's skull, the Russian going down, his pistol flying from his grip.

Bob ran past him to grab the pistol, but Yuri's foot snapped out at the last second, tripping him.

Bob slammed face-first to the dirt. Yuri was up quickly, trying to pin him down, clambering atop him to pound him into submission.

Bob flailed his left arm free, his hand searching the gravel and dirt even as Yuri's left fist caught him square in the right eye. Bob jerked his head away as best he could, the second blow striking his skull above his left ear. He bucked his body frantically, trying to shake the other man off, his hand still searching the cold dirt. *Gotta get loose, gotta—*

Yuri tried to shuffle forward, to pin Bob's arms with his knees even as his two-handed grip closed around Bob's throat, trying to wring the life out of him. Bob's fingers scratched at the dirt, his circulation cut off, blood pooling in his head, consciousness beginning to fade.

His fingers found cold metal, pressed against it. Bob stretched with all his might, bringing the pistol up off the dirt, turning it inwards, his index finger yanking the trigger. The blast was deafening, the bullet striking Yuri square in the ribs, the concussive force like a rabbit punch, the big man collapsing off his captive.

Yuri grasped at the wound. Bob rolled once, twice, three times, trying to get out of the other man's range. He leaned up, his own rib cage in agony again from unknit fractures, adrenaline driving him on as he raised the pistol and fired twice. The first struck Yuri square in the chest, the second through the middle of his forehead.

The Russian didn't give up, his heart still pumping though damaged. He tried to scramble to his feet. But brain trauma conspired against him, his body jerking spasmodically. He fell onto his back and stopped moving.

Bob tried to breathe evenly despite the pain. He pushed himself up to his feet and staggered toward the main building. He passed a steel Quonset-style garage. Liz's car was parked on the other side, he knew.

He rounded the corner and immediately raised the pistol.

Liz was standing beside the passenger door of her car. Mrs. Arbogast's little Honda was parked ten feet away, the senior standing behind Liz, forcing her to crouch slightly so that Arbogast could hold her via a forearm around the younger woman's throat, her revolver pointed at Liz's temple.

"That's about far enough, right—" Arbogast managed before Bob raised the pistol and fired.

Arbogast jerked slightly to the right, maintaining a grip on her captive. She glanced down at herself, then at Bob, realizing she hadn't been hit.

She looked up and met his gaze, shocked.

"By reputation, you're an incredible marksman, Mr. Singleton. I mean... blame the lousy light if you want, but I'm unimpressed, truly. Even I could hit you from here. Then again, maybe you like poor Liz a little too much. Maybe her being a hostage sort of... soured your aim. Now, put the pistol down, or I'll kill her."

Bob ignored the demand, keeping the gun level. "You shoot her, I shoot you. Why do you think I care if two Russian spies die instead of one?"

Arbogast grinned. "Because deep down, I can see it in your eyes. You're a bleeding heart. A weak man. People like you, Bob? You're why I've been at this so long. People who can't look beyond my gender or my age or my accent. People who think I'm a crass, stupid hick from Camden. People who can't keep their professional shit together. You won't take the risk, not when you've already missed once. You don't have the stones."

Behind her, a low growl sounded.

"Risk?" Bob said. "Nah. You're holding Liz, not me. And... I didn't miss. I wasn't shooting at you."

Arbogast heard the growl and frowned.

She chanced a glance behind her, in time to see the junkyard dog pushing open the gate to its cage, the remains of the padlock lying on the ground.

"Oh. Shit."

The dog charged.

Arbogast let go of Liz and turned to shoot at the dog, which was sprinting across the lot, the first shot wide, the second kicking up dirt just behind the charging beast.

"LIZ, RUN!" Bob yelled, taking off towards the car, his feet pounding the dirt as both tried to reach safety.

The dog leaped at Arbogast, its muscular body seemingly bigger than hers, its forepaws striking her above the shoulder, the pistol knocked out of her hand as it pinned her to the ground, fangs glistening from saliva as it tore at her throat and neck.

Bob yanked open the passenger door and let Liz in first. He slammed the door, then ran around the car's front end and climbed in beside her.

Liz glanced past him as the dog continued to ravage Arbogast, then turned away quickly from the grisly scene.

He backed the car up, past the shed. He got out quickly, the dog now a safe distance away. Bob retrieved the reciprocating saw from its position by the table.

Then he got back in and closed the door. He snipped Liz's wrist ties and hit the gas.

Bob glanced over quickly as they passed the scene. The dog was still tearing away chunks of flesh.

But Arbogast had stopped moving.

39

They drove back along Florida Avenue, Bob's foot on the gas, the brakes squealing as he stepped on them just ahead of the path down to Battery Steele.

Liz was out of the car in a flash, Bob hustling to follow her as she rushed down the path and past the treeline, the rain coming down steadily now, the damp setting in.

She found him about thirty feet in, halfway to the clearing. Tom had propped himself up against a stump, his chest heaving from a gunshot wound, another four inches lower. He was gasping slightly for air.

"DAD!" Liz ran over to him and crouched. "Oh God, Daddy..."

He peered down his nose, his eyelids heavy. "My lovely girl."

"Dad, hold on! We're going to get you help..."

He shook his head gently. "No. No... no way. Not for this." His eyes rolled around as he took in the dark woods surrounding them, raindrops rolling off the lenses of his glasses. “Besides... this is where I love. Always... always wanted to live here full time, in our little house, like you.”

Bob crouched. He winced when he saw the wound. “Gut shot and in the chest. He’s losing blood quickly.”

“DON’T YOU THINK I KNOW THAT?!” Liz snapped. “We need to staunch the wounds so that we can move him to the car.”

Despite his condition, the man who’d gone by Thomas Peters for most of his life managed to raise his right hand. He held her forearm. “No. I was selfish, Elizabeth. I should’ve accepted my fate, given you warning they were cleaning house. I... was an idealist, once, long ago.” He’d begun to pant audibly, the strength hard to maintain. “I believed in equality for all, that Marx would save us all. But I couldn’t. I couldn’t save the world.”

He stopped, unable to continue, his eyes dancing in their sockets.

“DAD!”

“I’m... just glad that I could save you.” He breathed deeply once more, then a long gasp, air expelled as the life left his lungs, his eyes suddenly vacant and dim.

“DADDY!” Liz hugged her father. “PLEASE!”

Bob put a hand on her shoulder. “Liz...”

She sniffed hard, tears streaming down her face. “I know.” She buried her head in the crook of her father’s neck.

Bob reached over and gently used his middle and index fingers to close the dead man’s eyelids.

Bob knew she needed some more time with her father. He wandered ten feet away but kept Liz in view.

He felt sorrow for her, but ultimately, he knew, she had to face up to her choices. Eddie Stone would demand that, at the least.

Stone. Bob thought of Arbogast, the handler known as "Uncle," lying dead at the community dump, her throat torn out.

He's going to lose his mind, coming that close.

Liz didn't deserve the shit storm she'd face at the agency's hands, not for a life that was out of her control. *Yeah, she could've turned herself in years ago*, he figured, *but they'd have gone after her family, her daughter.*

Then there was the coach. Eddie had been holding him for two days now, presumably cuffed to a bed, with his driver watching the former sleeper. *That guy's never done a damn thing to help the Russians. But you can be sure Eddie's not going to give a shit. He'll throw the book at him.*

Then an idea struck him.

Or... will he?

PORTLAND, Maine

EDDIE STONE SAT at the hotel bar and sipped a double shot of Laphroaig whiskey, feeling the soothing warmth as it kissed the back of his throat, familiar as a blanket.

They had a flight booked back to DC at seven thirty the next morning. He knew his boss, CIA Deputy Director Andrew Kennedy, would expect a full debrief within ninety minutes of his landing. It would not be pleasant and would start with a demand to know why Kennedy had been kept out of the loop.

At least we've got Ratachkov. At least he can explain this mess and wear the fallout in a nice, long jail term.

Working with Bob, trying to appeal to his sense of national pride, had been a mistake. He'd clearly been interested in the woman, Liz McGee, and in helping his friend. When the church was about to explode, he'd helped the traitorous baseball coach out, left Stone to fend for himself.

"A penny for your..." the figure sitting down at the next stool began to say. "On second thought, never mind. It'll probably cost me a lot more in therapy, getting inside your twisted head."

"Bob," Eddie said coolly. He downed the rest of his whiskey without turning to look. "I take it you're here with more threats to kill me and the usual dearth of scintillating news."

"Uncle is dead."

"Huh. Yeah... yeah, of course." He held up the glass until the bartender spotted him. "Same again," he said. "Then it was Liz McGee, in the end. You found her."

"Yes to the latter, no to the former."

Eddie waited a moment, but Bob didn't elaborate.

He turned the other man's way. "Boy... you're just bound and determined to force me to engage, aren't you? Okay, I'll bite."

"Sybil Arbogast, Liz's elderly neighbor."

Yeah, that's about par for the course. Didn't even look at her. His second whiskey arrived, and he toasted the bartender with a quick raise of the glass, then a swallow. "It's not going to matter, now. No Uncle, no chance Kennedy's hearing about most of this. Besides... we didn't come away empty-handed."

"You're going to prosecute Ratachkov?"

Stone didn't like the tone. He fixed Bob with a stare. "Yeah, Bob. I'm going to make sure we prosecute the fucking Russian spy. You got a problem with that, one that verges anywhere towards sanity and reason? Because this is the job.

This is what we're supposed to do, catch the bad guys, stop them before they stop us." He turned his head back to his drink. "Jesus H. Christ." He took another long swallow.

"He's not a spy, Eddie, not really. Do you have any evidence he's ever helped them in any way whatsoever?"

"They paid him for thirty years! He took that money. He knew what it was for, who he worked for. He could've turned himself in at any time, put his country before his bank account."

Bob scoffed so hard he almost fell off his stool. "WHAT?! Eddie, how many times over your career have you accepted some backdoor gift from an ally, some politician's favor!? When you were banking all that loot, were YOU thinking about your country? I don't think so. And at least he had a reason, a kid with medical bills."

"But I never played for the wrong team. That's what you never understood, Bob, what you still don't understand. It's not about the moment, it's not about the facts on a given day. It's about picking a team, defending it. It's 'my country, right or wrong,' remember?"

"Yeah... well, I'm never going to pick wrong just to feel right, or be accepted, or be part of the team, Eddie. Guys like you, you use that saying and lots of other jingoistic bullshit like it to suck in dim-witted people, get them to buy what you're selling on the basis of patriotism or loyalty. But the guy who originally said it wasn't saying deliberately side with wrong, just that it was still his country."

"That's your take."

"Another version came not long after, from Carl Schurz, a German-American statesman—"

"I know who Carl Schurz was, Bob."

"Then you know what he said: 'My country, right or

wrong; if right, to be kept right; and if wrong, to be set right.' I always liked that bit, about setting things right."

Eddie was tiring of him. He turned back to stare him down. "Why are you here? Why risk me calling Agent Hayes upstairs and us trying to take you in? In fact... let's skip all the prelim bullshit and get to what you're offering. Because you wouldn't be here if you didn't have a deal in mind."

"Simple: you let the coach go..."

"Not going to happen."

"And I'll make sure Liz McGee turns herself in."

That had his attention. "Really?"

"Provided she has a deal in writing beforehand."

Eddie let his shoulders slump. He was getting irritated, inclined to see how fast Bob could split town with more men from the Boston bureau chasing him.

But...

She probably knows a hell of a lot more than Ratachkov, an unused sleeper who seems privy to next to nothing.

Eddie figured he already knew Bob's answer, but he asked anyway. "And if I don't give her what she wants?"

"She's already arranged to disappear, permanently. You won't get to her in time, and you won't be able to stop her."

"Or?"

"She'll agree to ten years, no more. No life sentences, minimum-security pen nearby, where she can be visited by her daughter. And you let go Ratachkov/Jefferson go, with a letter thanking him for aiding your investigation and outlining his lack of culpability."

"That all, huh?"

"In return, she'll give you everything she knows about Uncle's ring, mostly learned from its biggest assets, her parents. That includes the locations and aliases of at least six more Russian operatives on the Eastern Seaboard alone, all of whom were due for cleanup in the next few weeks."

Eddie rubbed his chin stubble as he thought about it, though he knew right away he didn't have a choice. "You're some piece of work, you know that, right?" He sighed and took another slug of whiskey. He winced a little at the alcohol's bite. "And why is Dr. McGee making this offer?"

"She wants to stay close to her daughter, see her when she can. Rachel is the only family she has left. And she knows Chris Jefferson has a wife and kid."

He didn't like it. But Eddie knew he'd still be a hero in the department's eyes, even if he didn't get any dirt on Kennedy's duplicity from Uncle. And he knew Bob; he knew his former protégé wouldn't have offered the deal without being certain he'd take it.

"One other condition: he forfeits any money he received from them."

Bob rose from the stool. "Done and done. Her lawyer will be in touch about the details."

"And you turn yourself in as well," he added.

"Kiss my ass, Eddie," Bob said, as he turned to leave.

Eddie watched him cross the bar room toward the doors. Halfway, Bob stopped and turned.

"And, Eddie... if you ever go near Dawn and Marcus again, I'll find you, and I'll kill you."

"Not if I kill you first," Stone muttered as the door swung shut behind him.

Mike Schultz was waiting outside Rachel's hospital room when Bob arrived, as he'd agreed on the phone. He looked weary, Bob figured.

But then, he always looked weary these days, the weight of his career hanging over him.

"Bob." The police sergeant rose to his feet. He nodded towards the room. "She's asleep again now but was awake when I got here a half hour ago."

"Sorry, I had to stop and chat with an old colleague," Bob said. "You want the good news first, or the bad?"

"Let's do the good. The last three weeks have been a bugger."

"Your missing body is sitting in a morgue downtown, being prepped for burial. Its next of kin is willing to provide a statement as to how he got there."

"But... that's amazing!" Mike said, before realizing the subject. "I mean... that's terrible, of course, but... what's the bad news?"

"The bad news is her statements are all going to be subject to a sealed federal indictment, so your employers won't see an official copy for months. I can give you a copy of her statement to enter into the record with them before that seal goes in, but it'll probably put you into some sort of career limbo until the feds cough up the official record and confirm its validity. Is that enough?"

"Months?"

"Typically, three to six. Sometimes a year or more."

Mike smiled gamely, though Bob could tell he wasn't sure.

"My association's a good one," he said. "They protect their members. If they know the evidence is out there, and it's just time? Yeah. Yeah, I think it might be." He extended a hand to shake, which Bob accepted. "Thank you. Thank you for being a good friend, for doing this for me."

Bob shrugged, mildly embarrassed. "Eh, sure. It's sort of

what I do now, I guess." *Accept it, like Dawn said. You are who you are. Embrace it.*

"Bob?"

They turned towards the room. Rachel was awake.

It was going to be a difficult conversation, Bob knew, explaining her gramps's death, her mother's deal with the feds. She was going to have some tough days ahead, but she deserved the truth.

He knew he would be gone before she got out of the hospital. His soft-sided travel case sat in the passenger well of the battered Lincoln, in the hospital parking lot.

He also knew he'd miss Portland, just as he'd missed Tucson. Both had been something close to normal, for a while anyway.

But Eddie Stone couldn't be entirely trusted. The deals would be certified, on paper, but as usual, he wouldn't be part of the bargain.

That wouldn't stop Stone from sending men after him, trying to keep his agreement with his boss, Andrew Kennedy, to take the last survivor of Tehran off the board.

He had to keep on moving.

THE END

ABOUT THE AUTHOR

Did you enjoy *Body Count*? Please consider leaving a review on Amazon to help other readers discover the book.

Ian Loome writes thrillers and mysteries. His books have been downloaded more than a half-million times on Amazon.com and have regularly featured on the Kindle best-seller lists for more than a decade. For 24 years, Ian was a multi-award-winning newspaper reporter, editor and columnist in Canada. When he's not figuring out innovative ways to snuff his characters, he plays blues guitar and occasionally fronts bands. He lives in Sherwood Park, Alberta, with his partner Lori, a pugnacious bulldog named Ferdinand, a confused mostly Great Dane puppy named Ollie, and some cats for good measure.

ALSO BY IAN LOOME

A Rogue Warrior Thriller Series

Code Red

Blood Debt

Dead Drop

Hell Bent

Hard Country

Snake Eyes

Body Count

Made in the USA
Las Vegas, NV
19 January 2025

c41b6b82-e1d3-44b5-ab0c-727f503818dcR02